W9-BCL-367

The Intimates

The
Intimates

◆

Ralph Sassone

Farrar, Straus and Giroux ◆ New York

Farrar, Straus and Giroux
18 West 18th Street, New York 10011

Copyright © 2011 by Ralph Sassone
Distributed in Canada by D&M Publishers, Inc.
Printed in the United States of America
First edition, 2011

Library of Congress Cataloging-in-Publication Data
Sassone, Ralph.
    The intimates / Ralph Sassone.— 1st ed.
        p.   cm.
    ISBN 978-0-374-17697-6 (alk. paper)
    1. Friendship—Fiction.   I. Title.

PS3619.A813 I67 2010
813'.6—dc22
                                        2010024668

Designed by Abby Kagan

www.fsgbooks.com

1   3   5   7   9   10   8   6   4   2

To Peter Crowe Franklin and Lucy Blackwell

and to my parents

Part
One

• • •

Whenever Maize snuck away to see Hal Jamesley, there was always a blissful moment when she hardly recognized herself. It happened at the desk in the guidance suite where a smoked glass partition separated the secretary's cubicle from the counselors' offices. Maize would stop to check herself out in the partition before taking the extra five steps to loiter outside Hal's door, not knocking, just standing there until he noticed her shifting her feet on the carpet and summoned her forward for their next conference.

There were several mirrors Maize could gaze into during the school day—in the girls' bathroom or the girls' locker room, in the rearview mirror of her friend Lyla's car or the compact in her own pocket—but the smoked glass partition was her favorite. In its charcoaled and wavering reflection she was miraculously improved—slightly older and more cultivated, like Hal, with an urbane and faintly Gallic mystique she knew she didn't have in her real life at seventeen. Her brown hair went black and her perfected skin grew luminous in the constant midnight of the thick dark glass. She looked, she thought, like a memory of herself come blazingly alive, only stranger since it was a memory that hadn't happened yet.

Maize brushed her fingers against her cheeks or her forehead or her wavy hair whenever she stared, to verify that it was really herself she was seeing. The regular old Maize bobbed to the surface threateningly and then receded and rose again. She had to do it all extremely quickly or the guidance department secretary would glower from her computer and say, "Do you have an appointment?" startling her from her spell before she could move closer toward Hal Jamesley.

Mr. Jamesley's office was like the portal to a more intelligent life, the vivified existence she hoped she'd have someday, although the door to it was ugly and institutional and always shut. It was beige steel with a glass-and-chicken-wire insert through which Maize could observe what he was doing and brace herself until he beckoned her. She'd noticed that when Hal Jamesley was alone he'd mostly be staring at the ceiling or the green cinderblock walls with a faint grimace, as if in a seizure of insight or indigestion. When he was with another student advisee he'd gesticulate wildly while he spoke, his face thought-tormented, twisting and re-twisting a black phone cord around his hands as if failing to lasso his own interest.

He was her college counselor, a job at which he was incompetent. He made no secret that he was unqualified for the position and that he'd been hired under duress, as a last-minute replacement for Mrs. Franc, the college counselor who'd gone on a forced sabbatical after twenty years at the job. He had no experience as a counselor—he'd be the first to tell you that—having taken a teaching degree in studio art. In his other life, after school hours, he made collages and watercolors and paintings; he'd framed one small, blurry, burnt orange rectangle and propped it on his desk corner where the other counselors would have displayed bland smiley photos of their spouses and children. His fingertips were often stained with blue or red pigment like someone with an exotic circulatory disease.

So he was probably temporary, which was fine with him. The school had been desperate. Toward the end of the burnout preceding her hasty leave, Mrs. Franc had been known to tell students that it didn't matter how hard they worked or where they applied to college because they wouldn't be successful or happy in the end anyway. She scoffed at the prospect of future achievements. Specifically, what she said was "What? You think you're going to *escape* this whole mess-of-a-life just because you have good grades and nice manners and clean hair? Think again!" She'd said that to Maize, glaring toward her poster of Picasso's *Guernica*. Parents, not Maize's own, had started to complain.

"I'm hardly a font of knowledge about this stuff," Mr. Jamesley had said the first time they'd met. "I mean, when I was in high school, I wrote my personal essay on why my morose poetry was going to change the world, and then I wondered why I didn't get into Yale. I actually referred to my poems as 'my *friends*.' How lame!" He'd laughed and turned away, looking for something on his shelves.

Maize had watched him while he searched, sitting as silently as she did in all her classes. (*Maize is very bright and perceptive and an excellent writer,* her evaluations often said, *but she's shy and doesn't participate enough in discussions.*) She hid in the middle or the back of rooms—never up front unless forced—with her hair shielding her soft round face and her eyes bowed toward a notebook. Every now and then she pressed her fingers to the center of her full lips, as though suppressing an impulse to shout something rude. In her imagination she looked like nothing sitting there, and sounded like nothing and smelled like nothing, unlike Mr. Jamesley, who gave off a piney scent as he stalked around his office, rooting through drawers and cursing at the messy piles on his desk. "Where the hell is— I just had the damn thing in my— Yes! Finally!" he said with a gusty sigh. He handed her a thick book called *Endless Alternatives for Top Students.*

"Thank you, Mr. Jamesley."

"Hal. Not Mr. Jamesley. The only Mr. Jamesley I know is my asshole of a father. *Hal.*"

Maize had smiled wanly at the faint crease in Hal's forehead, estimating him to be between twenty-seven and thirty-two. Certainly not any more than that. He made it sound like he'd graduated from college in the past decade, listening to the same alternative music in his dorm that Maize had started playing in middle school. But she was clueless at guessing the ages of adults unless they were truly ancient. The last time her mother fished for a compliment by saying, "Tell me the truth, Maizie, do I look my age?" Maize surprised them both by blurting, "No, you don't. You look a lot older." Sometimes Maize had the brutal candor of quiet people who don't socialize enough; she'd noticed that about herself.

During that same conversation her mother had instructed Maize to pick three forceful adjectives to describe herself (college interviewers always asked that, she said) and warned Maize that one of those words had to be *ambitious* as in: *intelligent, creative, ambitious; sensitive, enterprising, ambitious.*

"Who the hell told you that?" Hal had said to her that first day, after Maize asked him about it. He'd glanced at her and squinched his silky black eyebrows.

"I don't remember." Maize had darted her eyes at her jeans. "I guess—I guess a friend of a friend."

"These days the questions are more abstract than that," Hal had said. "Do you know what I mean by 'abstract'? No—of course you do." He'd tapped her student file. "Extremely impressive. Your grades and scores are killer."

"Thank you."

"The only problem is that you have 'oral communication difficulties,' according to some teachers."

Which teachers? Probably the lazy social studies teacher who encouraged everyone to babble to fill the class time—especially the cute boys—and downgraded Maize for bad participation even though her written tests were flawless.

"Look, I can relate," Hal had said. "I was shy at your age—I mean, I'm *still* shy, really. I don't assert myself enough. To be honest." He ran his hand through his thin dark hair and yanked it in the back, as though snapping himself to greater attention. Then he tweaked his earlobe. "Lack of confidence, which in your case is unjustified. Ludicrous. I mean—" he waved his arm at the other student folders piled on his desk and rolled his eyes—"far be it from me to say that most of these kids, including the honor students, are imbeciles, but—well, enough said. Right?"

He had invited her to come back to his office once a week—at least once a week—to practice mock interviews with him. Although Maize liked him she didn't know if she wanted to do that. All she knew was that their initial meeting had taken longer than expected and that her best friend, Lyla, would scold her when she joined her in the hallway. "So where were *you?*" Lyla would say, but Maize would merely shrug.

She returned to Hal's office the following week, during free period, and then frequently during the weeks after that. Yet they didn't exactly talk about interviewing strategies and college admissions. They talked about the same things she talked about with Lyla: movies they'd seen, songs they'd downloaded, favorite books they'd read, and the lobotomizing vapidity of the suburbs where they lived. Or rather Hal talked and Maize mostly listened and he'd praise her for being so sensitive and mature. When she could slip away from Lyla at lunch without being noticed, she'd stop by Hal's office with an orange that they'd split as they talked, offering each other slices and putting the pits in Hal's Bennington College ashtray.

Sometimes if Hal was with another student when Maize appeared behind his door, he'd stop the other student in midsentence and tell him or her to come back another time. Once she heard Hal yell, "Enough already! *Basta!*" at Josh Kaufman, a ridiculously pragmatic future pre-med type who wouldn't stop talking about his chances at Johns Hopkins; he'd been talking about that since he was twelve years old. Maize was surrounded by kids who'd been prepping for college since they were toddlers—kids who'd been trained to describe every crummy playdate and softball game and summer job as an "extracurricular activity," who'd never really been allowed to be kids—and parents who claimed all they wanted was a *good education for their children* when anyone could tell that was just a line. They were like Maize's mother—snobs who lusted after elite colleges the same way they lusted for foreign cars and expensive handbags and giant houses. Josh Kaufman jumped out of his chair and scurried past Maize into the vestibule.

Inside his office, Hal coughed out a laugh. "Oh my god—for this I get paid. I get paid to talk to these little morons," he said to Maize. "Remind me of that. Please." He touched her arm, then quickly withdrew his hand.

"Okay. I'm reminding you," Maize said. A little more sternly than she'd intended. "This is your job."

"Right," Hal said. "Right."

She looked at Hal for a moment. He was handsomer than she'd first thought, with his silky black eyebrows and fierce dark eyes, and the fine hair on the back of his hands, and his Adam's apple like Ichabod Crane's, and she sometimes tingled a bit after she left his office, where Hal slumped in his desk chair inhaling the cigarettes he wasn't supposed to light indoors and blowing the smoke toward a tiny window screen, telling her about art between puffs. He expounded on abstract expressionism and

Dutch Master paintings and postmodernism. He told her that he himself was working on a series of post–Pop Art copies—fake reproductions he called *appropriations*—on weekends and after school hours. He would light up Camels and she'd breathe in his secondhand smoke deeply, as if ingesting wisps of his sophistication. The buzz she felt afterward was probably just the nicotine. In any case, she didn't tell Lyla about it.

"Sorry to bother you again," she sometimes said when she dropped by his office unannounced.

"No—glad you're here. Be with you in a minute, Maize."

"Thank you, Mr. Jamesley," she would say. She called him Mr. Jamesley in the hallway, where the secretary could overhear her, and Hal when she was behind his closed door. When she was with Lyla she referred to him as Mr. Jamesley again. She didn't want Lyla to find out about her special meetings with Hal; she didn't exactly know why, and she felt a little guilty since she and Lyla talked all the time—before school, during school, after school, and at night. Lyla leavened the damp humor of Maize's house with breezy reports of her sexual escapades. Maize especially liked to speak to Lyla after meals alone with her mother, at the table where Maize's father and ex-stepfather, Bruce, had once sat, where it was sometimes so quiet Maize could hear herself chewing. She'd grab the phone and let Lyla's words rush over her as though washing off the residue of misery itself, which would otherwise congeal inside her like something on a dinner plate.

Lyla told her everything intimate about herself. Seemingly. But no matter how graphic Lyla was about the details of her after-school adventures (*he bit my arm, we did it backwards, I blew him forever, he ate me out for days*), Maize knew there must be something missing. No matter how much Lyla told and told and told, the essence of what she did remained a mystery to Maize. It was a little like the feeling she had when she stood outside Hal's office and watched him, thinking she understood what was going on in there and inside Hal's head, which was filled with exotic things she hadn't learned, yet perhaps not knowing at all.

◆◆◆

Now it was Saturday morning. Maize was going off to her first college interview—an "alumni interview" for a Vermont party school, held at the apartment of a recent graduate who lived on the other side of the county. Her mother had been firing warnings at her all through breakfast: *"Don't be yourself. Don't be late which is typical of you. Get on the road in plenty of time in case you get lost and take a minute to fix yourself up once you get there. Your hair is always such a mess . . ."*

It was mornings like this when Maize wished her father hadn't died and her stepfather were still around, if only to tell her mother to lay off.

On Maize's way out the front door her mother shouted, *"Have your three words ready and remember to use ambitious!"*

Maize concentrated on blocking out her mother's voice. When her mother wasn't looking, she rolled her eyes. The whole application process was ridiculous when you stopped to think about it for two minutes. The colleges wanted to know all kinds of irrelevant information, like your mother's maiden name, a famous person you admired, whether you wanted to cure cancer or design toasters or dig fossils. As if you could really know for sure at seventeen or wouldn't be smart enough to simulate different ambitions for different colleges, like a stage actor changing costumes in the wings. On her application for the school in New Hampshire, Maize planned to present herself as a nature-loving cross-country skier; for the hippie college in Oregon, as a budding social activist; as a feminist bookworm with a special interest in archaeology for the famous women's college in Pennsylvania; and for the Big Ten university in Michigan, as a smart girl who knew how to cheer on a football team and handle herself at a frat party although she didn't know how to do that and disliked sports.

The smaller colleges wanted to get to know you personally during a forty-five-minute face-to-face interview like the one Maize had scheduled for today. The larger universities couldn't care less, though some of them pretended by asking you for a photograph of yourself.

Okay then, Maize thought, as she turned the steering wheel at the end of her driveway and glanced at the dashboard clock with a sigh. She was insanely ahead of schedule for this interview—two and a half hours—but it beat listening to her mother criticize her and then, between criticisms, remind her that she needed to project confidence. Her mother took Maize's applications more seriously than Maize did, offering to hire an SAT coach and an "essay doctor" and listing dozens of colleges under the headings REACH, COMFORT, SAFETY. Today's school fell under the category SAFETY, but you could never be safe enough for her mother, who'd been the first in her family to graduate from college and, as a result, considered herself unhappy and frustrated at a higher level than her relatives. She was hysterically vigilant, clutching Vuitton purses like body armor and never letting herself be caught in public unless she was dressed "professionally" in pressed clothes, and her pretty face was prematurely lined from the strain of all the effort. She acted as though with any misstep Maize would drop down the social ladder and drag her along with her. Suddenly their Audi would be detoured to a poor neighborhood where everybody had broken-down jalopies and cheap shoes and nobody could get out.

Her mother had been even more vigilant with her ex-husband, Bruce, whom she'd badgered for years, correcting his grammar in public and telling him to tuck in his shirttails at the dinner table and suggesting he lose weight and wear better neckties and take up a classy sport like golf, until it became clear to her that she'd never transform him into the gentleman CEO of her dreams. Bruce would remain obdurately who he was no matter how much attention her mother paid to remaking him. When her mother finally realized that, she'd kicked him out of the house.

It had come to the point that Maize could hardly go online when her mother was around. Her mother refused to let Maize file electronic applications or request information from colleges if it meant surrendering personal information besides her e-mail address. She refused to let Maize order anything off the Web with a credit card. Although she'd armed their P.C. with firewalls and spam blockers and spyware and every other kind of filtration device, she remained convinced that they were only a few clicks away from the horrors of identity theft: ruined credit, ruined reputations, ruined prospects that would take years to rectify while others ran amok with their data. Whenever her mother lectured Maize on these imminent dangers, Maize wanted to say, *Do you really think your identity's* good *enough to bother stealing?* but she didn't. They argued enough as it was.

Originally, Lyla was supposed to drive Maize to her interview. She was going to drop Maize off and meet up with her afterward at a secondhand store nearby, where Lyla liked to buy sleazy camisoles and teddies. But Maize's mother exploded when she heard that plan. If Maize wanted to drive to the interview with someone like her friend Jayne—a class officer who knew Wellesley's median SATs off the top of her head—that would be one thing. But the notion of Lyla driving Maize in her blowsy mother Bonnie's car (a dented red convertible with a license plate that read BON BON) was unacceptable.

"You'd never get there *in one piece*," her mother said. "Much less on time. God knows what would happen to you."

Her mother made no secret of disliking and disapproving of Lyla although the two girls had been friends since third grade, the same year Lyla flashed the boys on the playground during recess and got into big trouble for it. She feared that Maize would be vacuumed up into Lyla's world of unsavory things. She made up all sorts of excuses why Maize couldn't come to the phone when Lyla called (*Maize is in the bathroom, Maize is doing homework, Maize is indisposed*) and asked her daughter if it was really necessary for the two girls to speak several times a day. Her mother knew Lyla was bright but an indifferent student. Maize once made the mistake of telling her that Lyla cut study hall, and her mother seemed to intuit all the other things Maize didn't dare divulge: that Lyla napped during calculus; that Lyla rushed to the girls' bathroom at the end of the school day to change from her plaid uniform into a leather miniskirt; that she caroused with older men and underage boys she'd met in chat rooms; that she was pierced and tattooed in places Maize's mother didn't even want to think about, much less think about adorned. She eyed Lyla suspiciously as someone whose "gallivanting" would derail Maize's ambition and make it impossible to get it back on track.

She was partly right, Maize knew. Sometimes Lyla would cock her head at Maize when they were alone together, give her a long assessing look, and say, "You've got potential, you know," and Maize would say, "Oh yeah?" It was exactly what her teachers and guidance counselors had been saying to her for years—*You have such potential*—only Lyla meant something different.

Maize liked to think of herself as versatile and open-minded, befriending girls as utterly different as Lyla and Jayne, each of whom thought the other freakish. (Jayne on Lyla: "A sketchy nympho." Lyla on Jayne: "She'd wear navel rings if she could find clip-ons.") But secretly Maize knew it was only her own wishy-washiness that made the two friendships possible. *Nebulous, ambivalent, ambitious.*

"What? You're, like, actually stressing about this?" Lyla had said to her last night after dinner, when Maize admitted she was nervous about her impending interview. "A fourth-rate college in Butt Fuck, Vermont? Where the cheesehead students like to smoke up and tip over dairy cows? Come on, Maizie!"

"I suppose you could call it a safety school," Maize said.

"For you it's a safety school, yeah," Lyla said. "Not for me. I'm the one who should worry." Through the phone line, Maize could hear Lyla dragging on a Marlboro Red. "Imagine me there. Walking though the snow with the frat boys and sorority girls. Wearing mohair panties to get through the winter. Shit."

Then Lyla rang off. She had to primp for a date with a twenty-four-year-old she'd met on the train to the city. "Catch you at the lingerie place around three tomorrow," she reminded Maize.

"Aren't you going to wish me luck?" Maize said.

Lyla grunted. "Aren't you going to wish *me* luck?"

◆ ◆

As Maize drove through their hometown, she wished she could call Lyla again. The insouciance Lyla had loaned her had worn off overnight. Her mother's fears threaded into her own thoughts and tangled them. Her hand quivered on the steering wheel. She was no longer like Lyla, she was just herself again: a tall and dark-haired honor student who often got tongue-tied, whose almond eyes blinked and high forehead blushed when she had to speak in public, on her way to fail or succeed at something new. If she pulled over and used her cell phone Lyla would undoubtedly still be sleeping. It was only a few minutes before noon. On weekends Lyla was unconscious until at least two, her mouth dry, her long legs parted, her curls a lovely auburn cloud on the pillow. Maize had studied Lyla the times they'd slept over at each other's houses, until Lyla woke with a languorous groan to say, "Oh shit, babycakes. Is it tomorrow already?"

For a moment Maize considered calling Hal Jamesley. He was probably awake by now, wearing a smock or a spattered T-shirt and working on one of his paintings. He'd given her his unlisted home number during one of their conferences, swearing her to secrecy because no other student had it but telling her she could use it in emergencies. Yet even as he wrote out the digits on a scratch pad, Maize knew she'd never have the nerve. What were her opening words supposed to be? *Hi, what's up? Do you know the weather forecast today?*

In the village, Maize spotted a pack of classmates sitting on a bench outside the bakery: football players and the pert girls who hung around the boys scarfing down doughnuts the girls hardly touched. She stopped at a traffic light, looking straight through the windshield, hoping they wouldn't notice her. Not that they did normally. She remembered that the windows of her ex-stepfather Bruce's car were heavily tinted so she could see people but they couldn't see her, which was, she thought, exactly the way it usually happened. She didn't register very much for these people. For all her self-consciousness, she moved largely unnoticed through the hallways, speaking only when called on in class, and even then she mumbled. She imagined that years from now people would see her picture in the yearbook and think, *Who was she again? Did I go to school with her?*

On the bench outside the bakery, one of the girls threw back her head in laughter. Maize found herself looking for Bethany Campbell—the only truly pretty girl in the honors classes, and the only girl in honors who hung out with football players—before she remembered that Bethany had fractured one of her long legs in two places last weekend, during a ski trip to Aspen with her parents. Right now one of Bethany's gorgeous legs was in traction, according to the rumors that swirled around the school, and she might have to have surgery. Maize figured she should delight in a bad thing finally happening to perfect blonde Bethany, who was rich and popular and well-rounded, and whom even the female teachers looked at dreamily.

But Maize couldn't feel glee. She felt sorry for Bethany, whom she secretly liked as well as envied. The truth nobody wanted to admit—not the girls, at least—was that Bethany Campbell was genuinely lovely to everyone. She had a flattering personality. She wasn't stuck up and she wasn't competitive. She started almost every conversation with a compliment (*I like your blouse, I love your earrings, you're so good at French*) and she touched people's arms when she agreed with them. ("Right! Exactly!") She smiled and made small talk and congratulated classmates when they got higher test scores than she herself did. You couldn't go any further than that with Bethany ("Oops—gotta run!" she'd say before you could) but at least she made an effort. That was more than Maize could say.

The last time Maize saw Bethany they were standing next to each other on the cafeteria lunch line, and after Bethany told Maize she was looking really good ("I love your cheekbones") she asked Maize what colleges she was applying to. As it turned out, Bethany was also applying to the same school that was interviewing Maize today. "I'm not as smart as you, so it's kind of one of my first choices," Bethany admitted with her usual openness. "I don't know what I'll do if I don't get in."

"I wouldn't worry about it," Maize answered. She meant she didn't think it was a school worth getting at all worked up about, but Bethany interpreted it differently.

"Thanks. You're so sweet. Oh—listen," she said, touching Maize's forearm. "Wouldn't it be awesome if we both got in? It would!" She removed her hand to give a two-thumbs-up gesture.

"I guess," Maize said. But she'd glanced down at her plate of French fries and the rubbery burgers under the heat lamp, vaguely embarrassed. In truth, she didn't want any of her classmates to go with her to college. Not even Lyla. She wanted the chance to start completely fresh—dye her hair or throw her voice or change her entire personality and not have anybody complain, "That's not *like* you," with a look of gaping stupefaction.

"You know what, Bethany?" she heard herself saying. "Sometimes I think I'd just like to go to school in Alaska or something. Or someplace nobody else would even dream about going. You know?"

Maize had to stop herself from wincing. She felt herself blush. What did she think she was doing, talking like that on a lunch line? And to someone like Bethany Campbell, no less, whose dazzling blue eyes clouded in bemusement. They inched forward toward the cash register and retreated toward opposite ends of the cafeteria.

"I saw you over there with the Virgin Bethany. What the fuck were you talking to *her* about?" Lyla asked when Maize joined her at the lunch table. She was alert to any signs of defection.

"Oh." Maize touched her hair, feeling its coarse darkness more acutely after a moment in Bethany's soft blonde presence. She shrugged. "What would Bethany and I be talking about, Lyla? Nothing."

◆ ◆

The traffic light changed. Maize was clear of the village and passing a ramp to the town where Hal Jamesley lived. She made a left onto the cross-county road, following the simple directions the interviewer had e-mailed her. She studied the road signs with the intensity of an illiterate, narrowing her eyes at each of them and trying not to get distracted by the tassel swinging lazily from the rearview mirror. It was Bruce's tassel from his high school cap and gown; he'd hung it there for good luck, as if proof of education might save Maize from bodily harm. This was his old Subaru she was driving—one of the few things he'd left behind after the divorce.

Bruce wasn't so bad. Her mother had insisted Maize call him "Dad" rather than his real name, from the minute he'd moved in with them, but as she grew increasingly disenchanted she decided that Maize should call him Bruce again. "Stop referring to him that way. He's not your father," she'd said to Maize, a few weeks before she banished him from their house. "He's not your father. Your father is dead."

Maize and Bruce had gotten along well enough. He'd never been anything but kind to her regardless of how miserably things were going between him and her mother, helping Maize with her homework, making her lunch sandwiches, praising her compositions and art class projects as if she were a genius. He had a conspiratorial sense of humor about her mother's craziness, shouting, *"Silenzio! Silenzio!"* when she nagged them both at breakfast about how sloppy they looked and raising his eyebrows behind her mother's back. He was big and lumbering, sort of a goofball, but he had a stubborn streak despite his seemingly passive exterior. He repelled her mother's efforts to improve him by nodding in agreement with everything she said and then doing exactly as he pleased. Recently he sent Maize a photo of himself from California with nothing but the phrase "Why Is This Man Smiling? How Are You, Babe?" on the back. She hadn't told her mother about it.

"My stepfather used to smoke a lot of Camels, too," she said to Hal Jamesley, the week she got the postcard. "My mother's ex-husband, I mean. I always wanted to try one of them." She looked at Hal plaintively, waiting for him to reply.

"I don't want to be a bad influence on you," he said. "You know, some sleazeball pusher."

"It's all right. I won't tell."

"It's pathetic enough that *I* smoke, isn't it?" Hal said. But he paused for a moment, staring at his desk. "Okay—here." He pointed the open end of his pack at her.

"No. Just a puff off yours is fine," she said.

"I tend to lip my cigarettes." He extended it across the narrow space between them. "It's kind of gross."

"It's all right," she said, plucking the Camel from his fingers before he could say anything more. She drew on it sharply, without taking the smoke into her lungs, and exhaled a cloud quickly so she wouldn't start coughing. "Thanks." She smiled. "Thanks a lot."

Now she turned on Bruce's car radio to cut through the boredom, flipping through the stations rapidly but unable to concentrate. Overdubbed pop songs. Panicked-sounding commercials urging you to ACT IMMEDIATELY OR LOSE THIS OPPORTUNITY. Classical fugues. Talk shows hosted by reactionary zealots and condescending therapists. Christian programs that

sounded almost normal in the second or two before the an-
nouncer said, "Remember that come the Rapture we are one with
the Lord God Our Creator." It reminded her of the secular phi-
losopher her humanities teacher had made her class read recently.
He'd given them a take-home exam with a passage they were
supposed to agree or disagree with in an essay:

> In moments of great swollen emotion—anger or joy or passion—
> we become someone else. Someone only dimly recognizable
> from who we are in normal moments, who makes our normal
> self seem a ghostly shadow by comparison. This fleeting and
> vivid persona mocks our normal self; it seems more real or
> more true than our normal self because of its intensity, but it is
> not necessarily more true or more real. Our real identity lurks
> somewhere between the normal self and this engorged person-
> ality; it is more fleeting, more nebulous and elusive, more
> frightening and more irretrievable, though we sense its phan-
> tom presence like the strange wispy images that appear to us
> in the ebb moments between waking and dreaming, which we
> ourselves conjure but do not understand.

She'd read that passage over and over in her bedroom, in the
mornings and just before going to bed, and she still didn't know
how to respond although the essay was due in three days.

She turned off the radio. Fifteen more miles to go. She fidgeted thinking about the interview. What would he ask, and what
would she say? According to her mother you were supposed to
define yourself succinctly, pretend you weren't clueless about
yourself and living in a thwarted murk, the way air is thwarted
by smog. You were supposed to be a clearheaded Valkyrie who
planned to charge ahead in life no matter what, not just past

high school but also college, not just past college but your first job and your second job and the next in a fury of achievement, on and on until everybody you knew was left in the dust.

Maize broke a sweat. She looked to the left and the right of the county road lined with retail establishments, comforting herself with the banal sights. A trinket shop next to a liquor store. A pancake house next to a nail salon. An oil change center abutting the ranch-style motel where Lyla had had an afternoon tryst with an older guy who was a friend of her mother's. She'd arranged with Maize to give her a ride home. The No-Tell Motel, Lyla called it. But she had told Maize everything and now Maize remembered it, all the lurid details (the hot plate in the room, the crusty self-service coffeepot, the orange shag carpeting and the matching polyester bedspread), as if it were her own story and she had been there herself.

Maize remembered how Lyla had emerged from the corner room with the man while she waited and watched from the parking lot. The man patted Lyla on the shoulder in goodbye, as he might a niece or a business associate, and then the absurdity of it must have struck him because he hazarded hugging her right there on the gravel, while Lyla looked in Maize's direction with a strange, uncomprehending expression, as if she suddenly didn't recognize her. She loped toward the car and addressed Maize from a distance, as if her mind had run off with the man even though her body was now in the passenger seat. Maize had seen Lyla this way before, following her hookups; it took her an hour or two before she snapped back to herself, and then she tended to be distraught for a while.

"I mean, haven't you ever felt like you were *completely* at someone's mercy?" Lyla had asked once, when Maize commented that she was acting weird.

"No," Maize had answered Lyla. "Not even close."

She'd had to stop herself from grimacing. Secretly, she half agreed with her mother that Lyla took boys too seriously; it threw her into states of manic-depressive ardor and sapped her energy for other things. Desire was Lyla's chief ambition—something that kept needing to be fulfilled, unlike other ambitions or goals. It was like applying to the same college repeatedly; just because you'd been accepted once—even early decision—didn't mean they couldn't turn you away the next time. You had to apply over and over and over again. What a waste of energy.

Not that Maize was immune to its debilitating suck and pull. She'd had a few dates and she'd had sex, sort of. Once with a boy who'd rubbed a long-necked beer bottle between her legs in the dark of a movie theater, during the gory battle sequence of an action movie, and once in tenth grade with a bisexual guy named Robbie from her chemistry class, who'd wanted to dry hump when they were supposed to be studying valences together. Although she might have gone all the way with Robbie, he'd softened under his corduroys before they'd had the chance. But she'd liked him anyway and began to hang out with him after school, first at her house and then at his much bigger place, where his edgy mother took a shine to Maize right away, offering her soft drinks and the food her maids had cooked, guffawing at Maize's impersonation of their chemistry teacher, with his high squeaky voice, who complained whenever the whole class failed homework assignments he'd failed to describe clearly.

"Hah! For once you've brought home somebody smart! I like this kid," Robbie's mother had said to him right in front of Maize, and later she'd said the same thing more belligerently ("Say hi to Robbie's friend. *I like this kid*.") when she'd introduced Maize to her husband, as if ordering him to feel the same way about Maize as she did or suffer the consequences.

During their one humping session, Robbie had admitted confusion about his sexual identity to Maize; he didn't know who he was yet. But he desperately wanted to know and stake his claim on it. As if sex didn't erase you. As if it didn't make you, in the act itself, like everyone else who was doing it. As if it were a special talent instead of a handicap. As if it wouldn't hold you back if you let it.

Still, there were moments when Maize couldn't help herself, either. She couldn't always block men out to focus on more important things, the way she blocked out background noise while doing her homework. Attraction came up suddenly, unexpectedly, at the sight of a hunky cashier or a tall gangly postman, a nerd-boy in honors math or a sunglassed man in a passing car as she drove. Mostly she managed to keep it parallel to her life, something she could spot and dispatch by herself, something she could accelerate or pull away from slowly. But despite these efforts she occasionally caught herself leaning into the feeling, rubbing up against it the way Lyla leaned up against bars, brandishing fake IDs, until it engulfed her, made her part of itself, like an amoeba under a microscope.

Maize caught herself before succumbing to it. She wanted something to happen, but she squashed the desire whenever it reared inside her. She abandoned the hunky cashier's aisle. She focused on the blackboard in math class instead of the nerd-boy. She stared at her bedroom desk rather than outside at the postman. She threw off the bedcovers and took a shower instead of remembering Robbie.

"Oh—I'm sorry. I guess you'll figure it out," was all Maize could think to say to Robbie that afternoon they'd failed to have sex, when he confessed his confusion to her. And then, flushed, with mussed hair, they'd gone back to doing their chemistry homework as if nothing had happened, and became friends.

She seriously liked Robbie—he was brainy and funny and exceptionally well dressed—and if he'd stayed around longer they might have become close. Soulmates. He might have even replaced Lyla. But his parents split up and sent him away to boarding school before the end of the school year so that possibility vanished. They'd hugged each other goodbye and promised to stay in touch but they hadn't. She was a storage unit for Robbie's secrets, yet it meant nothing. Everybody moved on. They moved on and forgot. That's what college was about, never looking back.

Now she neared a final traffic light. In four blocks she would make a left turn, following the interviewer's instructions, but for now she idled. A restlessness jockeyed with the inertia the way it had when she was a child lying on the backseat and her parents were driving, their unhappiness drifting toward her like the chilled currents from the air conditioner.

Here's the sign the interviewer told her to look for in his e-mail. Here's the front gate with the guard station that has no guard inside it, which the interviewer joked about. She enters the interviewer's garden apartment complex and checks her wristwatch as soon as she parks. Still two whole hours before her appointment. How is she going to pass all the time?

Within seconds the car heats up and she can barely breathe. She opens the door and stands there in the wilting sun, just stands there not knowing whether to turn left or right. She imagines she must look retarded.

She decides to check out the interviewer's apartment complex. The buildings are brick and two-storied, with blue doors flanking a landscaped quadrangle. Teak benches line the courtyard, which has a large cement sculpture mounted at its center. A reclining figure with a human body's shape—two arms, two legs, and a head like a child's drawing of an adult, but no distinguishing details. She can't tell if it's male or female. There are no breasts, but still.

She paces the perimeter of the courtyard, reading the numbers on the doors and slowing when she gets to the interviewer's (#7A) yet not stopping fully. She checks her watch again. She touches her blouse and glances toward the parking lot, where heat waves shimmy from the asphalt and the hoods of cars. She sighs loudly. Since this is the shady side of the courtyard, she decides to sit on one of the benches until the time is right. She swipes a dead leaf off the bench before she sits. She crosses and uncrosses her legs. A tiny red spider mite crawls onto the back of her hand and, when she tries to brush it off, it smears on her skin like dried blood. Nice. A balding man crosses the courtyard and eyes her warily on his way to the parking lot as if she's a burglar. The sun flashes off the top of his bare head.

Last week, when she was in Hal Jamesley's office discussing everything except college admissions, he made an observation about the balding middle-aged physics teacher who'd recently progressed from a bad comb-over to a ludicrous toupee. "That rug of his is so distracting," Hal said. "Somebody ought to tell him. It's like a Yorkshire terrier's in the room taking a dump on the poor guy's head." Both of them fell into a paroxysm of laughter. Maize's arm flew up and landed involuntarily on Hal's forearm, which lay on his desktop, and though her first impulse was to yank it away she left it there, and Hal let her leave it there, saying nothing. He grinned demurely. He continued talking as though her hand wasn't there, real and palpable, and she pretended along with him that it wasn't there, keeping up her end of the conversation in what she hoped was a normal tone although their rhythm was thrown off. They each spoke in sharp bursts, galvanized by power surges while the other went dead, and when Hal's soulful gaze fell on her she had to stop herself from whispering the dopey thing she said next, which was "Hair's really funny." It was a relief when another student announced herself with three rattling knocks on Hal's door, giving them an excuse to separate.

"See you tomorrow?" he said when Maize grabbed her backpack and got up to leave.

She shrugged. "I guess."

"It's coming soon now," he said. "Your applications. We have to get at it."

◆ ◆

The courtyard bench is comfortable enough. Birds chirp in the trees and a wind swells though the maples. The moment Maize allows herself to think, *This is okay,* and closes her eyes, a wave of fatigue sweeps over her. Her spine slackens as she tilts her head skyward, letting it rest on the seat back, and she breathes deeply. What a way to begin the college interview process! Lingering outside this guy's apartment like a stalker! She could almost nod off. Last night she slept fitfully, jarred awake by weird dreams. Now one of them rides back to her until the random fragments of it regroup into a misshapen whole. She'd been in a foreign country detained by customs agents who suspected her of smuggling drugs inside her body. They'd thrummed their cold hands against her inner thighs, looking for packets of heroin. When they didn't find anything they put her on an operating table and cut her up, piece by piece, fruitlessly searching for contraband until there was nothing left of her. Even when she was dead from mutilation they hovered over her with their scalpels, saying, "There must be something here," and continued exploring. "Open the instep. Separate the kidney from the duodenum. There's no point stopping now."

"Hey—hi there! You trying to find somebody?" a voice suddenly shoots from across the courtyard. Maize opens her eyes and looks in the direction of the sound but sees nothing at first. Then a head pokes out a window one story above her—a male head, she can tell even from this distance, whose handsomeness flares and makes its unexpected presence even more startling. The head has a dimpled chin and full nostrils and light brown hair. When the man leans farther out the window, his shoulders look broad and square.

"Bet you're here for an interview!" he calls.

"Oh, yes—right. I am," Maize calls back. She stands and faces his apartment, remembering to smile, taking one step forward. "Sorry. I'm not exactly here at the right time."

"No worries! Down in a sec!" he calls, and his head disappears. When he opens the front door at ground level he's dressed like a surfer boy: electric blue shorts, faded yellow T-shirt, a string of puka shells circling his thick neck. His long calves are dusted with hair that's a shade darker than his head, his chest muscles ripple under his shirt, and he flashes a horsey smile full of white teeth.

He's a gelled version of the jocks who hang outside the bakery, around the cheerleaders, ignoring Maize so completely they make her feel like she's made of vapor. Just her luck.

Before she can apologize for being appallingly early he says, "Steve. How's it going?" and plants a big dry hand on her forearm. He pumps her forearm once lightly and says, "Come on up."

She follows him up a staircase, his beefy butt winking at her through the blue cotton of his shorts.

She's winded when she gets to his living room at the top of the stairs, partly from the climb, partly from the lingering surprise, and partly from the look of the place. There's a red futon with a white stain at one end, and a couple of folding chairs next to a huge silver TV and sound system on metal shelves. The walls are bare except for a college pennant from Steve's alma mater and a basketball poster of a player suspended in air during a slam dunk. Dirty sweat clothes huddle in the corner near the window. She supposes the packing trunk near the futon is supposed to be a coffee table, but she's not sure what to make of the electric guitar that lies on top of it.

Steve catches her eyeing the guitar, which he moves onto the dirty clothes pile.

"I'm not just a computer guy," he says. "I'm a musician, too. I play bass. See?" He picks up a framed photograph of himself from behind the pile of sweat clothes and shows it to her as proof. He's younger in the picture and his hair is longer and wilder. "See? That's from a gig with my old band." Then he takes the picture back and stretches his arms over his head, flashing his solid midriff, distracting her from the slightly sheepish look on his face. "But hey—gotta pay the rent, right? You want something from the fridge? I'm getting myself a drink."

He pads into an adjacent kitchen she can't see and calls back to her from there. She hears the suck of a refrigerator door opening. "Let's see: Coke, Corona, Gatorade, Heineken, club soda, Red Bull, tonic water, Bud Lite—no, scratch the tonic. It's flat. Regular water."

"That's okay. I'm all right," Maize says.

"What? Didn't hear you." He sticks his head out; his jaw is square and perfect and the cleanliness of the line, the incipient stubble on it, makes her sad. She could dress up and exercise and eat right for the rest of her life and she'd never have bones like that.

"Water would be great," she says. She sits on the futon, in the center, away from the white stain, and waits. She fidgets at the sound of liquid cracking over ice. She's nervous even though she doesn't care about getting into this school; something hums around her like a bee that followed her inside. Maybe it's the aftershock of being caught in the courtyard, loitering there with her mouth open and the befuddled look of a newly landed immigrant.

"Here you are," Steve says, handing her a tall and not entirely spotless glass that has already started to sweat. He's standing above her, his tanned bare thighs at her eye level, looking down at her.

She says, "Yes. Here I am. Thank you."

"Sure thing." He plops on one of the opposite chairs and a little of the liquid in his own glass sloshes out during the descent. Amber liquid. It's beer, she thinks. This guy is drinking beer in the middle of the day during a college interview. *Very professional,* her mother would say with a smirk. But Lyla would say, *Have a sense of humor, Maize, it's fucking hilarious,* and she'd be right. She can't wait to tell Lyla about it later at the lingerie store.

"Yeah. So." Steve takes a long swig of the beer, emptying about a third of the glass. "How you doing?"

"Fine. Thank you."

"Having a fun senior year?"

"Sure, I guess," she says. "It's fine."

"Had a blast my senior year. Almost as good as my senior year of college." He puts a bare foot on the crate between them, letting his legs fall open, and she ignores the peek of white briefs under the blue shorts. "Blows my mind that it was nine years ago. Wish I could go back," he says with a sigh.

"You do?" She can't believe anyone would want to return to

high school or remember it fondly. All she wants to do is forget about it like someone paroled after a long prison sentence.

"Oh yeah. Totally. You'd love my college. Believe me." He smiles a timid, inward smile and stares past her out the window, as if his glorious past lies just beyond the courtyard. Then he blinks and reaches for one of the manila folders on the trunk between them. "So anyway," he says airily, opening it. "Let's see what we've got here. Gimme just a sec."

"All right," she says.

While he reads she considers what he said: *You'd love my college.* She's noticed that third-rate colleges and party schools say things like that in their literature, emphasizing the student-teacher ratio and the picturesque campus and the social activities and whatever else helps sell the place, while first-tier schools are politely standoffish like the popular kids in school. She bets the interviewers from the good schools hedge their bets, saying things like *I'm sure you'd be happy at any number of institutions.* But she wouldn't be happy at this guy's school even if all the other colleges rejected her. It has fraternities and sororities and a physical education requirement, and graduates who hang sports posters in their living rooms. Her mother is such a fool for making her apply.

"Whoa. Tons of extracurriculars," Steve says as he reads. "Nice. They'll really like to see you've got school spirit."

School spirit!

"So let's chat about what made you apply here," Steve says.

My mother, she nearly says. Perhaps he would laugh. Instead she says, "That's hard to say. I don't really know." She shrugs for emphasis. "A lot of people say it's a good school. I mean, it has a good reputation."

"You're right. It's a cool place," Steve says. "But I guess what I mean is, you know, what exactly made you, Bethany, apply?"

The shock hits her like a wave of cold air and makes her sit more erect. The name flies out so fast she wonders if she imagined it. "Excuse me?"

"By the way—do you go by Bethany or just Beth?" Steve says.

"Excuse me? What?" She must look even more dazed than she did in the courtyard. "I'm not Bethany."

"Beth, then."

"Um, no." She puts her hands on her knees, about to stand and announce herself. She leans forward a bit, staring into his blue eyes and then at his full lips. The scent of him this close—beer and some sort of woodsy cologne—drifts over and distracts her. She should be thinking about the most graceful way to explain. Instead she notices he's beautiful, even if he's dim. As beautiful as Bethany/Beth or even more so. Anything she could say at this point (*You've got it wrong, there's been a misunderstanding, I'm really mortified*) will require her to admit that this mix-up is all her fault. She'll have to explain why she was wandering in his courtyard two whole hours early, like a geek who shows up to class before anyone else and lines up her pens and pencils on the desktop. She'll have to explain about Bethany's skiing accident and her mother. It will be so involved—the complications of it will fall over them both like dust motes in the room—that there will be no graceful way of explaining.

She stands and says, "Sorry. Could I use your bathroom for a minute?"

"Sure thing." Steve points left.

His towels are as unkempt as the underwear on the carpet. She turns the cold-water tap and lets it run hard while she stares ahead. She studies herself in the medicine cabinet mirror. Her face is pale, with beads breaking at her hairline. She leans into the sink and splashes her face with water, thinking this will make her more clearheaded, but it doesn't work. Now she's panting a little. She sits on the toilet after putting down the seat and flips the door lock next to her knees. She could just stay there. She dries herself with a green velour towel hanging on the back of the door before she realizes it's Steve's bathrobe. There's the same woodsy smell (maybe it's his soap?) and she buries her head in it for a second, taking a sniff and messing up her hair. She hears herself breathe into the cloth.

When she leaves the bathroom Steve is rotating his head in a slow full circle, with his muscular arms stretched behind him and his ropy legs flexed in front. He doesn't stop rotating his head at her return, as if to show her how relaxed this interview will be. She allows herself to glance at his shorts and the little bulge inside them.

"Hey there," he says. "Everything okay?"

"Yes. It's fine," she says. "Sorry for the wait." As she moves toward her place on the futon, her skirt brushes against Steve's forearm; the heat of it brands the back of her thigh. "I'm really sorry about this confusion."

"It's cool, Beth," he says. "So let's get back to that question."

What question? "All right," she says. She sits, looks at him and the floor between them. "But first I have something important to tell you."

"Yeah? What's that?"

She looks up at him now. He takes another sip from his glass and leans forward, smiling hazily at her from the beer buzz or something else. It's the same smile she's gotten from men at the mall a few times, before she walks away from them, secretly hoping they'll follow her but horrified at the thought that they might. Only Steve is better-looking than the men at the mall. She has never been alone with a man this good-looking, paying such close attention to her like a student poised to take notes, as though he'll later be tested on everything she says. She leans forward herself, and finds that she's whispering rather than speaking normally across the narrowed distance between them.

"It's really kind of funny," she says.

"What?" Steve leans back a bit, chuckling once, prepared to be amused.

She counts a few of the puka shells around his neck to focus her thoughts. A wooziness sweeps over her, carrying away her need to perform or project herself. She has nothing to lose. She can just be herself.

"My mother's the reason all this is happening," she says.

"Uh-huh? Is that right?" Steve says. He leans back farther.

"She is. I'm not a good match for this college, to tell you the truth. It's not one of my top choices. But it's nice meeting you, anyway."

"You mean you're not interested in my school?"

"Not really, no. To tell you the truth. But there's something important I need to clear up—"

"Don't sweat it," Steve says. "Your honesty's cool, you know? I totally appreciate it."

"No—but that's not what I meant to say."

"Dude, it's cool," Steve says.

"Oh god," she says. "Let me start over."

"Hey—no." Steve picks up another file. "You know what? This makes it easier. They gave me this list of questions I'm supposed to drill you with, but you know what?" He tosses the file on the floor in a gesture of practiced-looking whimsy. "Now we can just chill. Don't worry. It's all good."

He leans forward again and places his hand on her knee, making her expect a reassuring pat, but that doesn't happen. His big hand lingers there for a second and then another. She blushes. He says, "That okay with you?"

"Yeah," she says. "I guess. Sure. But listen—"

"Just a sec. I need a refill." He gets up and goes to the kitchen. Again she hears the refrigerator door and the shifting of bottles. When he comes back with another beer he sits next to her on the futon instead of the chair. He takes a swig of his replacement beer and says, "So what do we have here?"

Now that she's admitted she's going to another college no matter what, she supposes none of what happens matters anymore. Steve puts his leg up on the crate and they pause, relaxing into this knowledge the way he relaxes into the futon.

"I don't know what we have here. What do you think?" she says. She cocks her head quizzically and raises her eyebrows like Lyla. The sun streams into the room and strikes Steve's leg, bleaching the hair into a radiant fringe. "Maybe I should leave now. I think I should." She means to put her open hand on the futon, pushing herself off, but she miscalculates and her fingertips brush his hard thigh.

"No, don't go," Steve says. He takes her hand and lets it stay there, looking into her eyes and then at her face, her hair, breathing onto her, and she can't tell which burns more—her face or her hand—or whether she's blushing again. What she feels is like embarrassment, like ambition, like a traveling clot. *Modest, passionate, ambitious.* It's like all those things and not like any of them at all.

He says, "Don't go yet. I've got plenty of time to kill."

"You've gotten a totally wrong idea of who I am." She clasps his hand. "I—let me please explain."

"No worries," he says with a bright and idiotic smile. "No biggie."

She starts laughing then. Something unbuckles inside her and she cannot stop laughing. It doubles her over and makes her eyes water—this is so ridiculous—and when she undoubles the expression on Steve's face is fond, and the water in her eyes washes away any sharp malice or condescension. "Sorry," she says. "Oh. I'm so sorry." She touches the side of his face with her free hand, to show him she's sincere and there are no hard feelings.

That is when he leans forward and kisses her.

His kiss is gentle. He meets her, draws away to smile, draws back and leaves her puckering as though teasing her. The third time he does this she lurches forward, surprising herself, and wraps her arms around his neck, locking her mouth against his and hearing herself make a noise. He withdraws again, nibbles her ear, moves to her neck and traces, with his tongue, the exposed part of her chest. She gasps when he burrows his head under the top of her blouse. She is in the moment letting this happen and simultaneously not here at all; she is thinking how strange it is that ten minutes ago this wasn't happening and now it is; she's doing what everyone else has talked about, what Lyla has described, *I'm having sex now*, but at the same time she's watching it happen.

They are out of their clothes. Slowly he has helped her remove her blouse over her lifted arms, and unbuttoned her skirt, which he has tossed blithely next to his dirty underwear. He buries his head in the cleft between her breasts bearishly, like a hibernating animal, and unhooks her bra with his teeth as she pants and studies his broad back, his sharp shoulder blades, the perfect white moons of his buttocks flaring above his deeply tanned thighs. With one finger he pulls off her white panties and makes her yelp not only at the shock of it but the sight of his thing, hard and poking up from its nest of fur, like an animal springing out from a wood. He touches it, touches her down there with the heel of his hand, rubbing her slowly, then faster, gently, then with more pressure.

When he touches her hand again she closes her eyes and

suddenly imagines it's Hal she's with, Hal who slides off her underwear in one smooth practiced motion and grabs a condom
from under the futon like he's done it a million times, Hal who
parts her legs and moves his lips exactly as they are being moved
over her body right now, right here, slowly, inexorably, over her
jaw, under her chin, down her neck, to the small rectangular window of flesh that covers her windpipe, and lingering there, pressing, the way she's daydreamed she and Hal would press each other
though they never have, they never will, they wouldn't dare,
she's run off before they've ever had the chance. Why hasn't she
seen it sooner than this, as she lies here with every secret part of
her exposed and her emotions rearranging themselves the way
muscles rearrange themselves around a wound? It's only in this
stranger's bed that she can fleetingly admit it: she's wanted Hal
to do this from the first month, the first week, the first day.

She opens her eyes. From above Steve is looking at her with
shocking vulnerability, like a hungry child begging for food.
Despite his rippling muscles and stubble his face is a boy's face,
an innocent face. She could reach over and smother him or stran-
gle him and he would let her do it, he would be powerless to
stop her. She guesses this is what Lyla has been talking about:
the close animal presence, as when dogs strain instinctively toward each other on the street and greet each other with a stare or
a sniff before they're yanked away again. No wonder people go
crazy from it: they feel all this and then they're yanked away
again. It occurs to her that she's lived in this estrangement all her
life until this moment, unecstatic, unconsoled, unaware, and that
maybe now it's ending.

She understands he will enter her. He has been rubbing against
her groin in warm-up, reconnaissance, and now he is nosing his
thing around her opening, hazarding a few tentative jabs and

prodding her back into self-consciousness. She is a girl lying naked on some jock playboy's futon in broad daylight. His entering her is supposed to meld them but it does the opposite; it interrupts whatever communion she had begun to feel for an impersonal—what is the right word?—procedure. It delivers them freshly to themselves again. His thing might as well be an appliance they're experimenting with for the first time; its meaning detaches itself from their bodies as he aims and they both stare at it, with a dim scientific wonder.

The sudden sharp pain rips to the center of her, as if there are bones inside her that Steve's trying to stretch. Bones that will snap if he goes any farther. But he does go deeper, then deeper still, knocking the breath out of her, and it's only worse when he withdraws. She inhales and he plunges in faster; she moves against him through the pain until it crosses over into something else, not quite pain. They move together like that, in a rocking motion, until she hears the creaking of the futon frame. Then she rolls him over so that she's on top and she sits there on him, closing her eyes, scissoring her arms across her chest like someone in a yoga position when he bucks under her.

"Oh Beth," he says. "Oh shit—I'm getting there." Steve's eyelids flutter as he finishes. Then he lies inert beneath her for a while, breathing thinly, his face gone slack as if he's suddenly fallen asleep. She doesn't know what to do. It's a relief when he opens his eyes and pulls her off him and smiles. "Whew! Don't let anybody tell you high school girls don't know what they're doing. You've got a great little career ahead of you if you want it."

She drops the arm covering her breasts and the motion makes her shiver.

He asks her what time it is. She looks at her wristwatch (the only thing he didn't remove) and tells him. He says, "That was great. You're great, Beth. But we've only got another half hour. Tops."

He says, "I'd invite you to stay longer, honey"—honey!—"but I've got another interview after this." A mischievous grin flicks the corner of his mouth. He pauses, not sure if he should speak. "Actually, it's with somebody else from your high school."

She should be quiet now. Or she should tell him everything—tell him he needn't rush her out—and apologize or laugh, hoping that her laughter bridges him to the next feeling and he will laugh, too. But instead she says, "Oh yeah? Who with?"

"May?" he says. "May something? Weird name. I forget." He reaches for one of the folders he tossed beside the futon and opens it. "Here: Maize."

She hears herself say, "Yes. I know her."

He props himself up on his elbows so that his chest hair tickles her knee. Somewhere in her mouth is one of those hairs, curling around her tooth like dark floss. He says, "Oh yeah? What's she like?"

Blonde and pretty, Maize could say. Beautiful and brilliant. Very bold and sure of herself. Athletic and pragmatic and charming. Great sense of humor. Most likely to succeed. *Ambitious.*

She pauses a moment, looking at the blank wall above their heads.

"I don't know," she says finally. "I mean, I know her. But I don't know her well at all."

She stands up off the futon. She puts on her clothes with her back to him; now that they're no longer immersed in each other their nudity gives her goose bumps. She doesn't want him to see her anymore and she doesn't want to see him again, either, reclining there with one leg raised languidly, smoking a cigarette in a reverie and blowing the smoke toward the ceiling.

The rest happens quickly. She picks up her bag from the floor and sticks up her free hand in a rigid farewell gesture. She glances back in his direction only for a second. She's halfway down the stairs to the front door before he realizes she's leaving. "Hey, Bethany—Hey! Wait up!" Now he's standing at the top of the stairs, saronged in a blue towel. She still doesn't turn around until she gets to the bottom and puts her hand on the doorknob. She addresses one of the stair treads.

"Goodbye," she says. "You've got your next interview and I'm supposed to meet someone, too. Bye."

He inhales deeply as though he's going to say something important, talk a lot. "Okay. You won't?—Okay then." He exhales. "Later."

It takes her a moment to adjust to the sun in the courtyard. She blinks and squints, then everything comes clear again. She's a bit sore but she walks perfectly. Swiftly. She checks her wristwatch as she nears the parking lot, still running ahead of schedule. She can already picture her own consternated face when she meets up with Lyla again at the store, and Lyla's irritation as well, which will vanish as quickly as a baby's tears when she displays her latest secondhand find to Maize: an ivory camisole in imitation silk, with contrasting brown straps and one small, barely visible spot near the shoulder. Lyla will smile at Maize as she approaches from a distance, ignorant of the other ways her friend is joining her and hardly listening to Maize's lies about how well the interview went. She will raise the camisole so that it covers her face, drop it, raise it and drop it and laugh as in a game of peekaboo. At the very same moment, Maize imagines, Hal Jamesley will be at home finishing a painting or applying a fragment to a collage, grinning cautiously to himself in anticipation of their next long conference, unaware it won't be happening again, and Steve will be sticking his head out the window toward the desolate courtyard. Steve will search not for her but for a girl named Maize, wondering what she'll be like, whether she'll be pretty, a blonde or a brunette, dulcet-voiced or loud. He'll retract his head and go inside to check the clock on his kitchen wall, only to stick his head out again to scan the courtyard and the paths, the benches and the parking lot, as the sun starts falling and the wind in the trees makes them murmur an indecipherable language, like the first ghostly sounds of an arrival.

Part
Two

...

During the first days of his trip, Robbie was frantic to keep moving. He'd barely landed at Leonardo da Vinci before he raced off to see the Colosseum and the Circus Maximus, the Via Veneto and the Via Appia, the Aurelian Wall and the Arch of Constantine, the Sistine Chapel and the statue of Moses, the Spanish Steps and the Borghese Gardens, and walked or been driven past every famous square and fountain and basilica he'd highlighted in his guidebooks during the plane ride from New York. To each site he lugged a volume of Keats as if a little prodding voice were whispering, *Yes, this too will be on the exam*, while he scurried around, snapping a few pictures and trying not to look too much like a rube.

He had promised Maize he'd forward dozens of photos of Rome ("Pictures, Robbie, I want *pictures*," she'd demanded before he left) but so far he'd only gotten a handful of blurry and underexposed shots. In his frenzy he captured the outlines but not the essential details. He was too jumpy to hold the lens still long enough.

He'd also switched hotels three times within seventy-two hours of landing, moving from an *albergo* in the Parioli district (a room that looked out on a wall) to Via Barberini (too noisy) to a room near Piazza di Spagna that was adequate for now if also dangerously close to the crowds. At each rejected lodging he'd merely shown up at the front desk with his overpacked bag a few minutes before checkout time, informed the concierge of his departure, and walked away without warning to the next place, e-mailing home as soon as he got to his new accommodation. By the time he decamped to his third hotel Maize observed that Rome had made him even more skittish than usual, if that was possible. What she e-mailed him was, "My god, Robbie. You're acting like a fugitive. What's up with that?" All his mother wanted to know was how much this new hotel would be setting her back since she was footing the bills.

But even someone like Robbie—an underweight student with the metabolism of a hummingbird—had limits. On his third morning in Rome, in his third hotel, he woke so bone-tired he could barely pick up the bedside phone to order room service. And when his Continental breakfast arrived in the arms of an astoundingly handsome and amiable young hotel waiter named Carlo, Robbie lacked the energy to respond. He stood there jazz-headed in his tightly cinched seersucker robe, undoubtedly looking *molto americano*, and nodded catatonically as the beautiful waiter inquired, in alluringly broken English, where Robbie was from (Connecticut), how long he'd be staying in Rome (six days total), where he went to college (Rhode Island), and what he had been doing at night in the city "for amuse" (nothing much really). Unbidden, the waiter offered Robbie suggestions of bars and dance clubs Robbie knew he should make use of but wouldn't.

Was Carlo hitting on him or just being an excellent waiter? Robbie had such minimal experience with flirting he couldn't tell; it was like a core course he hadn't gotten around to taking. Over the past three years he'd been holed up in libraries and rare-book rooms while, it seemed, all his classmates were out screwing their way toward graduation. "Brother Robbie," Maize often called him, meaning a monk rather than the sibling she wished she had, the twin who shared her whole history and got all her jokes.

"Scusi," Robbie said repeatedly to the gorgeous waiter as he tried not to study his physique and his Roman profile, so chiseled and fine it could be on a coin. *"Scusi. Grazie. Scusi."*

He could have met this Carlo halfway if he'd had the nerve. He wasn't without some Romance language skills, having aced three semesters of intensive Italian back at college. Currently he was somewhere between introductory and intermediate levels, comfortable with *passato prossimo* if not *remoto* or *imperfetto*. But it was as if the ludicrous promise he'd made his mother before this trip—the vow that he wouldn't speak Italian with his father or his father's mistress—had tied his tongue altogether. A week ago, while hastily making travel arrangements, he'd imagined himself chattering with the natives and gesticulating as wildly as Giulietta Masina in an old Fellini film. Now he couldn't even bring himself to ask for simple directions when he needed them. As a result he'd spent the past seventy-two hours frequently lost.

Well, who could really blame Robbie? Was this entire situation his fault? In preparation for the trip, his mother had packed him full of suspicions the way other mothers made their sons take extra sweaters or a first aid kit. Again and again she'd warned him about how tricky the Romans were—vitally ingratiating on the surface, sure, but always working an angle whenever they got the chance. It was their innermost nature to be duplicitous, she'd said; they couldn't help themselves. The fact that Robbie's father's ancestors were Roman Jews—which made Robbie half-Roman—wasn't lost on them, but neither was it discussed.

"Trust me on this one, kiddo. They'll rook you in the blink of an eye," she'd told Robbie as they stood in his childhood bedroom and he struggled to close his overstuffed suitcase. She often talked like a suburban gun moll. "Keep your mouth clamped and pretend you're a native. Avoid close contact at all costs. Otherwise you'll look like a patsy."

So except for e-mails to Maize and his mother, and halting requests to taxi drivers and waiters and hotel clerks, Robbie had pretty much kept to himself since getting here. He was lonely and shamefully bored—in Rome of all places!—since he'd already covered all the tourist sites he'd wanted to see. He had four more days before his compulsory meeting with his father. What was he going to do with himself? There were only so many landmarks he could check off a hit list. There were only so many long-winded text messages and IMs he could send to Maize, assuring her that the food and the Roman men were as delicious as she'd heard. There were only so many times he could toss coins into the Trevi Fountain and repeat the wishes he'd made on the first day (*Please let this reunion be bearable* and *Please make J. leave me alone*) in case some pagan god hadn't heard his pleas the last time.

He was stranded for the duration. He had no choice in the matter. He would have to defy his nature and will himself to relax. He could relax if he really put his mind to it. Total incompetents managed to relax every day.

He decided the best way to start was with a long, languorous, wine-soaked, high-carbohydrate lunch among the idling classes. He strolled to a café on Piazza Navona and requested an outdoor table overlooking the square with its Bernini fountain. He looked at the fountain and reviewed the menu. When he caught himself poring over the first- and second-course offerings like rare manuscripts in the college library, he imagined Maize sighing fondly and shaking her head. *Once a grind, Robbie, always a grind.* Again he tried to surrender to the loose Italian spirit, letting the breeze play with his shiny straight hair, letting the burble of nearby water soothe him, letting the faint scent of chamomile (was someone having tea?) waft into his nostrils. But no sooner had he eased into the moment than a large bee hovered threaten-ingly around his face like an announcement: *Stop kidding your-self. Mellowness isn't your strong suit.* Maybe the most a high-strung person like himself could aspire to was fatigue.

It didn't help that he was marooned in Rome for a week when he could have gotten the trip over quickly. What had he been thinking? When his father had blackmailed Robbie into showing up for his birthday celebration—when he'd insisted on giving Robbie his senior-year tuition *in person*, after years of Robbie deflecting his letters and phone calls to the States with varying degrees of politeness—Robbie immediately had two war-ring impulses: to pop into Rome as briefly as an overnight busi-ness traveler and to explore the Eternal City as thoroughly as possible, since he'd never seen it before and might never be back.

He shouldn't have given in to the tourist side of himself, but he did. And his mother had encouraged him. When Robbie raised the possibility of a longer stay she seemed delighted by the idea that he'd be in Rome for a full week, just a stroll away from his father, though her ex-husband would think Robbie was there only for a matter of hours. "You know what, kiddo?" she'd said to Robbie as he debated the matter. "You're right. Have a vacation. You've been working like a dog." And when Robbie mentioned the extra cost she'd said, "I'll cough up the dough," and assured him it wouldn't be too expensive. She'd smiled as if glancing at a lovely postcard.

So Robbie consented to see his father. But officially, at least, only for his birthday. He lied that he would fly in and out of Rome within twenty-four hours because he had tons of thesis research to do and he was sorry, that was all the time he could spare. He figured if anyone could accept a workaholic's excuse it was his father. Although it was admittedly an odd situation, everything between them was strange—awkward, freighted, frosty. What the Italians would call *freddo*. In five years they'd barely spoken and they hadn't seen each other at all.

His father had abandoned them without warning—absconded to Rome with a pretty and decidedly younger designer from his firm, having relocated his textile business to Italy over a number of months, as if America weren't large enough to avoid the vestiges of his past or his ex-wife's endlessly radiating scorn. Robbie still didn't know what the bigger surprise was, the old man's sudden defection or his furtive and deranged interest in sex. While Robbie was growing up his father showed no interest in typical businessmen's fetishes—golf and sports cars, Cuban cigars and extramarital affairs—because he was too busy putting in sixteen-hour days at the office. But when he finally got around to philandering late in life, he made a diligent and serious commitment to it. Apparently he'd become as myopically focused on adultery as he was on his paperwork, to the exclusion of all else, so that anything short of abandonment would have seemed half-assed. Or so Robbie assumed.

After he left, the shock was like a vessel that opened up inside Robbie, an empty expandable vessel, and when Robbie saw it was there he felt obliged to fill it, and when he didn't know how to fill it, it became an all-purpose receptacle for every emotion, all his confusing love and longing, all his spleen and rage, all the humor and irony he could summon as a fifteen-year-old whose father had bailed on him.

Although his father had been financially supportive since leaving (lawyers saw to that), Robbie's mother had made the divorce extremely difficult and there'd been little contact between continents.

There were times when Robbie wanted to extend himself toward his father yet he found he lacked the limberness to do it, like a lame person with a madcap ambition to go rock climbing. He wrote e-mails he couldn't finish or even continue past the first sentence. He picked up the phone and dialed all but the last digit of his father's number, or dialed all the numbers and hung up at the sound of the European ring tones. And whenever his father made contact, Robbie found himself basically dumbfounded by a reverberating aftershock, unlike his mother, who if anything became more voluble after her husband's disappearance.

"Italy!" she'd said to Robbie the week her husband left, at a meal where she'd had too much merlot. "You're good with languages, kiddo. What's Italian for '*That sneaky bastard had a double life?*'" When Robbie reminded her that he was taking high school French instead of Italian she said, "Just as well. Don't tell me," and she'd swigged a little more wine. "On second thought, I don't want to hear a word of Wop spoken in this house by you or anyone. Ever."

During another desolate dinner for two that same week she'd turned to Robbie and said, "What do you need a father for, anyway? To hell with him. He was never around. Nothing's different. You don't need a father," and after a pause they'd both started laughing, hard and then harder, until they were breathless and red-faced, momentarily cleansed of resentment and grief and tension, and to Robbie's astonishment he believed her. He didn't need a father. He didn't have a father anymore so he didn't need one. His father didn't matter if they decided he didn't.

Now Robbie forced himself to order his entire lunch in Italian, pretending to be a native (or at least Continental) and trying not to overenunciate like a student. Certainly he could pass for Roman on his looks alone, his half-Italian blood giving him a head start. He had black hair, dark eyes, pale olive skin, and cool Milanese clothes even if he lacked an Italian's sportiness and outwardly sated demeanor. He chose three courses—risotto, bollito misto, and semifreddo—and was already on his second glass of prosecco by the time he ordered. He made a point of informing the waiter that he didn't need or want to rush through the meal (*"Piano piano piano,"* he said), which drew a *"Certo!"* and a smirk as if he'd just specified something ridiculously obvious, like the desire to eat with a fork.

He closed his eyes, breathed deeply, and counted to himself in Italian (*uno, due, tre, quattro . . .*), trying to smell the potted lantanas separating the restaurant from the square and struggling to be fully in the moment. But no sooner did he begin counting than he caught himself doing math—calculating exactly how many hours he had left in Rome (87), how many months since he'd clapped eyes on his father (62), and how many miles he was safely away from J. and the campus where they'd been staging their private little skirmish for the past semester (4,570). By the time he dug into his risotto, his head was buzzing like one of the Vespas that wove through the city.

Really, though. He should have more leisurely meals like this in America, especially now that he was going into his senior year of college. Both his mother and Maize had been encouraging him to take it easier forever. ("Straight A's are fine, but you should make an *effort* to get a C minus in something just to prove it won't kill you," his mother had said.) He'd had to admit to himself that he'd inherited his father's mechanistic work ethic—his tendency to labor robotically and sleep less than the average person—the same way he'd inherited his nose and the shape of his eyebrows. He wondered if his father had reformed since moving to a famously carefree country, but he doubted it. Otherwise, would he have scheduled his own birthday celebration for a weekday morning, as if it were a business breakfast meeting?

Just as well. Robbie hated dawdling. At college Maize could barely get him to hang out anywhere—the cafeteria or the student lounge or her dorm room one floor below his—before he jumped to more pressing matters. He was forever bolting from his seat to announce that he had to return to work. He always had research to finish, a term paper due soon, a test coming up. He studied his life away in the isolated quiet of carrels and stacks and other badly ventilated areas while his peers slouched at bars and concerts and film screenings. Maize joked that she'd become promiscuous solely because Robbie was forever leaving her alone—what else was she supposed to do with all her free time? What she didn't understand was that he'd have been dissatisfying if he'd lingered with her. When you got into the habit of leaving abruptly, staying put came to feel clammy and redundant.

Even if Professor J. hadn't indicated to Robbie—again and again, sometimes bluntly—that he wasn't keen on Robbie staying the night in his faculty apartment, Robbie would have fled back to his dorm before dawn anyway. But J. hadn't grasped that until the end, when Robbie left his apartment forever, and when he did understand he'd acted astonished and mortally offended.

Still, Robbie didn't consider himself a remote person. He wasn't. He was a cauldron of unexpressed feelings. And he did eke out time at night and on weekends to have long, careening conversations with Maize in which they recounted seemingly everything to each other. He listened to Maize, about her hookups and her hair dyes (currently she was a redhead), her first readings of Marx and Freud and Plath (whose work she was ashamed not to like as much as Ted Hughes's), and her attractions to a revolving series of men who Robbie thought weren't nearly good enough for her. ("Shucks," she would say whenever he voiced that opinion. "Pshaw.") She listened to Robbie, about the progress of his research, his taste in designer coats and tennis stars, his worries about life after college, and his latest conversations with his mother, whose house was so dingy the maid couldn't find the cobwebs she was supposed to sweep, though Robbie always saw them in any light, whenever he was forced to go home again.

He and Maize were like each other's human diaries, or as close to that as he'd ever come with anyone.

But as with real diaries certain things got omitted. Six months after the fact, Robbie still hadn't told Maize about his affair with J. He didn't know why, since Maize was trustworthy and discreet and she wouldn't blab to a soul. His reticence was admittedly perverse. The way he saw it, an affair was supposed to be a place to hide for a few hours a week, like a cheap motel room, but by being secretive he was still living there after the fact. If he checked in for too long it might start to look like his permanent residence.

J. was Robbie's first and only affair. Robbie had been a virgin beforehand. It was an event Robbie was doing his best to forget about now, like someone in posttraumatic shock, although it still came back to him in lacerating flashes that tore the lining of his consciousness. Letting Maize in on the sordid details—the seduction, the breakup, the excitingly awful recriminations that followed—seemed increasingly pointless as the months passed, plus there'd be the weirdness of explaining why he hadn't told her in the first place. He couldn't explain that plausibly. He himself didn't know why.

The only person who'd heard about the affair was Tonia Cantor, Robbie's flamboyant Italian professor. Signorina Cantor had introduced Robbie to Professor J. at one of her louche weekend cocktail parties, where she and the other dangerously bored junior faculty got crocked in the presence of undergraduates invited to join in the hoopla. The only reason Tonia Cantor knew was that J. had elected her his sob sister after Robbie had ended it between them. Certainly Robbie hadn't confessed anything to her first. At present he wasn't speaking to either of them.

"Nothing subtle about you guys," Tonia had observed one day after her party, where Robbie and J. had spoken solely to each other and tittered at anything even faintly amusing the other said. "I'm surprised J. didn't prop a pillow under his ass," Tonia had said, but Robbie had merely whitened and said nothing in reply.

Now he gulped the last of his prosecco. Better to forget about that for the moment. Better to relish every spoonful of his semifreddo and act airheaded like, say, the alcoholic drama major Maize had hooked up with recently and told Robbie everything about the next morning, once again making him feel like a tight-lipped nerd. Better to order a digestif with his espresso and gaze at the piazza and contemplate nothing more serious than an afternoon siesta.

"I would like the check, please," Robbie said in English before he caught himself—not only slurring his words but slurring in the wrong language. Although he tried to cover by saying loudly and clearly to the waiter, *"Mi fa il conto, per favore,"* the ruse seemed pathetically pretentious all of a sudden. This wasn't his homeland. He could try again next time if he wanted, but for the moment his cover was thoroughly blown.

◆ ◆

The next morning Robbie woke with a vaguely hangoverish headache. He made a point of showering and shaving and grooming himself pristinely before he ordered his room service breakfast. While he sat there in his creased pants and button-down, waiting for the waiter's brilliant handsomeness to fill the chamber like daylight, he texted Maize again. She was on lunch break from her summer job at a chain bookstore where romance novels and thrillers outsold serious fiction by twenty to one, counting the hours until her return to campus. So her patience was thinner than usual. When Robbie complained about his idleness she texted back, "Okay. We'll make a deal. I'll fill your empty time in Rome. You sit in a cinder-block basement all day stripping covers off paperbacks."

"Sorry," Robbie wrote her. He felt so bad about whining that he splurged on an international call his mother would probably object to having to pay for later.

"Why are you wearing a button-down, Robbie?" Maize asked when he called. "You should be lying buck naked on the bed humming 'That's Amore' or something when that waiter shows up."

Robbie barked a laugh. "Right, Maizie. Just my style."

Maize enjoyed lampooning Robbie's anal-retentiveness and modesty whenever she got the chance. She got a pass to do it because they went way back together, not only through three years of college but all the way through high school. She knew his parents from when they were still together and she knew a lot of his history. Not only was she aware of his teenage sexual fumblings, she'd participated in them to a degree and had never thought they were a big deal. Very little fazed Maize. She was precociously sophisticated for a girl who'd grown up in the suburbs, at least when it came to other people's lives.

So on his first morning in Rome, Robbie e-mailed her about the bad dream that had woken him the night before, bloated with misgivings—a nightmare in which his father and his mistress, Clarissa, guided him through the rooms of their apartment, pointing out antiques and paintings and statues they'd bought on shopping trips, before throwing open the doors to a light-soaked bedroom in shambles. The striped curtains were tattered, the sheets were violently disarranged, and strewn on the bare mattress were vibrators, handcuffs, dirty underwear, bloody rags, and bottles of lubricant. It had the raw air of a crime scene before it's cordoned off with police tape. When Robbie tried to avert his eyes, his father stole his arm around his shoulder and said, "*Ma che cosa?* What is this prudishness all of a sudden? We're family."

"Purely out of curiosity," Maize e-mailed him back, "were the vibrators big?" Robbie claimed he couldn't remember (in fact they'd been frighteningly large) and Maize let him change the subject. That was one of the many things he valued about her. She was still the shy and slyly insightful girl he'd loved back in high school, despite her recent tendencies to ask provocative questions and blurt out opinions. She knew just how far to push people and when to stop. If Robbie had the same talent, he'd never have accepted J.'s invitation to his apartment for a nightcap that turned into an all-nighter and a whole stormy semester.

"So if you're not hooking up with the waiter, Robbie, are you at least taking pictures of the fabulous Roman men for me?" Maize asked him now on the phone.

"Yes," Robbie said, though he hadn't. He hoped to rectify that today. He had no other plans besides using his camera, which was so tiny it fit in his palm. After breakfast he would wander around, soaking up the local color (Wasn't that what he was supposed to do?), and capture the sights for Maize and posterity. Even at twenty-one he was aware that without reminders he could forget entire experiences if enough time passed. People and places and bits of knowledge: all of it could get sucked into a memory hole like a lost language or the ability to play a musical instrument. It had happened to him already with certain details from high school (What was the symbol for manganese? Who had sat next to him in ninth-grade English?), especially the details from the year his father left.

Of course, these lapses could be helpful. With enough time he might eventually forget the sight of J.'s constricted face staring him down on campus after Robbie broke up with him, not to mention the scary and wearying things they'd done with each other's bodies before then.

"Oh Robbie, I'm so tired," J. had said to him that first night in his faculty apartment at 3:00 a.m., after they'd finished conversational foreplay and Robbie's attentions had gone rubbery from exhaustion. "I'm so old and so tired," he'd said with a sigh, a tumbler of scotch in his hand, and then he'd dared lay his big blond head on Robbie's shoulder haltingly, as if expecting a zing of static electricity.

It might as well have been a marble bust lying there; that's how heavy it felt to Robbie as he sat stricken on the sofa, unsure of what to do next. The air around him thinned and thickened as it would for an asthmatic at the start of an attack. Because he knew he had to respond—do anything to break the suspense—he patted J.'s fluffy hair carefully as if it were barbed wire, barely touching it, a gesture that struck him as more fraternal than erotic. It was as if he was comforting an older pal rather than inciting him to make out. He imagined that in another few moments he would rise with a neutering yawn and a dissipated smile and beg off, saying "To be continued" or something equally ambiguous, to signal that they might try again another night if the opportunity presented itself.

But he'd misread what was happening. Within seconds came the dull tickle of J.'s bearded lips exploring the column of his bare neck from its base, slowly, tentatively, then less so, trailing upward and up some more, until his lips fastened on Robbie's for a long first kiss with a thick tongue—J.'s tongue—darting and slithering so much it left them both speechless. When Robbie recovered enough to detach his mouth from J.'s he heard himself whisper, "I should go home," yet he'd either spoken too softly or J. wouldn't hear of it. J. was kissing Robbie everywhere he could now that his initial trepidation had passed—ferociously and randomly, on the mouth and the forehead and the jaw and the eyelids and the clavicle and the nose and the collarbone, and sticking his pointy tongue into Robbie's ears between kisses, making him yelp from pleasure or surprise, or the surprise of pleasure, and brushing the smooth boyish skin of Robbie's cheek with his bristly facial hair so that it soothed Robbie at the same time that it burned.

How bizarre it all was. No one sensation was allowed to dominate or fully take the lead. Every time Robbie began to feel excitement, it got displaced by discomfort or fear or a sense of his own clumsiness, migrating inside him as unpredictably as J.'s hands and his mouth moved over his body, leaving him dazed.

When J. started deftly unbuttoning Robbie's shirt, Robbie threw back his head and stared at the ceiling. He closed and opened his eyes. The room began to spin—jazzed by Robbie's hormones or mere confusion. He was enjoying himself both thoroughly and distantly, in the astounded way of someone stoned, J.'s kisses prodding through his numbness for a second before the numbness reappeared just as quickly. He assumed he could still get up and leave the apartment if he chose to; it wasn't too late to excuse himself without complete offense. But before he could commit to action J. had fully removed Robbie's shirt and his own polo and was towering over Robbie, asking him to get up and leading him by the hand to a corner of the room where a mattress wheezed as Robbie fell upon it.

"Beautiful, beautiful," J. said as he stood beside the bed, peering down at Robbie's half-naked body. "Every inch of you."

But in a second he went around the room, turning off all the lamps, and they were invisible to each other. Robbie's pupils throbbed at the sudden dousing of the lights.

The complete darkness intensified everything. Robbie felt the dense wet heat of J. licking the cleft between his pectorals, and then J.'s big hands stroking his torso in a circular motion, and then his calloused fingertips flicking and teasing his nipples, pinching them hard until they shrank and pebbled, and then him sucking and sucking at them like a demanding newborn needing sustenance, and then him outlining the bars of Robbie's rib cage and pressing his ear to Robbie's abdomen. With each application of J.'s fingers and mouth the rest of Robbie vanished; all that existed was the part of him that J. was working on at the moment, methodically, devoutly, while Robbie's own mouth formed an inarticulate O of disbelief. Flashes of horror coursed through Robbie along with waves of satisfaction and he supposed that these were inseparable, like freezing and scalding water that flowed from the same tap.

J. unbuttoned the top of Robbie's jeans, then the buttons of Robbie's fly. He lifted Robbie's torso and pulled the denim down over his legs, leaving him in nothing but socks and underwear— white briefs swollen and dampened by Robbie's arousal, which evidently had a life ignorant of Robbie's hesitation or more powerful than it. When J. asked him, *Are you ready for me?* and he didn't answer, he clamped his mouth over the flimsy cotton covering Robbie, gripping him through the cloth, panting heavily and heavier still like someone about to die. Finally he lifted the elastic waistband of Robbie's underwear and took him full in his mouth.

Robbie had never experienced anything remotely like it before. Not even after years of frequent and expert masturbation.

It felt like being fed into a tight, black, slick cave with trembling walls—not just his crotch but the rest of him subsumed deeper and deeper as J. continued, tracing with his tongue the thick dorsal vein that throbbed exquisitely, until Robbie believed he might pass out. It was like an abduction, this disappearance into someone else's body, this voluptuous surrender to pampering or capitulation, and he'd need to reclaim himself any minute now. When J. gagged Robbie felt his own throat spasm.

It was a relief when J. decided to take a breather. He stood and slowly removed the rest of his own clothes, folding them neatly on a chair, then draped himself over Robbie. With German fastidiousness he positioned himself so that their erections aligned and rubbed against each other and he thrust in simple, wonderful friction. Robbie moved against him for the first time all evening. Now that his eyes had adjusted to the dark he could see how magnetic J. was, with his big body and his milky rose skin covered in fur a shade darker than his head. He could appreciate the way J. dove at him again, even more violently this time, worshipping him and besieging him from all angles, up, down, left, right, sideways, with linear and corkscrew motions, nibbling and taking feral bites, and he could even enjoy J.'s orders to Be Still and Stop Moving So Much because he knew his compliance was temporary and this would soon be over. He'd be back in his dorm before morning.

Nevertheless Robbie found he was shaking. Had J. noticed it, too? He took deep breaths to stop himself from hyperventilating. He told himself to stay calm.

Just when he thought he'd settled himself down J. flipped him over on all fours and showed off more exotic skills. He ran his mouth over the backs of Robbie's thighs and the crooks of his knees, licking his palm and fondling Robbie from behind with his wet fist, burrowing his tongue in places Robbie hardly knew about, like the small secret area below his scrotum where J. poked gently and then not gently at all, withdrawing and then stabbing his tongue forward dozens of times like a switchblade, inflaming hundreds or thousands or millions of nerve endings, until Robbie heard himself cry out and felt his hips jerk and exploded helplessly onto the bedding.

J. flipped him onto his back again. Robbie was drenched everywhere and undoubtedly looked a wreck. He had to admit that what had just happened to him was amazing, and that he'd want it to happen again, but for now it was, thankfully, over. He wondered what time it was. He figured he would get out of J.'s apartment as quickly as possible and as soon as it was polite. He glanced across the dim room at J.'s front door like someone locating the fire exit in a strange hotel.

The problem was that J. was hugging him tightly now, kissing him at his sweaty hairline, and murmuring about how happy he was and how much he'd wanted Robbie, his voice gone watery with emotion and his eyes half closed. He was far more effusive in this delirium than he was clothed and Robbie merely nodded in response, as he would at someone talking in his sleep who probably wouldn't remember what he'd blurted out in the morning. He said "Thank you" as he glanced across the room at J.'s front door again.

As if sensing Robbie's departure, J. loosened his hold and stretched his arms over his head. He spread his long legs wide and then he smiled at Robbie rather curiously—waggling his thick eyebrows at Robbie with comic lasciviousness, like Groucho Marx. Robbie glanced toward the front door once again and waited for J.'s strange expression to pass. But when Robbie looked back he was still waggling his brows and grinning.

Was Robbie supposed to laugh with him? Was he obliged to thank him again for performing with frightening gusto? Was that the correct thing to do next?

It took two full minutes of J. smiling at him, spreading his legs even wider and starting to stroke himself, before he said, "So, my dear?" And it was only then that Robbie thought *Oh god* and grasped what had eluded him since he'd allowed any of it to begin: *He was expected to reciprocate.*

"Well, I hope you'll be taking pictures of your father's place when you finally get there," Maize said to Robbie now. "Whether or not it has the Bedroom of Horrors, I bet it's interesting."

"Maybe," Robbie said.

She'd always gotten a kick out of his parents, the way only someone who wasn't their child could. The few times she'd met Robbie's father she'd smiled wryly at his effusive greetings, as if they were part of a larger sales pitch for something she'd decided against buying. She adored Robbie's mother and considered her vulnerable—*achingly tender*, as she put it—not despite her crusty demeanor but because of it. Robbie wasn't sure he agreed.

Although it was natural that he'd view his parents differently from Maize, their opinions diverged even more after his father bailed. When Robbie allowed himself to think about his father at all, he remembered him as being mostly away at work but overwhelming in those rare moments he drew near, with his crushing vitality, his obliterating bonhomie, his boundless hunger for food, his grappling for money and success and proof that he was well liked. A hazel-eyed man who kissed startled strangers hello and took stairs two at a time. After his departure, Robbie convinced himself that everything about his father's expansive surface was calculated to hide his businessman's ruthless efficiency and clammed-up heart, whereas Robbie's prickly mother—who rarely embraced anyone, never used endearments, and found giving or receiving compliments as repugnant as self-pity—came to seem more openhearted and exposed to him, like a foolhardy soul who goes through the winter underdressed for the elements. He could see the devastation in his mother's immobile face, in the puffy skin under her eyes and the hollows of her cheeks. Occasionally her nose twitched as if freshly registering the shock of what her life had become. But in the photos Robbie's father sent back from Rome, he looked tanned and robust under the Italian sun—his gleaming health an unbearable rebuke to both of them.

"I don't think your dad's trying to piss you off," Maize said one day in Robbie's dorm room, when he showed her the latest photos to arrive from Italy and tore them up into confetti in front of her. "He's probably just sort of retarded."

"I know," Robbie said. "He's a phony."

"No, I think he's genuine," Maize said. "It's just that it's three layers down. There's what he shows you on the surface, and the stuff below the surface that has nothing to do with that, and the stuff below *that*, which is like the stuff on the surface only deeper."

"Huh?" Robbie said. "I don't follow." Next to her he often felt obtuse despite his superior grades—someone with a quick mind and a slow heart. "Fuck my father, who cares," he said automatically, and Maize had darted her eyes toward his wastebasket and shrugged.

He supposed he should listen more carefully when Maize analyzed people. Hadn't she pegged Tonia Cantor as hopelessly unreliable, months before Robbie himself had had to write Tonia off? She could have saved Robbie a lot of grief.

At his suggestion, Maize had enrolled in Tonia Cantor's Intro Italian class, but she dropped it quickly because she found

Professor Cantor charismatic yet loopy and incoherent. Tonia Cantor had shown up at the first meeting without a syllabus and regaled her students—in English, not Italian—with complaints about how lovelorn she was in their college town, how desperate for decent ethnic food, while her see-through blouse kept slipping off her shoulder, exposing her pink bra strap, and she made googly eyes at the boys in the front rows. Maize figured that if she stayed enrolled she'd learn a lot more about Professor Cantor's personal life than about irregular verbs and pronouns, so she switched to Intro Spanish.

It was true that Tonia Cantor was highly unorthodox and possibly even unbalanced. She was out there. But Robbie couldn't help having a soft spot for her. He secretly considered her something of a kindred spirit despite their glaring dissimilarities. Although Tonia exploded and Robbie tended to stew like a Crock-Pot, they both had inner heat. And he admired how bravely she paraded her feelings to everyone who'd listen without caring if they found her excessive. To hell with them if they did! She was the most wildly emotional adult he'd ever met. Her anarchic qualities would probably cost her tenure in years to come, but they were a relief on a campus where many of the faculty were brittle, sherry-nipping Ph.D.s who pronounced the words *basil* and *tomato* like Edwardians. ("Oh, please, speak fucking *American!*" Tonia brayed at one of them after a few vodkas, at the same fateful cocktail party where she'd introduced Robbie to J.) She had only the faintest sense of professional and personal boundaries.

Tonia Cantor's legal first name was Miriam, which was what appeared in the college catalogue, but she insisted that everyone call her Tonia, the name she'd adopted when she'd done graduate work in Rome. During conferences when they were supposed to be discussing Robbie's work, she identified herself as "just a Jewish girl from Long Island, trying to be cute," but since her erstwhile Roman holiday she found she "couldn't get arrested" by attractive men and was fast becoming "a single gal whose eggs are rotting" and "a frustrated love-o-maniac," meaning that she loved to be in love whether or not she had takers. She acted possessive of Robbie well after she'd radared his preferences. ("Oh, I get it, you like *boys*," she'd said. "Well, who the hell doesn't?")

He developed protective feelings toward Tonia Cantor, who was unguarded and wept like a faucet, just as Tonia had initially tried to remain protective of Robbie after the affair, when J. divided Tonia's loyalties. At least at first, she told Robbie that she disapproved of J.'s behavior and was "always, always, always on the side of youth in amorous matters." She claimed to be appalled when J. followed Robbie into the isolated and already scary art history stacks, where Robbie had gone to research a paper on Cézanne's apples, just so he could glower at him and shoot him the finger before retreating to his faculty apartment.

Robbie was afraid he had it coming. He'd left J. without warning, announcing his desire to end their affair on the phone rather than in person, and then he'd treated J. like a leper rather than someone he'd been involved with—someone he shouldn't communicate with in any fashion, like an ex-convict ordered to avoid all truck with other felons. He had been inexcusably awful to J., he realized, and arrogant to boot, yet he was also too terrified to waver in his resolve after dumping him; if he did he'd get sucked back into their morass and have to arrange his escape all over again.

"That's revolting! For shame! Shame on him! The library is a sacred place!" Tonia said when Robbie reported the Cézanne incident to her. "A temple of scholarship. That's practically a sacrilege. You want to borrow my car to get away from campus a little while? You want to hide in my apartment? I'll do anything to help you."

Tonia was a recklessly generous person—she really would do all that if Robbie asked her—but he shook his head no because he feared her lavishness was shot through with something darker, even if Tonia herself couldn't see it. A consuming and faintly proprietary urgency. If he allowed Tonia to spend too much on him he might find himself owned. After the initial high of feeling completely protected and wonderfully spoiled he'd wake up and discover he'd been branded with her initials.

"Your ex is acting like such a nimrod," she said. She grabbed Robbie's hand and stroked it in her office, as though it had been maimed along with his ego.

"Well, whatever." Robbie shrugged and withdrew his hand back to his lap. "It's no big deal. Really, it's all right." In the silence that followed he felt that he should say something more. "I mean, I ended up getting an A on that Cézanne paper."

Yet Robbie was even more rattled by J.'s behavior than Tonia. Until their breakup J. had been a paragon of self-control. From the moment J. had started flirting with Robbie at Tonia's party by standing close to him in her kitchen and quoting Rilke and asking him all about himself, he'd seemed an ideal starter lover— not only because he was erudite and experienced and tall and cute in a decidedly academic way, with his horn-rimmed glasses and tweed jackets and flyaway hair and blond beard, nor merely because he was ambitious and acerbically witty about his betters and colleagues (*Tonia is her own symptom*, he'd once said to Robbie), but most of all because Robbie guessed that J. wouldn't, unlike Robbie's peers, demand much of him beyond minor acrobatics a few times a week. He wouldn't get in the way of Robbie's studies. J. had every professional reason to treat their affair as a pastime rather than employment, since his main job was getting tenure and advancing up the ladder by being smart and politic.

There was security in J.'s single-minded careerism. It was

understood that Robbie wasn't welcome to stay for breakfast because that was when J. got his writing done and his students' German exams graded. It was understood that they'd never go out to a restaurant or a movie or even dine together at J.'s wobbly little bistro table because—leaving aside fear of exposure—they both had too much work. It was understood that whatever steamed up between them wouldn't encompass intemperate declarations about a future together because there was no future, their affair was fleeting and transitory for all its stimulation, like an interesting course that had to conclude at the end of the term, with final grades submitted and evaluations filed and everyone more knowledgeable and just slightly older than when they'd started.

Or at least Robbie assumed all that was understood.

But when J. started getting clingy (wanting to know what Robbie was doing on their nights apart and with whom, and suggesting that Robbie might stay in Rhode Island after he graduated), and when Robbie's high-Victorian reserve during sex in J.'s bed didn't abate, and when Robbie got bored stealing out of J.'s apartment at 3:00 or 4:00 a.m. like a burglar and impulsively declared that the affair was over, J.'s emotions rose like a fever he didn't know he had until it was too late. J. had rattling shivers and hallucinations of ardor. He started writing mash notes instead of academic articles and calling Robbie at all hours of the night, breathing into the receiver rather than speaking, until Robbie had to mute his cell phone before bedtime. Then J. started appealing to Tonia's sympathies and her attraction to drama, and before Robbie knew it he was in the middle of a riotous mess. Much as Robbie was homesick after three days in Rome, he was also pleased to be thousands of miles away from all that, in a place where J. would never think of tracking him and even his own father had no idea he was in town.

Yet sometimes Robbie had to admit—at least to himself—that he'd gotten something out of the J. affair anyway. Not just being relieved of his virginity, not just the cheap thrill of sneaking around and carrying on a secret life that nobody else knew about so nobody could question, but something bigger. In J.'s thirty-one-year-old presence, Robbie had never felt younger and more vital and full of possibility, precisely because he was lying next to someone whose own novice possibilities had already started to fade. Robbie brimmed with the cruel potency of being twenty-one, with his whole life ahead of him. He'd noticed that was something people didn't talk about or write about when older people took younger lovers. They battened on the predatory power of the elders and the innocence of the dewy subordinates. Well-educated people were familiar with Zeus and Leda, and David and Jonathan, and Socrates and Alcibiades, and Oscar and Bozy, and Humbert and Lo. But nobody dwelled on the ravishments of elders after their conquests—the bereft left to memories and sagging flesh while their young lovers skipped away toward the endless open vista of their own futures, where anything might still happen and anything could be built.

That had always been Robbie's advantage: his ability to move on. Robbie imagined his particular smell might have lingered on J.'s musty sheets for a few hours each time he left J.'s apartment, but if J. made an effort to inhale that scent it would disappear.

"Gotta go now, breakfast is here," he said to Maize after two knocks came at his hotel door.

"Take off that button-down, you stud!" Maize said with a laugh.

Robbie stopped at the mirror to smooth out his clothes, straighten his hair for Carlo, and practice a smile that would look welcoming rather than maniacal. But when he opened the door there was an old man carrying a tray on his bony right shoulder. In Italian Robbie inquired where Carlo had gone and in Italian he was told, he thought, that today was Carlo's day off. The plunging disappointment took him aback, but instead of giving in to it he gulped his black coffee and decided to avoid the hotel until evening, though he hadn't the foggiest notion of what he'd do with himself next.

◆ ◆

The exchange rate was terrible. He didn't have money to buy things but he could at least window-shop on Via Condotti, gawking at the sumptuous clothes and wondering whether his personality would improve if he dressed better, like a prince who felt entitled to cashmere socks and shirts priced like suits instead of a drudge who waited for clearance sales. All the supple tweeds and silky cottons and feathery wools inevitably reminded him of his father, whose mills had probably supplied some of these textiles and whose apartment was perilously close to this opulence. It wasn't impossible that his father's reflection might bob behind Robbie's image on the storefront glass, like a memory ember flashing through dark recesses of consciousness. But it was unlikely. His father worked in another district—Robbie knew that much— and at midday he'd be grinding away at his office the same way he had done in the States.

Maybe Robbie should do a dry run to his father's apartment— which his mother described as *luxurious* though she'd never seen it—so that he wouldn't get lost trying to find it in a few days. He'd always had a lousy sense of direction and he was dying to see what his father's block looked like, and his father's building, and even his father's sidewalk, though he didn't want to admit it.

If he didn't resist he'd be viscerally drawn to it like one of those displaced pets he sometimes heard about, who managed to find their way back to the master's house against all odds.

He wandered from store to store, telling himself he was merely moseying but also aware he was getting closer to his father's apartment, until he was on his father's block, which had no stores and no other excuses for being there. It was a purely residential, rather elegant street with imposing façades and balconies spilling with potted flowers and Lamborghinis at the curbside. There was almost no through traffic, as if this stretch had been cordoned off to all but rich people, so when Robbie found himself standing in front of his father's building, gazing up at the top-floor windows, he felt as conspicuous as a bull's-eye. With a shudder he dashed off to the nearest small square, which he'd never heard of and wasn't in his guidebooks, but which was lined with cafés and a newsstand.

It was lunchtime, so he bought a copy of the *Corriere della Sera* and took a table near a window behind tall planters, where he could observe everything safely without being looked at. As in much of Rome, there were legions of native men enjoying each other's company on this square—sitting at coffee bars together, walking arm in arm, laughing and conversing and using their hands to communicate—but strikingly few women, as if a female neutron bomb had been dropped. Where were all the Roman women? Home with *bambini* or chained to a sink? The few Robbie noticed had been working behind store counters or hotel desks or bustling somewhere, as if they had to make up for all the male leisure. Maybe the absence of native women was the reason the men here were famous for pouncing like wolf packs on any half-appealing girl who entered their territory. They seemed more ravenous for pretty women than they were for food, which was saying a lot in a country where the day was divided not into morning, noon, and night but breakfast, lunch, and dinner.

Robbie had read somewhere that a lot of these horny men were called *mammoni*—perpetual mama's boys who wooed women and bedded them but lived with their mothers way into middle age, letting them launder their clothes and make their beds and cook their favorite dishes with nary a flicker of worry about arrested development. Even if Robbie's own mother hadn't been a bad laundress who disliked cooking, he still would have considered these guys crazy. He couldn't wait to permanently get out of his mother's house, where the window shades were always at half-mast even in daytime and the pewtery air of depression was inescapable.

A petite brunette crossed the square in front of the café. Then a fleshy redhead. Then a bombshell in huge sunglasses. Although Robbie was concentrating on the *Corriere*, he sensed when each of these women appeared from the near silence that fell over the restaurant, plus the none-too-tactful shift of male gazes and craned necks in their direction before conversation resumed. It was like a soccer match where the men took shots and the women deflected their attentions like expert goalies. No one won but no one seemed to lose, either. He was reading the paper and lingering over his check and a double espresso when another silence fell and the heads around him turned even more dramatically— this time for a leggy blonde carrying a large shopping bag as she navigated the cobblestones on high heels. For a moment there was nothing except the clatter of plates and flatware as busboys cleared the tables.

It took Robbie half a minute before he grasped what he was noticing this time around; the awe made it register eerily late, like a delayed echo. What he saw emerged instantly yet slowly, as in a time-lapse photo of a plant rooting and budding and rotting with unnatural speed. The entire event passed before him in a matter of seconds that felt elasticized. Still, he didn't quite believe what he was looking at until he suddenly did believe it, and then his mouth dropped open as the chatter around him resumed.

The leggy blonde with the shopping bag looked exactly like his father's girlfriend, Clarissa—the woman his mother referred to as *that harlot*. It couldn't be her, yet it was: Clarissa from the misguided pictures his father had air-mailed to Robbie at college. Clarissa the plush and photogenic babe his father clutched to his side again and again like a severely overgrown child with his favorite stuffed animal. Clarissa in the flesh.

In person she was tall and lithe and athletic-looking, broad-shouldered as a champion swimmer, with bronzed skin and shoulder-length hair that curled into ringlets. Her silk dress had a bold green jungle-vine print that clung to her toned legs and shot up toward her prominent breasts. She looked Amazonian except for her delicate face and girlishly wide brown eyes. No wonder the whole restaurant had paused and a geezer near Robbie had sighed *"Dio mio"* as if his heart might give out on the spot.

Envy mingled with Robbie's horror as he watched Clarissa continue to stride across the square. Then he realized he wasn't feeling envy at all; it was stabbing disappointment that she was even better-looking than he'd imagined. Better-looking than his middle-aged mother and better-looking than himself and better-looking than just about everyone else on the planet. What a bummer. For years he'd hoped Clarissa would wear badly to make his father's decision look unwise. Now he crouched at his table behind a little potted cypress and merely hoped she wouldn't glance to her left.

Not that Clarissa seemed to notice anything in her orbit. As she gamboled over the cobblestones with a tan pocketbook banging against her hip, none of the men's leers reached her. She looked oblivious in the manner of gorgeous people who from childhood take in very little because they're used to being the focal point. How could you not dislike a person like that?

Robbie could only be grateful for Clarissa's obliviousness. It meant there was little chance of her spotting him as he stared in fascinated revulsion, or of her noticing as he threw euros on the table and rose tentatively to leave the restaurant. He was gripped by panic—the same galvanized enthrallment as when he'd run into J. after their affair, yet not the same because the person who spooked him now was a stranger. It was unlikely she'd recognize him. Even if his father had shown her old pictures of adolescent Robbie, they would have been outdated shots from when his hair was longer and lighter and his skin blemished. He wasn't that boy anymore.

He clutched his newspaper in one hand and his camera in the other as he prepared to leave the restaurant. He intended to flee in the opposite direction from Clarissa whether or not it would take him anywhere useful. But instead he found himself pausing at the threshold a few extra seconds, gazing at Clarissa's elegant retreating back and wishing he could get a better look. She got smaller and smaller and smaller as she receded into the distance, and he fell into a sort of trance where his next movements were his own yet someone else's. It wasn't Robbie who found himself walking in Clarissa's direction but some bolder, more foolish version of himself. It wasn't Robbie walking farther and farther away from the safety of his hotel but some phantom who resembled him. Nor was it quite Robbie who raised his camera and zoomed in on Clarissa's back before snapping a picture. It was a sleepwalker Robbie, a ghost Robbie, a ghoul.

Although Clarissa was nearly a block ahead now, the loudness of her green dress made it easy to keep an eye on her. At first Robbie picked up his pace but then he slowed to maintain a secure distance. Whenever Clarissa paused at a busy street corner clogged with Fiats and Volkswagens, he too stopped dead in his tracks until she moved again. He didn't concern himself with the other pedestrians bumping into him from behind, one of whom muttered what was probably an Italian curse.

She walked straight down the bustling Via del Corso for several blocks, before making a right turn and then a left onto smaller streets. By the time Robbie could detect where they were now, from a sign on a corner building, she'd made a few more turns and he lost his bearings again. He snapped pictures as they went along as if leaving a bread-crumb trail—shots of stores and cafés and *farmacie* and of Clarissa herself, an activity that had the advantage of making him look like a tourist instead of a spy.

Several minutes passed. Clarissa made another left, another right, another left again. Clearly they had moved into a whole new district now (vaguely near the train station, Robbie guessed), with wider streets and clots of young people ambling around holding cigarettes and notebooks. Somewhere in the distance a peal of bells announced it was two o'clock. Yet it didn't occur to Robbie that he was in an academic setting—practically his home turf—until he saw signs saying UNIVERSITÀ on a number of crumbling limestone structures and a few bespectacled, scholarly-looking men so distracted and ill-groomed they could only be professors. Again and again he also saw the word *sapienza* on buildings, but he had no idea how that translated.

If Clarissa had indeed led him to a university, how different this shabby quarter was from his own campus. His college looked like a country club, with a lushly landscaped quad and rolling lawns and playing fields, not to mention buildings so stately they seemed designed to make him wonder whether he deserved to enter them. For three years it had been Edenic until J. started pursuing Robbie down its bluestone paths and lush bowers, ready to alight at any moment like a pigeon bearing the message *I will not be ignored by you, I will not be dismissed.* And even when J. wasn't physically present he accosted Robbie with phone calls and e-mails and notes through the campus mail, now waxing sentimental about their bond, now calling Robbie a callous little prick, now apologizing for the bitterness of his last note, now telling Robbie he couldn't dump him as easily as he assumed.

After weeks and then months of this agitation, Tonia Cantor had gotten as worn out as Robbie, since J. was confiding his every move to her. She pleaded with Robbie to *reach out* to J. and *give him satisfaction* and *show him a little compassion* because J. was *really suffering like a wounded animal bleeding on the roadside.* But with each new salvo and plea Robbie got increasingly frightened. He became convinced that any response would give J. encouragement to think there was hope for them when there wasn't. Plus he was angry that Tonia had suddenly become J.'s pity pimp. Of the three of them, it seemed, he was the only one capable of being mature about the situation (the phrase *being professional* also came to mind, even though he knew it was wrong) and soldiering on in the aftermath of a huge mistake, although J. and Tonia both had a decade on him.

He came to wish he'd never met either of them. He came to wish they'd both return to their usual extracurricular activities (writing articles for obscure Teutonic journals in J.'s case, and reading *Cosmo* for advice on underwire garments and aphrodisiacs in Tonia's) and leave him alone. When they refused, he didn't know what else to do, so he severed contact with both of them, which shocked shocked shocked Tonia in particular and only made them closer allies.

Finally, Clarissa seemed to arrive at her destination. She stopped in front of a four-story apartment building with a massive wrought-iron front door, pressed a button on the intercom, and waited. Twenty or so paces away, Robbie pretended to read the newspaper he'd smudged with his sweaty hands and tried not to stare excessively. After a moment she leaned toward the intercom and said something while brushing away a strand of hair from her face. Then the iron door opened and she disappeared as it thudded behind her.

Robbie assumed she'd reappear shortly but she didn't. After several minutes he worked up the courage to inch closer and snap pictures of the unprepossessing façade, making sure to include the house number to the side of the entrance. He was standing directly across from the building now, a bit faint from his jumpy pulse. Only now in the idle moment did the recklessness of his actions hit him. At any moment Clarissa could reemerge to look straight at him—and then what would he do? In the meantime he loitered like a thief. He considered texting Maize to tell her what he was up to but decided against it. Strangers had to detour around him on the narrow sidewalk and a few shot him suspicious looks. Who could blame them? He was suspicious of himself.

While he waited there he imagined what his mother might say about the situation: *Turnabout is fair play.* It was one of her favorite expressions when it came to actions against his father. But in this case it didn't apply. This wasn't turnabout. If anything this was a pathetic imitation of J. in his obsessive phase, though to Robbie's knowledge even J. hadn't used a camera when pursuing him.

Another half hour passed outside the apartment building, and then an hour, and then an hour and a half. He paced up and down the street to prevent his legs from falling asleep. After two hours the tedium set in fully—he was thirsty and tired and faintly grimy from the diesel exhaust of passing cars—and he longed for a hot shower as if he'd been running several miles instead of loitering on the same block. He hadn't consciously decided *enough already* any more than he'd first decided to *follow that woman*, but when the next taxi rolled around he raised his arm and jumped in the backseat with a profound sense of relief. It was only as he gave the driver his hotel address that he remembered he wouldn't have been able to find his way back alone if his life depended on it.

◆ ◆

Carlo was back serving breakfast the next morning. Although Robbie hadn't shaved and his shirt was wrinkled, he felt better prepared this time. He'd rehearsed a few Italian sentences beforehand, making Carlo guffaw when he mentioned his impending visit with his father and the fact that they weren't close anymore. (Guffawing was an odd reaction, Robbie thought, but better than nothing.) Carlo reported that his own father was dead, having had what appeared to be heart sickness. (He pointed to the center of his muscular chest.) Then he asked Robbie, would he like a personal tour of—*How did you say it in English?*—happy places before he left Rome? Some night after Carlo finished work? Before Carlo had to return to his mother's flat in the suburbs? Yes? Would Robbie like the names of these places in the meantime?

Yes, Robbie said. In thanks he touched Carlo on his square

shoulder gingerly and he tipped him double the cost of his breakfast.

"Wow. That's totally random," Maize wrote him later, after Robbie texted her about having spotted Clarissa. "I'm not sure I believe you."

"I think it's a sign," Robbie wrote.

"A sign of what?" she wrote back.

"I don't know," Robbie replied. "I'll have to get back to you."

"Is Clarissa a student?"

"Not that I know of. She sure doesn't dress like one."

Robbie couldn't think of a single woman on campus who wore makeup or high heels or a slinky silk dress like Clarissa's, even at night. Dressing down was a badge of intellectual pride for all the females at their college, except for a few French teachers and Tonia Cantor, who sometimes went so far in the other direction she looked displaced and tawdry, like a chanteuse who'd stayed up so late she'd failed to notice it was dawn, she was still wearing a boa, and her mascara had smeared.

Maize texted him, "What I'm trying to figure out is why your stepmother was hanging out at a university."

"She is *not* my stepmother. They are *not* legally married," Robbie replied, as though typing in his mother's voice.

"Whatever," Maize wrote back.

Since last night he himself had been trying to figure out what Clarissa was doing near the university. The mystery of her actions—her phantom appearance and disappearance while Robbie's father was at work—gave him a thrill that didn't really kick in till he got back to the hotel, where he ate alone and gluttonously in the dining room. He was starving for greater knowledge. His desire to explore the situation and see where it would lead felt almost scholarly to him. But when he hinted to Maize that he might return to the same café at the same time today, in the hope of following Clarissa again, she wrote, "Robbie! Come on. Do you really want to do that? Creepy." And when Robbie didn't respond, she added, "You're in one of the world's great cities and you're headed back to teeny tiny Rhode Island soon. There are better things to do with your time. And it's not like you won't be seeing her in a few days at your father's."

"Of course," he replied. He asked Maize what she was doing to pass the time at the bookstore but he barely skimmed her answer. He'd already made up his mind to return before he signed off.

Clarissa did show up at the café again, albeit an hour later than the day before. She crossed the same square, drawing the same swarm of male gazes, and walked exactly the same route Robbie remembered, though this time she was more casually dressed, in linen slacks and a blouse and flat shoes that helped her move faster across the cobblestones.

When she reached the same apartment building, she didn't go inside. She buzzed and spoke to the intercom and waited, pivoting in Robbie's direction, so that he had to turn his back and walk away. When he got to a distant storefront window he feigned engrossment in the goods on display, which seemed to belong to a medical supply company. There were wheelchairs and crutches and walkers and canes—all the paraphernalia of paralysis—as well as a male dummy wearing leg braces and a youthfully jaunty cap while carrying notebooks. Was he supposed to be a student? Robbie kept staring intently like someone having the horrific premonition of a disabled future. He willed himself to keep looking and waiting a few minutes before he allowed himself to stop.

When he dared glance back up the street toward Clarissa, she wasn't looking in his direction anymore. Not in the least.

She was embracing a tall young man who kissed her on the forehead and the nose as she tilted her head upward toward him, smiling beatifically. Then she kissed the man back, welting his cheek with her rosy lipstick.

Clarissa laughed as the man held her close to him, his muscular arm scissored around her waist. She wiped her lipstick off his cheek with her thumb and forefinger, firmly yet tenderly, like a mother cleaning the face of child who hasn't yet learned how to eat. They looked straight into each other's faces and spoke as she continued to wipe, wetting her thumb with her saliva. In that brief custodial moment it was as if no one else in the world existed for them or for Robbie, zooming in on them myopically. Tall and handsome and pressed to each other, the two made a lovely little island in the middle of dun-colored shabbiness, casting breezes toward the shores of a less fortunate coast. It was hard not to be transfixed.

But then Robbie blinked, and the rest of the world returned, and she was just his father's mistress touching another man on a gritty street corner.

That was when he remembered to raise his camera and take a shot.

They didn't notice. They had turned away from him and started moving in the opposite direction.

He used his camera to record the way they strolled—arm in arm down the street—and the way Clarissa's head fell onto the man's shoulder now and then as they walked, and the way they held hands across the table when they stopped at an osteria for lunch. The big square diamond on Clarissa's left hand glinted whenever it caught the light. By the time they'd finished their meal, Robbie had gotten off a dozen shots from various angles. Still they didn't notice him.

Robbie guessed the man was even younger than Clarissa—in his late twenties or thirty at the most. He had an unlined forehead and black hair and aqueous blue eyes that were especially striking in someone with dark coloring. His fine profile was nicely spoiled by a coarse nose, and his body was beefier than most of the men Robbie had seen in Rome so far. It looked like a body that made the ground shake if you were close enough to it. Although his leather jacket and jeans and T-shirt were nothing special, they gained stature from cloaking someone so big. Even if this man and Clarissa weren't so handsome together, they'd probably look superior due to their height alone.

Robbie felt his groin thrum. It titillated him whenever the man grasped Clarissa's hands in one of his big paws. At the same time it made him queasy. Desire had always rattled up a maelstrom in him—lust combined with fear combined with envy combined with a sense of utter hopelessness—but it was even more complicated now, looking at this magnificent specimen overshadowing his father, who was older and shorter and whose honor was being violated while his son watched.

When Clarissa and the man left the restaurant and walked back to the apartment together, they didn't embrace anymore. It was as if they'd spent their ration of affection for the day. Robbie decided he didn't need to see anything else for now. But he did follow Clarissa the next day and the day after, infused with a sense of tingling anticipation. When Maize e-mailed him, he wrote that he was "soaking up the local color" and "doing this and that" while he waited around for the reunion.

Clarissa didn't meet with the man again, as it turned out. But it hardly mattered to Robbie. The daily hunt gave him purpose and he had photos to prove he wasn't imagining what he'd seen. At night he asked the concierge to lock his camera in the hotel safe as if it were an heirloom.

◆◆

As it happened the pictures turned out wrong—oversized and in a weird format. Through miscommunication or willful misunderstanding on the part of a Via Barberini photo processor, the shots of Clarissa came back as mock postcards rather than regular prints. They were thick as cardboard, with the image of Clarissa and her man on one side and a blank space on the flip, bisected for addressing and writing vacation messages. A tacky tourist gimmick Robbie hadn't asked for—at twice the price of regular prints. And to make matters worse, the processor had made three copies of everything instead of the single set Robbie had ordered.

How annoying and frustrating that Robbie lacked the capacity to argue about it. In that helpless moment at the photo store it seemed his whole life could turn out that way—having just enough vocabulary to get embroiled in situations without knowing how to extract himself. He wished Tonia Cantor were around to help him with his meager language skills just then, to tell him the things he didn't know how to say. When she'd tipped her allegiance to J.—a switch she'd called *simple human sympathy for a complex and troubled person*—Robbie hadn't understood why and it scared him. It scared him even more when she divulged how J. had enlisted her help with an ambush: he'd asked Tonia to invite Robbie to her apartment for dinner so he could be there waiting, to have it out with Robbie in person.

It was good of Tonia to warn Robbie about that. But when she did it seemed imperative to get away from both of them as fast as he could.

"Why the *fuck* aren't you returning my calls? You're freaking me out here," Tonia said in one of her increasingly long-winded voice mails. She left five or six at a time because Robbie didn't answer her and because his machine kept cutting her off. Finally she got the drift and stopped calling.

Now he pored over the ridiculous pseudo-postcards, battening on details instead of the larger whole: the rose of Clarissa's lipstick; the shine of her gold earrings; the leather strand around the man's strong neck; their toned arms wrapped around each other's waists and shoulders as they strolled toward the osteria; the plumpness of their kneadable backsides; their mouths yawning in laughter when one of them said something amusing; their hands—the man's big and veined, Clarissa's smooth and long— touching each other's forearms for emphasis as they spoke. How superfluous. They were clearly enjoying each other's company without any hand signals. They were obviously hanging on each other's every word.

And all that lovely time, there was Robbie just outside their nimbus of contentment. Trying not to draw too close to be noticed. Watching and waiting for what would happen next, like a demoted god who saw everything but lacked the power to steer events.

It gave him a chill as he sat in his hotel room; it was like he'd been spied on rather than the other way around. Maize was right. It was creepy. It dredged up dank and unseemly emotions. Despite the fact that his philandering father deserved to be cuckolded by his much younger mistress, Robbie was offended for him. Clarissa was betraying not only his father but everything he'd cast off to be with her: his country, his house, his wife, Robbie himself. She was saying that none of those sacrifices mattered, that she could do anything she wanted to his family and they'd roll over. They were that weak and passive. The joke was on them.

Robbie felt his blood pressure spike as he contemplated it. Anger pulsed in his throat like something ready to rupture. At that moment Carlo rapped on his door with breakfast, making Robbie start in his seat. He took the knocks as a signal—an announcement from his conscience or someplace deeper than he could identify, calling him to action. He broke into a light sweat. *"Un momento, un momento!"* he shouted through the door. He paused a few seconds. Then he pulled off his shirt and pants and examined himself in the bureau mirror. He greeted Carlo wearing nothing but a towel around his waist, at once proud of his unusual brazenness and worried that he was acting half-deranged like Tonia Cantor—Tonia, whose entire demeanor more or less said, *Here I stand naked before you. How do I look?*

Carlo's eyes bugged at the sight of Robbie's bare torso. He was too startled to chirp his usual *"Buon giorno."* He hesitated before crossing the threshold into the room.

Slowly Robbie turned away from Carlo, showing him the smooth back that matched his hairless chest. He walked toward a window that was covered up like the windows in his mother's house. When he parted the curtains he felt his towel loosening. He resisted the impulse to tighten it and stood there bathed in the morning light. And when the towel fell to the floor he let it fall. He turned fully exposed to face Carlo, who had set down the breakfast tray and was moving toward him now with a widening grin.

◆ ◆

Although he had two full days to figure out what to do with the postcards, he couldn't fix on anything definite. No sooner did he imagine himself telling his father "Your girlfriend is a whore" than he pictured himself saying nothing and simply laying the postcards of Clarissa and her man on his father's lap, letting them speak for themselves. No sooner did he imagine this than he saw himself delivering the postcards anonymously to his father's office in an envelope marked CONFIDENTIAL, or leaving them behind in the apartment where his father would find them later—in a file folder or suit jacket or sock drawer—before he remembered that he didn't *know* where his father's suit jackets or sock drawers were anymore, and couldn't very well root around the apartment looking for them.

As Robbie trudged down Via Condotti toward his father's apartment for their reunion, he was still turning over his options. The postcards bulged in the breast pocket of his sport coat and beat against his chest like a second heart. Although it was too early for tourists to be out in force, he already felt claustrophobic from plowing through his own crowded thoughts. It didn't help to be passing one of the hotels he'd abandoned earlier in the week, wondering if anyone there would notice him looking even more dissatisfied now than when he'd left. When one of the valets nodded in his direction, he lowered his gaze to the pavement and picked up his pace.

That was how he'd responded whenever J. had flared into sight last semester. He'd stare at the ground intently as if searching for a dropped coin, not caring if he bumped into anyone so long as it wasn't J., whose survivor's instincts as an untenured professor stopped him from accosting Robbie in public. He kept walking myopically toward his destination. And he did the same thing when he saw Tonia, only he had to practically jog away because she cared far less about protocol than J. Rather than avoiding messy scenes, she embraced them.

How ironic it was, Robbie stalking Clarissa so soon after he himself had been pursued by J. Maybe surveillance was a condition of ardor: Robbie tracking Clarissa; J. and Tonia pursuing Robbie; Clarissa looking into the eyes of a man who wasn't her husband; Robbie's mother staring blankly out her living room window as she tried to chase thoughts of Robbie's father from her memory. Maybe that's what love was, a roundelay of hunts and substitutions, and who you ended up with wasn't your fated partner but whoever happened to be around whenever your energy gave out, as when the music died in a game of musical chairs and you pounced on the nearest seat. If there was a chair available at all. People wrote about love, and talked about love, and sang about love, and made metaphors about love all the time. But they didn't know what love was.

◆ ◆

Now he rang the buzzer of his father's apartment. Now he entered the elegant marbled lobby and took the gilded cage of a metal elevator to the top floor. When his father threw open the double doors of his penthouse, light flooded the corridor and half-blinded Robbie. All he could discern for a moment were three heavily backlit silhouettes in front of him, and before he knew it the largest of these was engulfing him in a bear hug while he stood there stiffly, worrying about the postcards getting crushed against his chest, nearly suffocating. When Robbie reminded himself to breathe, his father smelled exactly as he had when Robbie was a child, of talcum and cotton and some sort of evergreen. Tears sprang to his eyes as if his father's arms had squeezed them out of him by brute force. He was curious what he himself smelled like to his father. Was his scent familiar to him, too, or had the hormonal changes of adolescence rendered him unrecognizable?

"Roberto!" his father was saying loudly into his ear. "Roberto! Robertino!"

Finally he released Robbie and introduced him to the other two silhouettes on the threshold—first Concetta, the aproned maid, and then Clarissa, who startled Robbie by kissing him on both cheeks. "We're both so thrilled you're finally here," she said in a deeper voice than he'd imagined her having as he'd watched her. She took him by the forearm and guided him inside gently, as if he were a handicapped friend who might otherwise crash into walls.

Their apartment wasn't what he'd expected. Although it was large and expensive-looking, with many high-ceilinged rooms and thick moldings and open views toward distant hills, the furnishings didn't match his father. Gone were the brooding antiques Robbie remembered from the old man's offices and private rooms back home, replaced by streamlined sofas and chairs in light, soothing fabrics—ivory linens and cream velvets—with pale wood tables, tan cashmere throws, and bright silk pillows that popped against the neutral tones surrounding them. The long Italianate windows had no curtains or shades, maximizing the sunlight, and the doors to the terrace were open so that lush air wafted through the rooms, swirling over the inlaid floors and bouncing off the tall white bookcases, which were stocked with surprisingly serious titles—books Robbie had read in college or hoped to read in the near future.

Was this truly his father's home? Did his father really live here? *Lavish*, he could hear his mother say bitterly as if she were spitting, though its luxuriousness was more understated than that. In any case, Robbie had to admit to himself that it was appealing.

"Clarissa decorated this whole place herself," his father said, "from top to bottom, with nobody else's help."

"Oh, that's not true, Philip. Don't shortchange yourself."

Clarissa touched his father on the shoulder and turned a wide rectangular smile on Robbie. "Your father has great taste, but he thinks it's unmanly or something to care about furniture. He had a much bigger hand in this place than he admits."

Robbie returned Clarissa's smile. Clearly she was lying. The only room that looked at all like his father was his "home office" at the back corner of their apartment, which was exactly like his home office back in the States. It had none of the cool gliding modernity of the rest of the interiors. Instead there was a massive, ornately carved mahogany desk topped by a brass banker's lamp, and a tufted Chesterfield sofa in cognac-colored leather, and Louis XIV chairs in dark green chenille, and a Persian rug with muddy brown and ocher tones. The office windows were swathed three ways—with shades, sheers, and heavy curtains—just like the windows in his mother's house, and here too the shades were three-quarters down although it was daytime. At home almost all the natural light got sucked up by the décor, making it hard to read or eat or even breathe without turning on a lamp, and giving the whole place a clandestine quality, like a temple.

"Wow," he couldn't help saying as he looked over his father's office. "Let me guess who decorated *this* room."

Clarissa chuckled. "Yeah. We call it the grizzly bear's den, where your father hibernates with his bills and papers and invoices. No one is allowed to enter it, on penalty of death. Not even poor Concetta. She's forbidden to tidy it up."

"Drives Clarissa crazy," his father said.

"I don't care as long as we don't get bugs or mice. Everybody should have a room of one's own. At least one room." She rolled her eyes and scowled. "Would you listen to me? Like that's my original idea."

Robbie smiled wanly and nodded, recognizing the allusion.

But he couldn't look Clarissa in the face now, after staring at her so intently for days. When they returned to the dining room and the maid served them a breakfast frittata, it was Clarissa who gazed at him for a long moment. Then she said, "Is it terribly forward of me to say you look a lot like your father? I mean handsome, of course."

"Oh—thanks." Robbie glanced at an empty dining chair across the table and pursed his lips. "Most people say I favor my mother."

"They do?" his father said. "You're not at all like your mother. You don't even have her coloring."

"She must be a beautiful woman, then," Clarissa said.

"That's what most people say." He'd forgotten that Clarissa and his mother had never laid eyes on each other because his mother had so many negative opinions about Clarissa, whom she alternately called *your father's marital aid* and *the fair-haired nightmare from Cleveland.*

Robbie glanced over at his father, who had grown red-faced.

"So you're getting your degree this year?" Clarissa said. "Your father says you're a remarkable student."

Robbie said, "I don't know about that."

"Robbie is studying English," his father said. "The all-purpose major."

"That was my major in college," Clarissa said. "I'm the black sheep from a family of scientists. My parents run a research lab and all my siblings are doctors except for my brother, who's getting his master's in comp. lit."

"Her brother's a ladies' man," his father said. He winked at Robbie. "How are things going for you in that department?"

Robbie fidgeted in his chair. *That department?* They'd never discussed Robbie's inclinations before—it was one of a thousand uncovered subjects from the past five years—yet somehow he'd always assumed his father knew about him, and he wasn't about to blurt out the information now in front of a stranger. The one time he'd broached the subject with his mother her response was "I figured that," as if he'd revealed a preference for beef over chicken or dogs over cats or boxers instead of briefs, and they hadn't said another word about it. He understood most families didn't discuss sex. Yet the whole topic seemed especially sealed off by his father's wayward carnality, the way families of alcoholics rarely discussed liquor.

"Oh god, Philip. Please don't embarrass your poor son." Clarissa rolled her eyes and touched his father's forearm. "Nobody wants to talk about romance with his parents. I certainly didn't. Right?" She turned to Robbie.

"Who wants to talk about romance with *anyone?*" Robbie said, trying to mimic Clarissa's breezy tone. He could only be grateful to her for extricating him.

His father scowled and squinted simultaneously, as if constipated. Robbie recalled the expression. That was how his father looked whenever he needed something and got frustrated. It was oddly comforting to see it again. Then his father cracked a smile.

"All right, then, I'll rephrase it," his father said. "Do you have any *special friends* back at school?"

"Sure. My friend Maize," Robbie said. Strictly speaking, it was true; Maize was his most "special friend" by a mile. He could already imagine the conversation where he'd describe everything about this moment to her—not only this stilted exchange but every other detail he could summon, down to the ironed damask napkins.

"*Maize?*" his father said. "Is that a girl? What kind of hippie name is that?"

"It's very interesting," Clarissa said. "It sounds Native American."

"It sounds like *produce*," his father said.

"It's not Native American. Actually you've met her," Robbie said. He stiffened in his chair as if his own name had been insulted. "Back when you still lived in our house. Maize and I went to high school together."

"No—I did?" Like a child who'd been lightly slapped, his father raised his chin and blinked in mystification. The first time he'd met Maize years ago, he asked Robbie the very same question ("What the heck kind of name is that for a girl?") after having greeted her with a big smile and a hug hello in their living room. Later he commented to Robbie that Maize was a "cutie-pie" by way of heterosexual encouragement, and Robbie had stared at him flatly. He didn't want to recall any of that now—it still made him cringe—but it came back to him anyway.

Apparently his father had blacked out that whole episode like countless other things from his past life. *Out of sight, out of mind*, as Robbie's mother often said with fake stoicism when she spoke about her husband. But that was just something she said. That was possible only if you were the one who'd escaped; the people who stayed behind were left to dust the same old memories again and again like unpaid janitors.

"You really should hear your father brag about you," Clarissa said, startling Robbie out of his reverie. "He tells everyone you're at the top of your class. He says you never stop working, just like him. Chip off the old block and all that."

"Oh," Robbie said.

"He just made Phi Beta Kappa and he's in the running for valedictorian," his father said.

How on earth did his father know that? Had the dean of students sent a copy of his congratulation note all the way to Rome? Certainly Robbie hadn't told him. He hadn't even said anything about it to his mother or Maize.

"So you're brilliant *and* modest," Clarissa said. "That's refreshing. Pardon me for saying it, but so few gifted young men are. They don't know how to handle it. They offer up their genius for your admiration and heaven help you if you don't genuflect." She laughed softly. "It's sort of funny if you're in the mood for it."

Robbie shrugged at the silver candlesticks. When a silence fell over the table except for the distant clatter of Concetta in the kitchen, Clarissa asked about his impending thesis and he suddenly felt obliged to fill the void. He talked about his senior project on *Ulysses*, the Molly Bloom soliloquy in particular, and the parallels between that final section and the opening chapters of Proust. He described his research on early modern painting and the Dada manifesto and threw in asides about Tristram Shandy and Svevo (whom he'd never heard of before Tonia Cantor) and he chattered about ready-mades and Beckett and Duchamp. As he heard himself rambling he blushed, shamefully aware that he was acting like one of those young men Clarissa had just mentioned, not merely defeating the silence over the table but also, he suspected, justifying his expensive education to his businessman father, who worshipped productivity and loathed the idea of wasted time.

Why did Robbie still care about pleasing him? Old force of habit? Years ago his father would come home from the office, bear-hug Robbie, and greet him with the question "What did you accomplish today?" instead of simply saying hello. Robbie had learned to have an answer even if he'd done nothing.

By the time he stopped speaking Clarissa was leaning toward him over the dining table, bright-eyed and alert as a bird who'd located something shiny and delectable. His father sat erect with his nostrils flaring in a barely suppressed yawn. How ridiculous that the sight of his father's boredom could still wound Robbie's pride. How absurd.

"What amazingly complicated connections," Clarissa said. "Amazingly sophisticated. It's hard to believe you're an under-graduate." Her fingers drummed on the table and her voice rose in excitement. "You know, Virginia Woolf put me off Joyce more than she should have years ago. She was such an awful snob about his work. Do you know what she called *Ulysses*? Underbred! Can you believe that? You make me want to reread it immediately."

"That's amazing," Robbie said.

"Are you going to go to graduate school?" Clarissa said.

"I'm not sure." Robbie looked back at the tabletop and hoped the subject would drop. But his heart was also fluttering pleasantly as if a cheer had gone up in his chest. Clarissa seemed genuinely fascinated by his outburst—a real audience—and she was stimulating to talk to, unlike his parents, who'd always regarded his cerebral side as an impediment to common sense. They always seemed to be waiting to point out how naïve he was in the world outside of books.

"Graduate school in English," his father said. "That wouldn't get you anything except a job as a professor."

"You make yourself sound anti-intellectual, Philip." Clarissa raised her eyebrows. "I think it would be great to be a professor—having a captive group of bright young people write down everything you say like apostles."

Was that how J. and Tonia had viewed Robbie? At least at first, when Robbie was so eager to learn from them? What a shock it must have been when he announced he didn't require their instruction anymore.

"I'm just saying," Robbie's father said, "that's it's useful to join the real world and trim your eyelashes."

"I guess you could say that." Clarissa turned to Robbie again and said, "You know your father. Ever the pragmatist. Wake up and smell the espresso."

Robbie nodded and grinned. He didn't completely disagree with his father, much as he sometimes fantasized about an academic life. When he considered J. and his fusty colleagues, what had once seemed romantic now looked like slow desiccation. It reminded him of the line about Mr. Casaubon in *Middlemarch*: that if you put a drop of his blood under a magnifying glass you'd find nothing but semicolons and parentheses. No wonder someone juicy and fervent like Tonia Cantor was going crazy in such an environment.

"I was thinking maybe I'd try to get a job in publishing," Robbie said.

"Book publishing," his father said, "or new media?"

Robbie was stumped; he didn't know the answer, having never given it sufficient thought, so he said, "Books."

"Hmm." His father laid his fork on his plate. "They don't pay much in book publishing except at the top levels."

"I don't care. Book publishing. Yes. Books." Robbie tried to fix a hard, challenging stare on his father but then his eyes flickered away to the tablecloth. "Or maybe, um," he said, "maybe magazines."

"The important thing is that you do what you love," Clarissa said. "Right? You'll succeed at whatever you're passionate about."

"Right. Sure." Robbie nodded twice. As he watched Clarissa take his father's hand, either in solidarity or a gentle warning to lay off his son, he wondered what she herself was passionate about. Why would a young, pretty, intelligent, and—he had to admit it—thoroughly charming woman like Clarissa throw in her lot with a workaholic businessman who made her move to another continent? Why would she consent to be the woman from his father's ugly air-mailed photos—the blonde who embraced her shorter lover and smiled broadly again and again, but who never looked quite at home in her surroundings? If her motive was mere gold digging, as Robbie's mother claimed, she'd sold herself cheap. His father was hardly a captain of industry. On a strictly mercenary level she could have done better.

No. It couldn't be that simple, much as he wanted it to be. Clarissa must have really loved his father—at least at the start— to sacrifice so much of herself. Now and then you came across heedless souls like Clarissa and Tonia Cantor, who splurged their emotional currency without worrying about future impoverishment. You had to admire them even if they scared you to death.

Then again, Clarissa wasn't pure at all. He touched his jacket so the postcards scraped against his chest again. He leaned toward her heat and then leaned back against the chair as she spoke.

"Your literacy will be useful whatever you do," she was saying. "I admire erudite people like you, with the drive for scholarship." She sighed and shook her head. "Though I read a lot—"

"She reads constantly," his father said.

"—I'm not good at writing about it or doing what you just did, Robbie, you know? Synthesizing things. Something essential always gets lost."

"Clarissa is a painter," his father said, as if that explained it.

"Sort of. Not an accomplished painter," she said.

"She's terrific."

"Ah, sweetheart?" She turned to Robbie and said, "Your father's a *wee* bit biased." She laughed.

"See for yourself. Those are two of her paintings there." His father pointed to the left wall.

"Oh." Robbie dimly recalled his father mentioning something about Clarissa's paintings in one of his letters, as if selling her artistic side to his cultured son, but at the time he'd ignored it. Even now he found it unwelcome—information he didn't want to synthesize—like the undeniable current of kindness in practically everything Clarissa had said today, and the fact that she was easier to converse with than his father or his mother. Her gentle wit and self-deprecation reminded him of Maize's. They might have been friends if she weren't his father's girlfriend.

A small shudder quaked in him from someplace mysterious. He opened his mouth to ask Clarissa about her training, then he stopped himself. He followed his father's pointer to the dining room wall and found something unexpected—not the dilettante paintings Clarissa had prepared him for, with sentimental nature scenes of waves and sunsets or muddy abstractions. Instead there were two matching portraits of a young man and a young woman against pale gray backgrounds. The outlines of their heads and bodies were at once clear and indistinct. Competing lines reverberated around their heads like loose haloes and inside their torsos, too, as if Clarissa had multiple ideas of who she wanted the figures to be, drew the boldest strokes around her original perceptions, and let alternative ghostly versions coexist alongside them on the canvas. The two portraits looked finished yet forever in flux—evolving and subject to change. The only part that seemed solid—crisply etched and fixed—were the legs raised in forward motion, as if this boy and girl could walk from this canvas to another any minute they decided to make the leap.

Robbie's gaze lingered. For the moment he lacked any response besides "Huh. Huh." It was one thing to say flattering things about the apartment furniture and another to exclaim over Clarissa's talent.

Clarissa spoke to break his focus. "Wow. Look at the time!" she said. "I'd better go check on Concetta. I can't imagine what's taking her so long with the dessert." She rose and wrapped her arms around Robbie's father's shoulders from behind, like a soft sweater. "My poor birthday boy, having to wait for his cake."

"Hold off on that for now," his father said. "I need a moment alone with my son. We have a private matter to discuss."

"We do?" Robbie said.

"Okay. Whenever you two are ready," Clarissa said.

"Man-to-man business," his father said. "Not for a woman's ears." He grinned.

"Right-o." Clarissa cupped her ears and turned conspiratorially to Robbie, speaking in a southern belle accent. "Mah *delicate* woman's ears just shatter at the sound of anything serious, according to Big Daddy here." She smiled and said, "I'll go get lunch started while you chat."

"Don't—no," Robbie said. Alarm was buzzing through him suddenly. Did he really have to be alone with his father now, after so many years? "I can't stay for lunch."

"No?" Clarissa looked startled, like a little girl whose new doll had just been snatched from her hands. "No? I thought we'd have the whole day with you."

"My flight leaves this afternoon," Robbie said.

"Well," his father said. "It's a workday, anyway. Come along then, Robbie." He gestured stiffly like a receptionist in a doctor's waiting room. *This won't hurt a bit.*

Robbie followed him to the back of the apartment, toward his office, his legs quivering as he walked. He hoped this was only about handing over the tuition check and nothing more. In the long hallway he touched the photos in his breast pocket and he thought, *Now or never,* only Clarissa's wounded expression had made him even more muddle-headed than when he'd arrived.

His father closed the office door behind them and said, "Sit down, Robbie. Let's have a heart-to-heart."

Heart-to-heart, man-to-man: the kind of cheesy phrasing Robbie heard only on bad TV or when his father went into patriarch mode. Clarissa was smart to mock it; after all these years it still made Robbie wince.

He sat primly in the corner of the office, on the Chesterfield sofa, and waited for his father to speak. Momentarily he considered extending his arm over the space between them and passing his father a photo. But his father broke his concentration by moving even farther away toward his desk.

"Before I forget," his father said. He opened a drawer and drew out a large leather-bound ledger onto his desktop. He carefully tore out a check from its perforated binding, but he didn't hand it to Robbie. Instead he left it there and joined him on the sofa. The cushion sighed as he lowered himself on it just a foot or so away.

"Well," he said. "Here we are, father and son. I'm grateful to have this moment alone with you."

"Yes," Robbie said. "Sure." But apparently that wasn't enough assurance for his father.

"Grateful to have my handsome and brilliant son with me again today, on my birthday, after so much time." He began to reach over toward the top of Robbie's head, with his hand curled, but he paused as if unsure of himself now that Clarissa wasn't around to smooth things over, and Robbie recoiled as if avoiding a jab.

His father cleared his throat. Robbie leaned back against the arm of the sofa to clear his head. He touched the stiff photos in his breast pocket again as if they were armor.

"I hope you know that I've missed you," his father said, "and that I love you. And you know that your mother loves you more than anyone. You will always be our son no matter what has happened."

"Well," Robbie said. "Obviously." His throat tightened. This seemed like a warm-up for a performance he didn't want to attend. "Well."

His father inhaled deeply and said, "How is your mother these days?"

"She's fine," Robbie said. "Considering."

"Is she getting out much? Seeing people?"

"Sure," Robbie said automatically. What he meant was that she was keeping company with him during school vacations, and with her maid five days a week, and with herself the rest of the time. After the separation she'd cut herself off from her few friends. But when Robbie saw the expectant look on his father's face it occurred to him he'd misunderstood the question.

"Are you asking me if Mom's, um, seeing *men*?" Robbie had to stop himself from scoffing. "Um, no. The answer to that is no."

The last time Robbie had broached that subject with his mother she'd said, "Men? You must be joking. I'd rather have a root canal."

"I'm sorry to hear that." His father frowned. "I'm genuinely sorry to hear that. It's high time your mother moved on with her life."

"It's not easy for everyone." Robbie shrugged, then felt his blood pressure rising. What the hell did he mean to signal with a shrug? "You know, especially after being so badly screwed."

There. After years of waiting to say something like that, it had slipped out easily. He didn't know quite how it happened—how he lost the self-control he'd maintained since the separation. Perhaps it was mere proximity or maybe his father's sudden turning up of the heat—all his mawkish declarations of love love love—had gotten him woozy. Whatever. Yet now that Robbie had said it he was flabbergasted. He was supposed to pick up his check with minimum fuss and deposit his postcards and leave. But since his dining room monologue he'd gotten unmoored. He heard himself breathing and looked down at his hands, which had curled into fists.

"I will admit that I could have handled my departure better—much, much better," his father said. "I'll be the first person to admit that." He nodded gravely. "I want you to know that I asked your mother for a divorce several times before Clarissa came into the picture and she refused me. Did she tell you that? Several times, and she always said no. I felt trapped. I don't know—I panicked."

"I'm not sure I believe that," Robbie said. He felt himself shrug again. In a small voice he said, "But I guess none of it matters now."

"Yes it does, Robbie. It matters a lot. Listen to me. I didn't want it to turn out like this. I always wanted to be close to you and your mother, but I thought I had responsibilities that came first. I didn't get to finish college like you, you know. I had to drop out of Columbia because my father was a drunk and we couldn't afford it. He died with huge debts I had to pay off for years and I never wanted that to happen to you. I know I was obsessive about that—I admit it. I wanted you to have everything. Everything I didn't have. So I worked two full-time jobs when your mother and I had you, and when I started my own business I thought if I just worked hard and made enough money everything would be okay. We would always be safe. Things would take care of themselves . . ."

"Dad," Robbie said. He put up one hand like a stop sign and then the other. "Please. Don't."

What was his father doing? Why was he doing it now? Why had he saved it all up for this moment when he'd had five whole years to put it in a letter or something, and how could Robbie stanch it? He supposed he couldn't, any more than he could stop himself at the dining table when he'd had an audience.

". . . Your mother and I were happy for a while, and when we couldn't get along anymore I thought, *At least I have a son. I have my son.* But by the time I left you would hardly say hello to me anymore, no matter how much I tried to hug you, like you'd taken your mother's side and I was already the enemy."

Robbie felt himself start shaking. What his father said was true, true enough. Robbie wished he would stop. His words spilled out in a torrent, and maybe they were Robbie's fault because he'd dammed them up for months and years by refusing to communicate—refusing to give his father what Tonia Cantor cloyingly called *satisfaction*. Had Robbie foolishly thought he could get away with that forever? That all of it would just go away if he ignored it long enough?

". . . But it wasn't always like that with you," his father was saying. "Listen to me, Robbie. Are you listening? When you were little you could never get enough of me. You'd sneak downstairs when I ate late suppers and cling to me while your mother slept. You had these pajamas—these baby blue pajamas with the feet attached. And I thought, *Whatever else happens at least I have a son. I have my son. My little Robbie. My—*"

His father's voice broke, and his throat clogged, and before Robbie knew it great heaving sobs were emanating from his father's lungs and his face was an utter mess.

This was not what he'd come here for. He'd come here for his education—the funds to continue his education so he could graduate. His impulse was to stand up and leave the room, at least until his father got hold of himself, and perhaps go further and leave the apartment completely. But he still hadn't gotten his check and his father kept weeping more and more loudly—some wounded-animal sound from the center of his gut—and instead Robbie found himself inching toward him slowly on the sofa, as cautiously as if approaching an electrified border fence, close and then closer still, until his father's hand was resting on the top of his head like a benediction.

All of it was happening, yet it wasn't. There was a sense of unreality, a little the way nights with J. had always felt to him, because during them he'd think how strange it was that moments ago he wasn't doing anything of the kind and in another moment he'd be back in his regular life, which had nothing to do with them. And always the same numbness afterward—not only because it was 4:00 a.m. and he was walking back to his dorm in the dark, but because the solitude that puddled around him scared him even more than anything he'd just done with his body, and he felt alienated, as if in a foreign country he couldn't escape, and he wanted to cry out.

He leaned toward the noise—his father's hand and his threatening body. He let the top of his head be stroked. His father's hand was hot. Something was breaking loose above him and for a second he thought of a chick straining toward a lightbulb in a hatchery, arduously, messily freeing itself from a shell.

He closed his eyes and willed himself not to think about anything for a second. He didn't want to think and he didn't want to remember. But there were the blue pajamas his father mentioned, and his father stroking the little boy's head the way he stroked it now. They were alone together. His mother was asleep and his father was eating dinner from a hot plate. Robbie was standing beside the kitchen table in his pajamas, sucking his thumb and observing his father raptly. And then the mirage evaporated and another one emerged: Robbie pacing the dark house in the middle of the night years later—was it ninth grade?— and approaching the home office, where he discovered his father weeping more violently than he wept now, as a television set chattered obliviously on a console. Robbie had stood there unnoticed and paralyzed in the hallway, not knowing what to do and terrified of knowing more. A sepia glare surrounded his father, a morass of complication and regret beyond the threshold. What was he crying about? Robbie hung back. Quietly he'd tiptoed to his room and gone to sleep as if he'd never seen it. His father left a few months later.

"When is Dad's flight getting in?" he'd asked his mother that afternoon when she'd picked him up from school.

"That's the thing," she'd said, staring straight through the windshield at the parking lot. "It isn't."

He didn't cry then. He wasn't crying now. But something inside him spasmed as he sat folded against his father's chest. He heard himself making strange little sounds—sighs and gasps—and he supposed he should speak to extract himself, but all that came out was "Daddy" mumbled into the old man's dress shirt like a secret.

It was Clarissa who rescued them by knocking lightly on the door and calling, "Hello? Everything okay in there?"

At the sound they separated. His father cleared his throat and wiped his eyes. In a new and chipper tone he called, *"Avanti."*

The door opened a crack and Clarissa's smiling blonde head poked into the office. "Sorry to interrupt you guys, but you have a birthday surprise that refuses to wait." She withdrew her head and whispered something into the hallway before a different head filled the gap again.

The moment Robbie saw it, he drew in a breath so sharp he nearly gasped.

It was the man from the photos in Robbie's pocket. Clarissa's boyfriend. Her lover.

"Look who's here. Late as usual," his father said.

"Happy birthday, Philip," the man said in a rich baritone. "I'm far too polite to ask how old you are." He flashed a smile full of big white teeth.

His father laughed and said, "You son of a bitch. You nearly missed my cake."

Robbie started laughing, too, but differently from his father— loose and trilling and nearly hysterical. He couldn't help himself. His father and Clarissa darted their eyes at each other in curiosity.

"I made up for my tardiness by bringing you a nice gift." The door opened fully and the beautiful man strode into the room, wearing the same jeans he had in the photos, which Robbie had the wherewithal to shove deep into his pocket. He was carrying a small gold-wrapped package the size of a book. He gave it to Robbie's father before turning to extend his hand. "Hello. Pleased to meet you," he said. "You must be Philip's son. I'm George."

"Clarissa's late brother," his father said.

"I prefer *errant* to *late*," George said. His large pillowy hand engulfed Robbie's. "Your father makes me sound like a visitation."

Clarissa followed him into the room and said, "My little brother's doing graduate work in Rome this year, before he returns to the wilds of Berkeley, California."

"My studies are a dodge—a pretext," George said to Robbie, still smiling. He drew closer so that he stood with his waist at Robbie's eye level. "An excuse to have a university pay for me to hang out with my big sister in Europe."

George grabbed Clarissa and embraced her exactly as he had on the street. But this time Clarissa smirked.

"Yeah, right." She slackened against her brother's hip like a Siamese twin. "Don't believe it, Robbie. George is very ambitious. He's been working extremely hard this year."

"Even if what he does isn't a real job," Robbie's father said.

George left Clarissa's side and threw his arms around Robbie's father like a lover, kissing him noisily and repeatedly on both cheeks. Between kisses he said, "I adore you, Philip, even if you're a philistine." His father laughed at the insult and said, "You slovenly rat," pretending to punch George in the ribs, as if this were a comic routine they'd performed many times before.

Robbie realized he hadn't said anything since the interruption. He was stupefied. He should say something. But when he willed himself to speak all he could manage was "Oh—oh."

"You'll be getting a degree soon, too, right?" George said to him.

Robbie nodded. He twitched out a grin. He felt himself listing to the left. He told himself to sit down and compose himself before he remembered he was already sitting.

The bantering voices—his father, Clarissa, her boyfriend who was her brother—caromed around Robbie like projectiles he needed protection from, with George's words registering the sharpest. *Jesus,* Robbie said to himself, *wait till I tell Maize about this,* at roughly the moment George was saying, "I can't believe what a morbid room this is, Philip. Like a funeral parlor. I'm amazed you get anything done in here without falling asleep. My birthday gift to you should've been a halogen lamp." In a jocular tone Robbie's father told George to mind his own business. He wasn't changing a thing. His office suited him fine exactly as it was.

It was a relief to be following them out of the office and down the hallway, though Robbie's legs were still shaking. They walked back to the dining room, where a large white cake lay waiting, studded with many candles. The maid lit them while Clarissa got fresh napkins out of the sideboard. Clarissa rested her head on his father's shoulder, appreciating the flaming cake, and when she reached her arm in Robbie's direction he flinched— as if she were accusing him rather than inviting him to join them on their side of the table.

Clarissa thanked the maid in Italian and asked her to take a picture of all of them. Even with his faulty language skills, Robbie could understand that much.

He might have positioned himself on his father's flank, but instead he stood next to Clarissa. Gently she pressed herself against him.

The flash went off. How soft and warm Clarissa's body was, with a sweet scent that wasn't overwhelming—vanilla or almond or a combination of the two. Robbie found himself on the end of a chain of linked torsos, one body over from his father, who was being embraced by George again. The maid pantomimed for them to huddle closer so she could get all of them into the shot behind the cake.

Three times the flash fired. Robbie supposed he was smiling. He was dazzled and he'd had little experience with this kind of huddle. Again and again the flash went off.

His father looked over at him and said, "I am going to need your help," and for a hot second Robbie didn't know what he meant. In his stupefaction the simplest things eluded him. But of course he was talking about the candles.

One final flash. The four of them were leaning over the cake with puckered mouths, extinguishing the tiny flares together. Or that's what it looked like, that's what the photograph would show for posterity. But only his father and Clarissa and George were making wishes as they sent little gusts in the same direction. At the moment the maid froze the image Robbie was somewhere else—already anticipating his impending exit, the hugs at the door, the promises not to be a stranger, his father's murmured exhortation to please remember what they'd discussed, and the tremor in Clarissa's voice as she said, "This was too brief! We didn't get enough of you! Promise you'll come back soon, promise!" and Robbie pushing away with thanks and claims that he must go, really he must get to the airport, sorry but it was time.

At the moment the picture froze Robbie wasn't blowing on the candles like the others. He was still holding his breath.

◆ ◆

Robbie was dazed when he hit the open air outside his father's building. Now that it was midday the streets simmered with tourists and genuine Romans carrying parcels, calling out to the children who outpaced them, bustling to offices or appointments on exquisite shoes. The sun struck everything equally with a pitiless light. There was no cooler side of the street to retreat to for a stroll, so Robbie supposed he should head back and finish packing.

He resisted taking the same route that had led him to the apartment, although the familiar way would certainly be more efficient. His thoughts were still muzzy—bleary as if wadded up with batting. He lacked the will to text Maize and file a report about the reunion at the moment, which might have been just as well. Only when he was several blocks away did the details start to sink in, through the glaze of fear and surprise that had coated him while they first appeared: The way Clarissa and his father had touched each other whenever they spoke, just the way she and George had done in the postcards Robbie was still carrying. The way Clarissa and George sandwiched his father in an embrace as they'd joked with him and leavened him, summoning a blissful childish look on his face that Robbie had never seen before and had probably never worn himself.

No wonder his father wanted to be around Clarissa forever. She made it all seem so easy. Some people had the gift for intimacy while others didn't, despite their other good qualities like brains or taste or a knack for numbers. The talent for intimacy wasn't parceled out equally or rationally. It appeared in unlikely places yet it was absent where it seemed likely to thrive. Not that it was a necessity. Not that you couldn't live without it. But like liquor or a first kiss, once you got a taste it was hard not to want it again, even if you were incapable of handling it well. Outside its fragile aura the rest of life looked drab.

Now Robbie stopped in his tracks and took the postcards out of his pocket. He leaned against a stony façade to study them again. Photos were supposed to be documentary evidence, but Clarissa and George looked different in these pictures than they had close up: sexier for their strangeness yet less vibrant. They looked like simulations of themselves, the stereotypical blonde and the hunk. All Robbie had captured accurately was the unstinting affection they felt for each other, the unselfconscious ease with which they touched and smiled and raucously laughed and leaned close as if listening to blood secrets. Their deep animal connection requiring no fear or vigilance—something Robbie had confused with sex—as when members of a species reunite far from predators to move gracefully as one body.

Robbie had never had that with anybody. Not even with J. in their most private moments together. Not even with Maize. Not even briefly.

When his towel had fallen in front of Carlo, he hadn't done what he'd intended—turned to show himself fully with the light streaming around him. A sudden chill hit his naked torso. Carlo took a step toward him and Robbie grabbed the towel off the floor to cover himself again. He said *"Scusi"* and dashed past him to the bathroom to look for a robe. He closed the bathroom door and locked it behind him, repeatedly calling out, "*Scusi*, excuse me, *scusi*, excuse me," through the wood until Carlo understood and finally left him alone with the breakfast tray. Even with the bathrobe on he continued to shiver.

One of the last things Tonia Cantor had said into his message machine was "You have a cold streak, you know that? You need to look out for that."

And just before he'd escaped J. forever—left him so cruelly and brutally it made the backs of his own teeth ache—J. had said, "You know, I don't think I can love you the way you need to be loved," in the darkness of his bedroom, and Robbie had been too dumbfounded to reply—pretended he was asleep and hadn't heard him—and J. had let him say nothing, as though one of them had farted in bed and they'd silently, politely agreed to let it dissipate into nothingness.

Maybe J. had loved him and Robbie had ignored it, simply because he had nothing to give back. Maybe he had felt for Robbie painfully but Robbie had been too distracted, staring at his schoolbooks and term papers and anything else that would keep him from it as well as certain truths about himself. His cowardice. His laziness. His immaturity. Robbie could see that possibility now, for a fleeting moment, as distinctly as if it were an object before him to be captured by his useless camera. He could see that J. deserved more and also that, given the chance to replay their affair, he'd probably do nothing differently despite everything he'd learned.

Now he kept moving. He passed one of the hotels he'd stayed at before proceeding to his current accommodation. Perhaps any fool would have noticed before now that with each new room he was drawing nearer and nearer to his father's apartment, but Robbie hadn't. He crossed to the opposite side of the street, blushing slightly and hoping no one from the staff would recognize him as he moved swiftly past. He didn't know exactly where he was. Take a few unfamiliar steps and he could end up anywhere.

He got lucky, though. When he reached the next street there was his latest hotel in the distance. He made a beeline for it. He was as focused on it as when he'd been following Clarissa, whose perfume lingered in his nostrils and whose image remained in his sweaty palms.

But he didn't go inside just yet. He sat on a travertine bench outside the hotel, looking at the postcards again, finding nothing new but deciding that he didn't want to be alone with them in his room all the hours before departure. He didn't want to carry them around anymore or travel with them but he didn't want to throw them out, either. He kept staring.

On the next bench over, some other tourist was being photographed. In German or Dutch the photographer called out something, probably instructions to smile.

Robbie imagined that if someone snapped a picture of him right now it would look like this: a young student tourist in Rome. And under that picture another picture: a tourist in the life that came before and the life that came afterward, innocent of local customs and insecure about his command of alternate routes and idioms, no matter how many books he read.

The midday sun continued burning down. Robbie was sweating. He stood among the passersby who didn't acknowledge him. His heart was pounding and he felt a jagged edge of panic about to surface. But there was no reason for it. He had no reason to rush. Maybe he should wander to a store and buy himself something with his spare euros while he still had the chance.

Instead he sat on the bench with the postcards and took out a pen. A week ago he might have defiled these useless images of Clarissa and George or tossed them into a garbage can. Now he turned them over to the flip side and addressed them. Two to J., two to Tonia Cantor, one to himself at his college address, and one to Maize, who'd get the whole story if not the other things he'd promised her before this trip. In a moment he'd dial her cell or leave a voice mail for her saying, *I failed and I have something important to tell you.*

Although it occurred to him to write something like "Wish you were here" on the postcards, he left the message portions blank. He would send them incomplete. He could picture J.'s and Tonia's bemused expressions as they flipped the cards over again and again, studying them, vaguely understanding that they'd received a souvenir but not quite knowing of what.

Of course there'd be a long delay before the cards reached them. The mail in Italy was notorious. Robbie would be home and back in his regular life before anyone got his message.

He didn't know the first thing about the Italian post, so he surrendered the cards to the hotel's front desk. He tipped the concierge lavishly to distract him from looking at them in his presence. The concierge was pleased to receive his cash, and when he leaned over his desk to shake Robbie's hand and assure him that his mail would go out *subito*, immediately, Robbie noticed a lavender carnation pinned to his starched white dress shirt and a lavender necktie that matched the flower.

He recalled that lavender and white were Tonia Cantor's school colors. He knew it only because Tonia Cantor had waylaid him in her academic robes at last year's commencement ceremony, where she'd marched in the procession and loudly cheered the Italian majors taking their degrees. Robbie had attended to avoid going home to his mother's house for a few more days before the long hot summer began.

That was fourteen months ago. All three of them had been there that day, Robbie and Tonia and J., and they were all still speaking to each other because nothing bad had happened between them yet.

He remembered that as he packed up his little silver car and prepared to leave the campus, Tonia had bounded up to him carrying a spray of lilacs browned by the sun. She looked flushed with excitement, as if it were her own graduation, and it made Robbie curiously sad before he pushed the feeling away.

"Look at these! Look how lovely!" she'd said, pointing to the lilacs and raising them above her head like a torch. "They match my gown, you see? The colors of my university. Now I'm giving them to you as a present on this wonderful day."

"Oh," Robbie said. "Thank you. Are you sure?"

"Of course I'm sure."

He thanked her again though he knew they wouldn't survive the long drive ahead. Tonia Cantor kissed him on both cheeks, in the European fashion, and then did it again for good measure.

"We must stay in touch next year, Robbie. We must!" Tonia said. "And now that you're no longer my student you must call me Tonia."

He promised her easily, and nodded. He slammed the trunk of his car shut and got in the overheated driver's seat. Tonia was still talking as he closed the door behind him, turned on the ignition, and revved the engine. He smiled at her and lowered the window halfway to be polite. He heard himself agreeably chirping, "Yes, yes," to whatever she was saying, not knowing if it was the appropriate response to what she asked, but from the look of her it was. Even as he pulled away she continued speaking to him and he kept saying *Yes.*

He gave Tonia another look as he shifted gears and engaged his blinker and rolled down the long driveway that led from campus, picking up speed as the distance between them grew. In the rearview mirror she was gesticulating in his direction— waving at him and waving some more. The wind lifted the flaps of her robe and the light shimmied up from the asphalt. She looked wild and beautiful in that moment, like a classical hero- ine or the priestess of a minor religion. As he drove ahead she got smaller and smaller, and from far away it was hard to tell if she was bidding him farewell or welcoming him in.

Part
Three

···

Robbie's mother assured Maize the tasks would be simple: identify and separate, discard and pack up. On the phone she'd told Maize that they'd ransack the fourteen rooms of her house (including the maid's room and the basement) like methodical looters, but they'd leave the dining room and kitchen and one of the living rooms intact because she needed someplace to park herself before the big move.

Maize considered her orders manageable—a cinch compared to the work she'd been doing the past year—yet it still made her fidget the closer she got to the house. As she rode in the taxi from the train station, wedged in the backseat with Robbie and his new boyfriend, the backs of her sweaty thighs stuck to the vinyl beneath them. An early summer breeze lashed the car windows yet no one was saying much, and the cramped pneumatic silence felt like riding in an elevator with strangers rather than her best friend and Daniel, who'd jockeyed to take the aisle seat next to Robbie during the train ride up and who now held Robbie's hand as he stared fixedly out the taxi window at the sliding scenery they rolled past, a blur of foliage interrupted by houses with stone walls and brick walls and split-rail fences, by velvety green lawns and midnight blue BMWs, by banks of red and white and coral impatiens flaring in the breeze like tiny flags from unfamiliar nations.

It was a startling sight even to Maize now, coming from the

gray-and-brown city block where she and Robbie lived. You didn't see crisp, stark colors like this outdoors in Manhattan or probably in the heathery countryside, either. They were the colors of someplace in between.

"So there it is—that's it," Robbie said when the taxi reached his mother's long, winding street. He pointed to an unfamiliar white clapboard colonial about fifty yards back from the road and said, "Close but no cigar." The driver misunderstood and thought they'd reached their destination—jerked to a sudden stop so that Robbie had to apologize and tell him no, not just yet, five houses farther down on the opposite side, he'd let him know when they got to the right place.

In Maize's many years of captivity in this town, through elementary school and middle school and the slog of high school, she'd never noticed the house Robbie had just pointed out—the house where his mother would be moving soon—though she'd undoubtedly passed it many times when she'd visited him: a perfectly tidy if shrunken facsimile of his mother's current residence, as if it were a scale model of the life she thought she'd be living, within easy walking distance of the grander place she was giving up, which was comforting or dispiriting, depending on how you looked at it.

Maize glanced over at Robbie, who was smirking at the new house from the backseat. Over a month ago, when he'd informed Maize that his mother had, in her wisdom, up and sold his childhood home without consulting him and was buying another property in the same town and the same neighborhood and on the same street, just a few doors down, he twitched so much telling her that he looked like he was having a seizure. Maize insisted he sit on the Ikea sofa in the kitchen (which was also their living room) while she poured him cheap wine and cobbled together a pasta dinner for them both, although she herself had just had another awful day at work and was tired.

"Five doors away," Robbie had said to her that night. "I mean, why bother?"

Maize had shrugged. "I guess your mother wants a change and figures it's better than nothing."

Robbie had rolled his eyes and slouched deep in his seat—a position that reminded Maize of her coworker Eli, though otherwise the two looked nothing alike.

To Maize, Robbie claimed that what angered him most wasn't the sale of his childhood house—he wasn't as attached to it as you might assume—so much as the insouciant way his mother had told him about it after the fact. She was forever doing things like that, he'd said, which seemed like an overstatement to Maize. Yet she knew that his mother tended to announce major events in an offhand manner, after a delay, as if their relationship were taking place via satellite. His mother reported traumatic events like a dame from a black-and-white movie—one of those women whose expressions remained unflappable behind a cigarette smoke screen—perhaps to convince herself and Robbie they weren't so bad after all. "Doctors did a little housecleaning" was how his mother described her hysterectomy to him, phoning on the day she came home from the hospital. "Mother's Day shopping will be lighter this year" was what she said by way of mentioning that his paternal grandmother had died and left him savings bonds. (Robbie, away at college and still estranged from his father at the time, hadn't even known his grandmother was ill.) And when his guilty father tried to check on Robbie's mother's welfare after defecting to Italy, she'd changed their phones to new unlisted numbers and forgotten to tell Robbie until friends complained they couldn't reach him. "So you missed a few calls, what's the diff, this isn't 911," she'd said when he complained, refusing to concede how odd it was.

"Slow down, okay?—Thanks," Robbie told the driver now. He bobbed on the taxi seat twice, like a restless child about to jump. "Here's where you turn. Right here—here!"

"He heard you, honey," Daniel said to Robbie, squeezing his hand, though he also twitched as if the nervousness were contagious.

Robbie's mother's house loomed larger and larger as the taxi progressed down the semicircular driveway. It was a big three-story structure that sprawled over three wings, with black shutters and a slate roof and a bluestone porch, dormer windows on the top floor, and a decorative cupola over the garage. It had a broad side lawn on the left and, on the right, an incongruous rock garden with a Japanese maple that, Maize knew, Robbie's father had planted before he'd split for Europe. She also knew that behind the house was a glittering pool hidden from the front, and behind that a rarely used tennis court that always seemed in need of a sweeping.

None of it was a surprise to Maize as it would be to Daniel; she knew this house nearly as well as her own childhood home a mile and a half away in a lesser neighborhood with smaller lots. But coming from the four-hundred-square-foot hovel she and Robbie had been sharing for the past year, it did feel more gargantuan than she remembered it, and she had the impulse to turn around and flee.

Too late to back out now. Robbie's mother was already striding down the drive toward the taxi with a wad of cash in her hand, presumably for the driver. She'd promised to pay Maize and Daniel generously for their work, but not till the end of the week, and Robbie wouldn't be compensated at all for his labors. It was what he loftily called his "filial duty" to be here. ("You know what I mean," he'd said when Maize had asked him to elaborate. "Filial duty. Like in the House of Atreus.")

"Get a load of you, kiddo!" Robbie's mother said to Maize after she paid the driver. "So skinny and gorgeous! And that hair!" His mother wrapped her arms around Maize while she was still holding her suitcase, making for a lopsided embrace. Maize had never known Robbie's mother to be physically affectionate before. If anything, she was the opposite: a toughie despite her fine-boned face and delicate features, her big brown doe eyes (which Robbie had inherited) and her glossy dark hair, her good legs and her fragile-looking collarbone. To Maize she had always looked like Audrey Hepburn's plumper and more world-weary sister, her wide mouth likelier to scowl than bloom into a dreamy smile. "I owe you one for helping me out," she said into Maize's hair now.

No sooner had she hugged Maize than she pushed her away, as if snapping back to her regular personality. She nodded hello in Robbie's direction. Then she stuck her hand out at Robbie's boyfriend sharply, like a foreman greeting a site worker.

"And you're David," she said.

"Actually no, ma'am." Robbie's boyfriend met her assessing gaze. "It's Daniel."

"*Right,*" she said in a protracted syllable, sounding skeptical, as if Daniel might not know his own name. "I'm the old battle-axe Robbie's told you about. Don't believe everything my son says about me."

"Robbie hasn't said a thing, ma'am." Daniel blinked at her and took a step backward. "Well, almost nothing."

"Good."

"Yes, Mother," Robbie said, filling the space between them. "Considering how we detest each other." When no one replied he said, "So."

"Yep. So." His mother slapped her hands lightly against her hips, like a cowgirl spurring a slow horse. "We've really got our work cut out for us, don't we? Let's get you kids settled in." She turned to Maize. "Etta fussed so much over your guest rooms, she didn't make my bed or put sheets on Robbie's mattress this morning. You'll probably find mints on your pillows or some other nonsense."

Etta, Maize remembered, was the family maid. The soft-spoken woman Robbie's mother had hired after his father left, having fired the maid they'd had for many years before, as if banishing eyewitnesses to her marriage.

"Mints on the pillows. Yum," Maize said. She'd always taken a saucy tone with Robbie's mother, from the moment she'd met her many years ago. They'd always gotten along, and she suspected that Robbie's mother liked her far more than her own mother did. "I trust that means we're getting room service, too?" Maize said.

"Hah! Don't press your luck," Robbie's mother said.

"Your cleaning woman really shouldn't have bothered herself," Daniel said. "I can stay in Robbie's room."

"No, I insist that you and Maize take advantage of my guest rooms while I still have them," Robbie's mother said. "My next house won't."

Maize grinned. She knew that Robbie had been out to his mother for several years and that his mother claimed she couldn't care less. But Maize also knew that when Robbie informed his mother that her third helper this week would be his boyfriend, not merely another friend from the city, she'd paused a long moment before saying, "Hmm. Is that so," and then skittered on to other topics. Robbie had been on speakerphone in their apartment so Maize had overheard.

"We saw your new place on the way here," Maize said to his mother now. "It looks terrific."

"It'll do. Lower maintenance."

His mother strode forward. Daniel splayed his hand between Robbie's shoulder blades and Maize watched Robbie close his eyes and sink into Daniel's palm for a moment, with the pained yet beatific look of someone being massaged before he yanked himself away to proceed down the driveway. She scrambled to keep pace with Robbie's mother while lugging her heavy suit-case. Again Robbie's mother took Maize's arm in hers as they neared the front door.

More touchy-feeliness—what was this? Maize squinted while the bare dry arm pressed against hers, not unpleasantly, and they climbed the porch steps. Perhaps his mother was rattled by having a disarmingly handsome stranger like Daniel around during a week when she'd be packing up her life, although she'd supposedly encouraged Robbie to corral as many day laborers as he could and said she'd pay them lavishly for their trouble. Or perhaps his mother merely needed reassurance from someone familiar besides her son that Daniel was what she'd call a "good egg."

If that's what she was looking for, Maize wasn't the girl to do it. She found herself fatigued by the trip and overwhelmed by the occasion and she didn't know quite what to make of Daniel, either. Not just yet. He seemed nice enough—buff and bright and commandingly attractive, and he gazed on Robbie intensely, like a doctor with an unseemly interest in one of the patients he was examining—but she had learned hardly anything about Daniel besides the fact that Robbie had the sloppiest crush on him that she'd ever known her friend to indulge. Robbie stammered and flushed the few times he'd mentioned Daniel to her, but he'd pretty much kept them apart in the ten weeks since he and Daniel started dating.

"Nothing's changed here. You'll find it all the same," Robbie's mother said to Maize as she opened the front door. "Except soon it won't be mine."

Maize surveyed the interior details now—far more precisely than she had when she was a teenager hanging out here with Robbie. She supposed it was one of the many occupational hazards of having toiled in André Gilbert's real estate office for the past year: no longer being able to enter someone's home without assessing its features and impediments and resale potential. She was still in her honeymoon of loathing André Gilbert purely, before any complicating emotions intervened. It bugged her to think that André might have a permanent effect on her now that she'd been brutally cut loose. Yet she couldn't help registering the size of the rooms and the high ceilings and the condition of the oak floors, or stop herself from counting the number of bedrooms (6) and baths (4) and half baths (2) and fireplaces (3), or regretting that all the windows were covered with shades and sheers and curtains that blocked out the natural light and would be bad for showings to potential buyers. She could almost hear André saying, *Good bones here, but a gut job.*

The only place where Maize could turn off her attention to housing details was the apartment she shared with Robbie. And that was defensive. Even before it was stripped bare by burglars, Maize had been aware of how grungy and grubby her own living space was—a world apart from the luxury properties she'd shown to André's buyers. If she went looking for depressing features of her own home there'd be no end. It could practically be her next career.

Knock it off, she scolded herself now. *Nobody asked you for a market evaluation.* Robbie's mother's house was already sold and closing next week.

And as if thumbing her nose at André Gilbert, Maize studied the pastel blue Formica countertops and outdated appliances in the kitchen—which Robbie said his parents remodeled the same year his father left, nearly a decade ago, as if in an effort to refurbish their feelings about each other—and announced, "I love this room. It's wonderful. I've always adored this kitchen."

"It is very nice—enormous," Daniel said, yet no one answered him as they moved toward the staircase.

"So this is yours, Maizie," Robbie's mother said, leading her to a chamber with pink walls and a floral bedspread and a sewing machine, as if decorated for an imaginary daughter. It was right next door to Robbie's old bedroom, which eerily looked as it had in high school: a sparse white cell with a twin bed and Radiohead, Mozart, Schoenberg, and Joni Mitchell CDs fighting for space on crowded shelves with tomes like *The Magic Mountain* and Augustine's *Confessions, The Brothers Karamazov* and Dante's *Purgatorio.* Robbie had been bookish above all else for as long as Maize had known him, reading compulsively the way other people smoked or drank too much, scanning poetry and comparing translations of prose, which sometimes left him befuddled when he looked up from texts at the decidedly less artful life that surrounded him. He was confused when his experience didn't conform to what he'd read somewhere.

Like right now, Maize thought. Now that his gorgeous boyfriend was here in the mix, poor Robbie didn't have a clue about what to do with him. He kept sidling close to Daniel and then swerving away, like a bad driver who couldn't keep to a lane.

As Maize glanced between them, she noted again how physically similar Daniel was to Robbie. It was practically narcissistic for the two of them to be sleeping together. Although Daniel was a more gleaming version of her best friend—taller, more muscular, and more sure-footed than Robbie—they both had nearly black hair and wide eyes (though Daniel's were blue) and strong chins, not to mention smooth chests and hairy legs. The significant difference was their ages—only three years, but Daniel seemed a lot older than Robbie if not as cerebral, or at least that's how Robbie seemed to see it. The few times he'd allowed Maize to go out with them for an evening, Robbie hung on Daniel's words as if his boyfriend were the only adult present, though he did his best to hide any tremors of inferiority around him. He maundered on about subjects Daniel didn't know about and stared longingly at Daniel only when he wasn't looking back, like a starving man eyeing a banquet table for what he could furtively shove into his pockets. Noticing this made Maize flinch—not merely because Robbie seemed to be surveying a future that didn't necessarily include her, but because it saddened her how hard it was for Robbie to relax into his hunger, and it brought back her own hunger and solitude before they'd first stumbled toward each other in high school and then rediscovered each other at college.

Now his mother pointed down the long hallway past two chandeliers and a series of heavy paneled doors toward the opposite corner of the house. "And David—sorry, *Daniel*—" She thumped her forehead comically as if to dislodge the stubborn fact of his true identity. "That's where you'll stay. Robbie will show it to you." She took a few steps toward the staircase to the third floor and her own bedroom before freezing as if she thought better of it. "Go ahead, Robbie. I made our reservation for seven, so drop your bags and amuse yourselves until then." She winked at Maize. "Only don't do anything I wouldn't do."

◆◆

For their first meal together, Robbie's mother drove them to a French restaurant a few towns away. It had faux-rustic farmhouse touches like stippled stucco walls and primitive exposed beams and uneven wideboard floors and dim overhead lanterns, to distract you, Maize supposed, from the formality of the service and the decadent cuisine that seemed to emanate from a culinary time warp: chateaubriand and coquilles St. Jacques, vichyssoise and steak Diane, potatoes Anna and foie gras. The kind of gout-inducing food that was probably fashionable decades ago, although the prices were very au courant—what Maize's mother would have called highway robbery.

Maize fidgeted in her seat. She and Robbie and Daniel weren't well-enough dressed for this restaurant. Robbie's mother looked inappropriate, too, Maize thought, in her denim shirt and khakis, but she seemed not to care. She encouraged the three of them to "order up a storm" because they'd need their strength for the week ahead, and she was equally generous with the burgundy she poured for everyone except Daniel, who clapped his hand over his glass each time she pointed the bottle his way and said thank you, he was fine with mineral water.

"So how's your job, Maizie girl?" Robbie's mother said. "Still rampaging though the world of zillion-dollar lofts?"

"Umm. No. Not exactly." Maize took a sip of wine and shook her head.

"Maize is taking a little leave from real estate at the moment," Robbie said.

Maize scoffed and said, "A leave? Let's face it." She turned to his mother. "What Robbie means is, I got fired."

Since it had happened a month ago, Maize had been telling everyone except her own mother the same thing—*I got fired*—feeling a surge of power and shy pride every time she announced it, like someone who'd survived fire or flood or terrible surgery yet still had the pioneer pluck to be plowing forward. She didn't feel bad about being sacked except for the lost pay and the lost sight of Eli, whom she'd gotten used to observing furtively whenever they were both in the office. It was *working* for André Gilbert that had made her feel pathetic and weak, she now realized; whatever followed was the opposite.

"Really. That guy must be nuts firing a smart girl like you," Robbie's mother said. "Unless you didn't show up to work or were your usual uppity self."

"Thanks," Maize said. "It was complicated." There was no reason to go into the fact that André had threatened to call the police when Maize was cleaning out the belongings from her desk that final day—as if Maize would take something that wasn't hers on her way out—and that Maize had said, "Go ahead, André. I dare you. I have a few things I'd like to tell the police myself," and that André had wisely backed off.

"I agree that Andy was unwise to let you go," Daniel said.

"André," Robbie said. "Not Andy."

"Thanks, Daniel," Maize said.

"Robbie mentioned your boss was a pip," his mother said. Then she turned to Daniel. "And he tells me you're a medical student. I guess you have a specialty since no one wants to be a regular G.P. anymore, right?"

"Um, well—yes, ma'am." Daniel sat up and the caned dining chair squeaked under him. "Nephrology, probably."

"Sorry," she said. "What's that?"

"Kidneys," Robbie said.

"More or less," Daniel said.

"Right. Kidneys. Of course." Robbie's mother daubed her mouth with a starchy white napkin and said, "Robbie's father passed a few kidney stones a while back. Excruciating pain. Not that he didn't deserve it."

"Robbie never mentioned that," Daniel said.

"No, he wouldn't have." She looked off toward an empty table next to theirs before turning back to Daniel. "In any event, I appreciate your coming up here with Maizie to help, but I'm surprised you can manage it. I thought medical students never had spare time. Slept thirty seconds a night and all that."

"I'm in a gap period between medical school and my internship at the hospital," Daniel said. "I have three weeks off before I start up again."

"Hmm," she said. "You kids sure have a lot of gaps these days. Some of them seem to last years."

Robbie drummed his fingers on the damask tablecloth and said, "All the new interns start together as a group on the first of July. Across the country, right?" He appealed to Maize rather than Daniel for verification but she shrugged.

"That's right," Daniel said. He lifted the burgundy bottle and said, "We show up every summer like a swarm of locusts in white coats. Would anyone like me to pour more wine?"

"No, thank you," Maize said, but Robbie and his mother merely shook their heads.

How polite Daniel was, Maize thought. A tall, blue-eyed Virginian with a Southern boy's genteel manners. He'd raced from his side of the taxi to Maize's to open the door for her when they arrived at the house today, and he held out the chair for Robbie's mother at this restaurant before anyone on the staff could do it. Maize had also witnessed him lighting a strange woman's unlit cigarette although he didn't smoke. He'd probably resist letting Robbie's mother pay when the check came before gracefully conceding.

"You're undoubtedly thinking, *Too bad he's not straight,*" Robbie had said to Maize some weeks ago when she'd commented on Daniel's courtliness. "Women are dying for halfway decent behavior from guys these days, right? And he is a gentleman and he is wonderful—don't get me wrong." Robbie bit his nail. "But he can be different with men."

Maize had supposed that was true. She'd seen Daniel flash the rigidity you heard about in Southerners: a hardness just under the velvety surface, a readiness to size up and dismiss with a word or a cutting look, especially around males his own age. As if life were a big locker room and there could be only one winner at each event. She'd witnessed him being peremptory with a waiter and a cashier the one night they'd all gone out together. But Robbie seemed to get a special dispensation from Daniel's testosterone surges, like a physician's note excusing him from gym class.

"What an expert Robbie's becoming on internships these days," Robbie's mother said now, rolling her eyes, and she took another bite of her entrée.

Robbie had told Maize his mother wasn't thrilled by his internship at the downtown weekly newspaper when he could get a real paying job someplace else. On the day he'd finally landed the position after months of rejection, having been told he was too inexperienced or too brainy for other entry-level positions, his mother's reaction was: "Terrif, Robbie. You spend years getting honors so you can type and file and run other people's errands for forty hours a week. And for free."

"You're correct about that, ma'am," Daniel said to her now.

"Robbie is becoming quite an expert on interns. Right, sweetheart?" He brushed the top of Robbie's hand with his long fingers and it jumped reflexively before, Maize noticed, Robbie stared at his mother, willing himself to keep his hand there while Daniel stroked it. Maize was proud of Robbie for doing that—showing affection publicly; at the same time her throat tightened at the sight of it.

But Robbie couldn't manage it for long. After a second he picked up his water goblet and took a long swig to free his hand again.

"Well then." Robbie's mother smiled. "Now that I've been warned, please remind me never to need an emergency room on Fourth of July weekend."

"Excuse me?" Daniel said.

"Nothing personal," she said. "But it'd be scary to have some rookie be the only thing standing between me and the cemetery."

"We're very closely supervised," Daniel said. "I can guarantee that."

"Of course," Robbie said. His hand inched closer to Daniel's again. "Of course you are. Mom—"

"I'm sure. No offense." She pointed at the nearly empty bottle and asked Robbie and Maize if they liked what they were drinking or wanted to try something different.

Robbie shook his head, his face reddening as if in delayed reaction to what he'd already swallowed, and Maize said, "No, this is fine." She hadn't gotten this buzzed since her night out with Eli over a month ago. "It's delicious."

"More of the same then," his mother said. "Never mix, never worry and all that." And she summoned the waiter back to their table.

◆◆◆

It was at that precise moment—when Robbie's mother blithely shifted the subject after making a jab at someone—that Maize realized why she'd been experiencing a fluttery sort of déjà vu since stepping out of the taxi earlier. It was like being around André Gilbert again—a suburban, less employed, distaff version of André, but André nevertheless. Or perhaps Maize was merely so haunted by André and the shame of their connection that lots of unlikely things would resemble him from now on.

It made Maize bite the inside of her cheek. She wanted nothing more than to escape the memory of André now that she'd fallen out so badly with him. She didn't want to add André to the list of people who would seemingly haunt her for life. She already had a long enough list of those people: her dead father and departed stepfather; Hal Jamesley, who'd left his counselor job after she'd graduated from high school and was now at large somewhere in the universe; her stern freshman English teacher, who said she was a potentially brilliant writer yet fatally unfocused and too daydreamy to get anywhere; her old friend Lyla, who, she'd last heard, was now living in an RV with a boyfriend in Portland; the slyly captivating Eli, who'd engrossed her for months by doing nothing more than sitting at his office desk and whom she'd been avoiding for the past month; the dorky college basketball player who'd given her rolling waves of orgasms for several weeks during sophomore year until, out of nowhere, he simply stopped texting her or speaking to her, as if he'd finally noticed they couldn't make even the smallest of small talk about the weather when they weren't having sex, leaving her relieved despite a roaring raw hunger for his body, because she didn't want him to enter her imagination the way he'd entered her physically. No, not another one in the gathering of ghosts she traveled with; it was already crowded in there.

But the basketball player had shown up in her thoughts anyway, whenever she was walking down the street and noticed someone freakishly tall: a beacon of something, though she didn't know what.

She'd told Robbie about the basketball player and the rest of her hookups and fleeting attractions. She'd glancingly mentioned Eli to him, and the dead-eyed receptionist in the real estate office who'd never once greeted her in the morning or wished her good night at the end of the day. She'd told him about her mother. She'd told him about André Gilbert. She'd told him at least a little about pretty much everything, though nothing about Hal Jamesley, whom Robbie had never met and never would. Hal had shown up during senior year of high school, after Robbie had been shipped off to boarding school, and now it was as if the statute of limitations had run out on the misdemeanor of him. She figured even the most confessional types had to have a secret or two for themselves. Hal Jamesley was hers.

And it wasn't as if she didn't regale Robbie with details about the rest of her life. In the past year alone, she'd given him enough details about André Gilbert to fill three of her blank journals, which she'd written in more and more voluminously in the weeks since getting axed.

She'd met André just before their graduation last spring, through a flossy college classmate who was going off to a deb job at a literary magazine in Belgium and who'd found Maize amusing. This girl, Chandler Sloane, had a mother who'd sold her enormous apartment on Park Avenue and bought an equally enormous loft in Tribeca through André, who had just fired his assistant and was looking for a replacement with the right tone for his clientele. When Maize and Chandler Sloane had been briefly paired by their semiotics professor on a project—decoding Godard's *Alphaville*—Chandler decided that Maize was wonderful because she did all the work for both of them. Chandler mentioned to Maize that André Gilbert was "this adorable gay guy" as well as "a trip," and something about André's former assistant being a kleptomaniac from Bryn Mawr or something equally ghastly. She said her mother could make a phone call to André for Maize, if she liked.

Robbie didn't understand why a clever girl like Maize would take a job as André Gilbert's office robot when she could make money waitressing or temping, or doing something that required a less steady commitment until she found fulfilling work. But then Robbie didn't have a mother like Maize's mother, who'd transmitted her fear of poverty the way other parents passed on phobias about dogs or airplanes or aging to their children, and who'd repeatedly warned Maize that she expected her to support herself from the second she graduated college. Maize's mother was convinced that paying your dues, in the form of demeaning and inane grunt jobs, built character, although from what Maize could tell it was just as likely to grind what minimal character you'd developed down to a nub.

On the morning of her interview with André Gilbert, her mother had called Maize long distance to remind her to wear *a suit* and *jewelry* and *makeup* and *perfume*. As if she were going to a wedding. As if she were an idiot who might otherwise show up to a Manhattan luxury real estate agency in sweat clothes.

It surprised Maize that André Gilbert didn't question her about her name the first time they met. Almost everyone who encountered Maize for more than two seconds asked something about it. (Was she Native American? Was it like the corn or the puzzle? How exactly did she spell that?) But André hadn't. He couldn't seem to care less about that or anything else involving Maize's personal life. Beyond glancing for a second at her résumé during the interview and saying "fancy schmancy" when noting the college she'd gone to, André didn't concern himself with Maize's history, either. He signaled clearly through his lack of chatter that all he cared about was Maize's potential as a worker. He wanted to know how nine-hour days, six days a week (including Sunday open houses), sat with Maize. He asked her if she had a suitable wardrobe for the job—crisp and professional—because he wouldn't tolerate the kind of "whore schmattas" college girls wore, especially in downtown offices like his, where it was even more inappropriate since all the men in the place were big sissies. The only time André looked directly at Maize was when asking whether she'd be fussy about not having a lunch hour (there was no time for that in this business, he explained; when you were on you were *on*), and then he stared so intensely at Maize, narrowing his eyes and leaning forward over his desk and passing his tongue over his upper lip, that she had started to feel a bit like lunch herself.

"That'll be okay," Maize chirped before thinking about it. "I never eat much during the day, anyway." She took a breath and looked at her ragged fingernails. "I guess I could have a bigger breakfast before I come to work."

"Whatever," André said, and then informed Maize that the job came with health insurance but no pension plan.

The tenor of their meeting made Maize want to squirm. Weren't employment interviews supposed to be superficially friendlier than this? Weren't you both supposed to see if you had some kind of rapport? She'd usually gotten along famously with gay men since there was no sexual tension to muddle things. She supposed it was possible that André had already prescreened Maize through Chandler Sloane, but there was no way of checking because Chandler had left no contact information when she'd decamped for Brussels.

Maize shuddered inwardly at André's lack of warmth or interest in her. But then André surprised her by offering her the job on the spot and she convinced herself that his aloofness was liberating. If André remained indifferent to who Maize was beyond the most basic facts, Maize was free to be whomever she wanted, at least while she was at work. She would be free to reinvent herself and become a new Maize—new and unexpected and presumably improved. Wasn't that what the most vibrant people did when they came to this city? Wasn't that the promise of youth, or at least the promise of someone with a brand-new B.A.?

Still, the old Maize couldn't resist making some sort of personal contact before she left the office. If André wouldn't ask her anything about herself, Maize would turn the tables.

"André," Maize said, when they were both standing and the interview was wrapping up. "That's an interesting name. I assume you're Russian or French?"

"Nope," André said. He touched his perfectly streaked hair. "André's what I go by instead of my real name. Which is Abbott. Abby. The ugliest old schnorrer name on the fucking planet."

"Oh, I don't know about that." Maize laughed, delighted that he had exposed a self-critical side in a semipublic place; it was like being in a dressing room with a friend who asked if certain jeans made him look fat. "I consider Abbott very distinguished," she said. "I believe Abba means 'father' in Hebrew and it's the male version of Abigail, which means 'gift from God.' And since an abbott's the head of a monastery, I can't help wondering if there's a connection to the name Abelard, like Abelard and Héloïse. You know? The inspiration for all those beautiful twelfth-century love letters."

She felt very smart and bright saying all that, imparting what she knew like an enthusiastic high school teacher or Robbie in one of his scholarly fugues. Robbie would be so proud of her! For a moment it seemed her impeccably impractical education—in which she'd learned about Middle English and Duchamp's urinal and sub-Saharan droughts but had never been taught how to apply for a credit card or answer an office phone—wasn't useless after all. She expected André to praise her or at least indicate, with a plucked eyebrow, that he'd registered his new assistant's sophistication. Instead André went dead behind the eyes.

"Right. Abbott, Abelard, blah blah," he said. "I still hate that name. Don't ever call me anything but André or I'll have to kill you. Okay? We clear on that?" He smiled widely at Maize for the first time that day.

Now Maize squirmed on the guest room mattress in Robbie's mother's house, replaying that moment and the variations on *I'll kill you* that she'd heard André deliver to other brokers in the past eleven months, all of them involving pirated body parts: *I'll cut your heart out, I'll cut you off at the legs, I'll leave you with nothing but a bloody stump.* She was alone with her memories— her fragmentary recollections of André and Eli and her ugly green desktop and the company's hectoring e-mails about deportment—in a dark silence. She ordered herself to broom-clean these items from her consciousness and go to sleep. She had a big week ahead of her. She had a different boss now. Even if Robbie's mother turned out to be a fascist shrew, this would undoubtedly feel like a spa vacation compared to André's office.

✦ ✦

Next door on the following morning, Robbie woke in his childhood bed to spasms of guilt—not merely because Daniel had sneaked into his room overnight and they'd gleefully messed up the sheets, which Robbie would have to launder later on, nor because Robbie had thought about J. while lying on his old twin mattress beside Daniel, but because he felt a thousand times more at home in his mother's house than he did in his city apartment. Between rapturous rounds with Daniel, for the first time in months he'd slept as soundly as someone comatose, his dreams untroubled and vivid, his deep breathing in sync with his lover's, the breeze through the window screens filtering sounds of crickets and tree frogs instead of sirens and car alarms. He hadn't experienced the slightest twinge of longing for the life he and Maize had left behind for the week, though he knew he should have had at least a few twinges.

Since the burglary their apartment was denuded except for a cot in his bedroom and an air mattress in Maize's and some paper plates in the forlorn kitchen cabinets. Even before it had hardly been comfortable: a first-floor hovel in a crumbling tenement on a grubby stretch of lower western Chelsea that had resisted the gentrification of the rest of the neighborhood. In place of smart restaurants where steaming hunks cruised each other and ingested excessive amounts of protein, Robbie and Maize's block had a corner bodega and a Jamaican jerk chicken stand that doubled as a check cashing parlor. In place of clever shops where men bought overpriced lamps or underwear on their way back from the gym, their block had a welfare housing project caged with rusted cyclone fencing.

Robbie remembered how proud Maize had been about finding the apartment online and getting it for them a year ago, before the competition pounced. A rental in downtown Manhattan rather than Inwood or Bushwick or New Jersey where many college graduates had to start out. It had been advertised as a two-bedroom when in fact it was three dark closet-size rooms, the kitchen doubling as the living room. The second "bedroom," Maize's room, was in the middle of the apartment and looked out on a grimy brick wall six inches away, as did the bathroom and the living room/kitchen. There was no natural light except in Robbie's room facing the street, where his view was of an Aztec-looking man with high cheekbones and a sleek black ponytail selling drugs from the front stoop to people in passing cars. Robbie watched through his barred windows, feeling less like a resident of the city than one of its inmates.

But the worst part was that their apartment had two front doors, both inches from the building entrance—one to the living room/kitchen and a second, hollow-core number to Robbie's room so flimsy that a five-year-old could have kicked it in during a tantrum. Day and night, whenever anyone was buzzed into the building through the squeaky metal security door, whenever the tenants used their keys, it sounded like they were entering Robbie's bedroom directly from the street. Which in retrospect seemed a warm-up for the actual invasion that had happened a few weeks ago.

"Hey there, Robbie, wake up," Maize said now, bursting into his childhood bedroom with only the slightest warning knock. Forward and impolite, maybe, but nothing new. They had no privacy in their railroad apartment so they'd gotten used to walking in on each other at all hours. But when she discovered Daniel lying shirtless next to Robbie she gasped and stopped dead in her tracks on his mother's blue shag carpet.

"Oh my god—sorry!" she whispered. "I didn't—I thought—you know—"

Robbie beckoned her forward with his hand. He realized she wasn't used to finding him in bed with anyone. Although he'd slept around since his senior year of college, making up for a late start, none of his dates had stuck before Daniel and he'd never

brought any of them home to their apartment. Not even for dinner or a drink or a snack before the main event. He told them he
wanted to spare his roommate the sight of half-naked strangers
plodding through her room, but in truth it was his own room he
wanted to keep them from. He wasn't ready for the semblance
of domesticity with anyone besides Maize yet—having his bed-
mates wake expecting breakfast or conversation or fresh towels
for a shower or a spare toothbrush. He hadn't advanced to that
stage even with Daniel, whose confidence cowed Robbie, whose
virility made him light-headed, and who'd met Maize a few times
in restaurants but hadn't yet spent a single night under their
roof. In recent weeks Daniel had started asking Robbie about
that, a little and then frequently, which was one of the reasons
Robbie had invited him up here to Connecticut. That and the
fact that his mother needed another laborer.

"I want to spend more time together with you," Daniel had
said to Robbie a few weeks ago. "I want to be your boyfriend."

"That's very sweet," Robbie had said, and he'd remembered
to smile. But even as he spoke he knew his reply was inadequate—
not merely because it wasn't the answer Daniel wanted to hear
(*Of course I really want to be your boyfriend, too*) but because he
couldn't relax his face after Daniel had made his announcement, the same way Daniel sometimes didn't unstiffen even
after they'd both climaxed. He'd covered by giving Daniel a
long deep kiss to compensate for the emotion he couldn't express
otherwise. Since he'd begun hooking up with men after J., it
continually amazed Robbie what an all-purpose zapper sex could
be, temporarily annihilating tensions and judgments and unanswered questions and obscuring how you didn't look at a lover
the right way or communicate with him when you were fully
clothed. It was as if lovemaking displaced your frustrations and
disappointments with each other and set them somewhere else,

like an object thrown hastily on a bedside table just before you tumbled onto a mattress. But when you opened your eyes and woke again it was the first thing you saw sitting beside an alarm clock.

Robbie had made tremendous progress with Daniel, he thought, nonetheless. Daniel was not only Robbie's first overt longer-term partner (ten weeks and counting now) but the first man he'd ever felt an intense visceral connection to during sexual aerobics—the only man who rendered Robbie febrile whenever he touched him, and caused Robbie to salivate at the sight of his body like a drooling dog with a beef bone, and made Robbie's skin hum whenever he straddled Daniel and devoured him head to toe (even pulling at his pubic hair with his teeth), and who provoked grunts and shouts and bestial noises Robbie had rarely heard before, much less out of his own mouth. With previous men sex had been part recreation and part physical therapy, the sensual pleasure of the exercise tainted by a sense of hygienic usefulness. But never with Daniel, right from the start. Daniel was exceptional.

"Shouldn't we be working already?" Maize whispered to Robbie now. "It sounds like your mother and Etta have been packing for hours."

"I guess," Robbie whispered back. He yawned and nodded toward Daniel's bare torso and closed eyes. "I'll see what I can do."

"Could we maybe get some coffee first?" Daniel said in a regular voice. He rubbed his eyes and sat up in bed, exposing his statuesque midriff as he stretched his arms toward the ceiling.

"Daniel—hi. How are you?" Maize said. "Good morning."

"Good morning, Maize." Daniel yawned and draped his arms around Robbie, laying his head on Robbie's T-shirt. "And good morning to you, sweetheart. Ready to labor like a he-man today?"

Daniel's arms tightened around Robbie's torso and his hot breath grazed Robbie's earlobe. When Robbie glanced at his groin he noticed he was starting to tent the top sheet—right in front of Maize—so he raised his knees to hide himself.

"I guess so," he said to Daniel. "I'll be ready in a minute."

The three of them spent the whole morning in the basement, sorting and stacking and packing things that probably hadn't been touched in years. On the main floor, Etta was doing much the same thing with Robbie's mother. Daniel said he was starving, but Robbie didn't respond. Although Etta had made them a bacon-and-eggs breakfast Daniel had said, "Thanks, but I'm afraid I get queasy if I eat this early. I'll just have one of the power bars I brought with me later on."

Robbie's mother had ordered them to separate her belongings into two piles—keepers and discards—and she'd make the final decision about what stayed and went after they were done.

"I certainly vote for tossing this," Daniel said, holding up a small Murano vase that Robbie recognized as one of his mother's old anniversary presents from his father.

"I assume you're joking," Robbie said. "That's Venetian glass."

"So?" Daniel said. "Just because it's Italian doesn't automatically mean it's valuable."

"But look at the detail. It's so elegant," Robbie said. It truly was exquisite, Robbie thought, with thousands of intricate flower shapes in dozens of colors. Robbie imagined an artisan working quickly and fervently on it, frantic to do something impressive with the molten material before it cooled down on him. He said, "That vase has got to be worth a lot. And even if it's not expensive it's just plain beautiful. It's like—you know?—a Flemish tapestry made of glass or something."

"All right, all right. I guess I missed that art history class when I was taking organic chemistry." Daniel squinted like someone in a conversation where the other speaker suddenly starts jabbering in a foreign language.

Robbie's eyes darted to Maize for a confirming nod, but she quickly glanced down at a box of flatware she was packing. Clearly she wasn't going to second him, nor had she made a peep earlier when Daniel had voted to cast off china sets and framed photos and books in favor of old ice crushers and rotating fans and Mixmasters that probably didn't work anymore. Robbie supposed she was too smart to take sides about something that didn't matter much in the long run. Maybe she even thought Robbie should fake sharing Daniel's opinions just so they could move through the piles more quickly. That would be like Maize, Robbie thought—she had an absorbent personality—and of course she was right. His mother would have the final veto power, anyway.

But Robbie knew he'd never been as big a person as Maize and he feared he'd become even smaller in the past year. Frustration had been puckering his spirit. Since he'd graduated from college his intelligence had been underused to the point of atrophy; he couldn't casually relinquish his taste on top of that. It was one of the few things Robbie still had to offer the world and that he specifically had over Daniel, whose pre-med course work was far more practical than Robbie's education and whose father had taught him manly things like how to rewire a lamp and chop firewood and sail, unlike Robbie's father, who'd instructed him on the proper width of lapels and the length of shirt cuffs and the gaucherie of wearing black tie before six. In the short time they'd known each other, Robbie had noticed, Daniel had enjoyed lording his macho skills over Robbie although he also seemed to find Robbie's helplessness amusing, as if Robbie were a kiddie savant who could name the square root of any prime number off the top of his head but lacked the sense to knot his shoelaces.

When Robbie rambled on about poetry or dance or the visual arts Daniel nodded and yawned politely, or stroked Robbie tenderly and said, "You're adorable, you know that?" which had the effect of making Robbie feel like a windy young fart. At Robbie's instigation they almost always made love immediately afterward.

Robbie knew he had a tendency to drift off into aesthetic monologues and effectively disappear into the intellectual ether, especially when he felt insecure. Maize was too simpatico to drag him back down to earth. He supposed he needed Daniel's groundedness and he admired Daniel even if his proclivities were more than a little mundane. Whenever Daniel planted his big hands on Robbie's shoulders and shook them, saying, "Earth to Robbie, Earth to Robbie, come in please," Robbie was secretly grateful, though he was too proud to show it.

"It's a fragile thing, Daniel," Robbie said when he saw him swathing the vase he'd just spared from the scrap heap in newspaper. "Shouldn't you be using bubble wrap?"

"That might be a good idea," Maize murmured.

"Not necessary. Not if you know what you're doing," Daniel said. And to show them he wrapped the vase elaborately, making deft use of scissors and cross-hatched tape, as carefully as he might stitch a wounded limb. By the time he was finished the vase's outlines were so blurred that Robbie was sure it would have to be completely unwrapped for anyone to understand what he was holding on to. It was a small, tight mess.

◆ ◆

Nevertheless, Robbie reminded himself as he and Daniel and Maize hauled boxes to the front wall of his mother's house for garbage collection later that day, even if Daniel was unintellectual and had little feeling for art, he had plenty of excellent qualities. He was smart in the sciences and hardworking and responsible. He was handsome—so handsome that on certain days Robbie couldn't look at him directly, for fear of becoming tongue-tied—as well as athletic and physically stronger than Robbie. He played basketball and soccer and bicycled and jogged and he didn't even break a sweat now as they moved heavy boxes together, carrying a number of them by himself on his broad shoulders like a teamster. And his steely ambitions matched his hard body. To hear him tell it, he'd had a Doric certainty about what he'd wanted to do with his life since he was seventeen and he knew exactly how to make it happen, his career path toward the M.D. clearly marked at every stage. First college, then medical school, then an internship, then a residency, then a hospital position, then a burgeoning private practice. To an underemployed person like Robbie, Daniel's careerism was nearly as big a turn-on as his blue eyes and lustrous hair and nicely shaped calf muscles and naturally bronzed skin, which was usually hot to Robbie's touch and sometimes smelled faintly of the peanut butter he ate to keep up his energy during shifts.

But if Robbie was going to be truthful with himself, he'd have to admit that his overwhelming emotion about Daniel was base naked animal lust. It was an inebriated state that made Robbie's flesh prickle and his brain sweat. Daniel's body was so perfect it could have illustrated one of his medical textbooks, and he knew how to use it everywhere. So Robbie took Daniel's lead and gave himself over to the carnal sensations he'd resisted with J. and his other lovers: all the stirrings and flutterings, all the churnings and glidings and burnings, all the scrapings and frictions and burnishings and swoonings that made Robbie himself feel exponentially more desirable. From the moment Daniel had first leaned over and kissed Robbie full on the mouth, his two-day stubble a wondrous warmed sandpaper, his doctor's hands exploring Robbie piece by piece and part by part and limb by limb with thrilling authority, and Robbie's back had arched toward rising pleasure—from that moment Robbie was fiendishly hooked. He couldn't get enough of Daniel after suppressing his lust for the better part of a decade, channeling it into cerebral pursuits. It seemed like life's comic revenge on him for overcultivating his intellect at the expense of his libido. Now that he'd emigrated to the Dictatorship of Sex, he was one of its serfs.

It was humbling yet undeniable. There was nothing of Daniel that Robbie didn't want to devour or take into himself— nothing. Not just Daniel's lips and Daniel's mouth but Daniel's long fingers; not just his fingers but his toes and the undersides of his huge feet; not just his feet but his shell-like ears; not just his ears and the small of his back but the parabolic curves of his buttocks; not just his buttocks and his pits and his cavities and his holes but his shoulders; not just his shoulders but his ropy bare arms, which enveloped Robbie in embraces where Robbie momentarily ceased to exist as someone separate.

Yet with a shudder or two it was over and Robbie was forced to return to his own comparatively flawed body. Rattled and dejected with all his usual emotions colliding around inside of him. And when Daniel reached out to him with the same arms that had excited him a moment before, Robbie had to stop himself from squirming.

Robbie reassured himself that he'd gotten closer to something momentous with Daniel—whatever you wanted to call it—than he had with any other man, even if it felt like being the sole witness to a small miracle.

It was a problem with intimacy. Whether it involved a kiss or

a hug or patting the back of someone's hand or cradling someone or getting slammed against a floor for a bruising rough fuck,
or merely whispering *Yes, yes, I get it, me too* from a near distance
that felt like no distance at all, it always passed too quickly and
you were abandoned to the rest of your life, bereft and a little
disbelieving.

"Congratulations. A hot doctor. He's a catch," Maize had
said to Robbie after he'd introduced them for the first time.
She'd said it without a trace of jealousy though she had no boyfriend of her own, and Robbie had found himself weirdly let
down. He didn't want Maize to grow competitive, but he realized
he needed the spark of her envy, or something like it, to jolt him
toward greater feelings about Daniel. Daniel was a catch by
most people's standards and superior to the other men Robbie
had dated, but there was still a blankness whenever Robbie
asked himself whether or not he could fall in love with him—an
unanswered question that kept faintly echoing (*Why not? Why
not now?*) like ambient noise unless he was around Maize.
Whenever he recognized the perversity of that, he wanted to do
something rash and declarative, like sign a lease with Daniel or
buy him a ring or, at the least, invite him up to his mother's house.

As he glanced over at Daniel now he thought, *And yet another good thing about my boyfriend*: he dressed well but never
preened like the many men Robbie had met in the past few
years—men whose vanity was like a tacky mirrored partition
between them and Robbie, a wall they had to shout over to be
heard during their brief encounters.

Generally speaking, Robbie's dates after Professor J. had fallen
into two categories: dull guys who became psychically invisible
as the night wore on, nattering about clothes and celebrities and
personal trainers, and desperately smart young things who were
all too present, with an immediate surface dazzle that didn't go

farther, or that did go farther only to reveal more and more surface, like the antique Chinese boxes one of them collected, which
were said to have hundreds of layers of lacquer.

When they dropped another load of boxes outside his mother's front wall, Robbie looked over at Daniel's bad eight-dollar
haircut from a barbershop in the East Village and a fresh surge
of affection coursed through him. Robbie should be grateful
he'd landed someone as versatile and driven and fetching and
unvain as Daniel at all considering his helplessness in the dating
department. He'd hooked up a lot during his senior year but
when he got to the city he still felt as vulnerable as a junior high
school kid overwhelmed by zits and his first palpitating crushes.
He reflexively looked away like a maiden whenever men nodded
at him or tried to hold his gaze on the street, as if they were pin-
pointing his shortcomings. He stood rigid and silent and stricken
in bars, gripping sweaty drink glasses too tightly and wondering
if he was sipping correctly, his self-consciousness a force field
that repelled anyone within striking distance. And when he
screwed up the courage to place his first online personal ad and
asked Maize to look it over, she was stunned by his cluelessness.

"LITERATE SEEKS SAME?" she'd said incredulously, reading the
headline on Robbie's computer screen while leaning over his
shoulder. "How hot, Robbie! Are you shitting me?"

Robbie had stiffened in his desk chair. "What's wrong with
that?"

"Nothing if you're hoping for a pudgy old scholar who reads
Sanskrit. I thought you said you wanted to get *laid*."

"I do. Really, I do." Robbie squinted at the screen and then
looked up at her with widened eyes, biting his lower lip. In the
months since they'd moved in together she occasionally adopted
the commando tone of her horrible boss, André, whom she'd
complained to Robbie about—barking and authoritative and

quick with criticism no one had asked for—as if she'd been embedded in a war zone too long and was picking up combat language.

"Okay, dear," Maize had gone on in a softer voice, as if she'd heard how she sounded and decided to correct it. "What picture of yourself are you using with the ad?"

"I'm not posting any pictures. I figured I'd have a better chance of attracting serious guys that way."

Maize blinked and jerked back from Robbie's desk chair. She looked like she might stagger. She also looked quizzical and frightened as if realizing for the first time in their long friendship that he was psychotic. It made Robbie look back at the computer screen to see what she'd seen, through her eyes: the literacy headline, followed by no description of himself beyond saying he had dark hair—nothing about age or height or weight or body type—followed by words like *sincere* and *diligent* and *bookworm* and *considerate* and *depth*, as if he'd spent the past twenty years sealed away in a cave like a newt. And no picture.

He looked away from the screen again. Maize was gripping her forearms, kneading them—a gesture Robbie had never seen her make before—as if to restrain herself from slapping him.

"All right then," he said. "Rewrite it for me. Pimp me out."

She gave it the headline HOT ITALIAN 22 YR OLD and included all sorts of immodest details about his "toned smooth swimmer's body" and "bedroom eyes" and made him upload her favorite digital picture of him, and within two hours his in-box was flooded.

He'd had dozens of lackluster dates since then, ranging from underwhelming to godawful, until the grind of them got to him like a bad job. By the time Daniel came along, Robbie was losing hope that he'd ever meet anyone compatible—or at least someone who'd distract him from his dashed hopes for himself with an obliterating besottedness. He'd imagined that kind of febrile intimacy as the most secret, dangerous thing that could happen between people, in the dark and under the covers, away from the eyes of others who'd never be privy to exactly what had happened or how, as if it were a perfect crime. Yet until Daniel his dates hadn't risen beyond the level of minor traffic violations.

In flashes Robbie thought he loved Daniel, and he grasped at the feeling like a firefly until it slipped through his hands again. It wasn't at the moments he'd expect—when they held hands in the dark or had sex or listened to Dinah Washington together. It happened at odder junctures, when they were merely sitting watching TV or a movie or reading separate books, saying nothing and not needing to say anything, or when Daniel stopped on the street to admire flowers in a townhouse's front garden, bending down to smell them through a wrought-iron fence, or when Daniel stopped to give homeless people bills instead of spare change and wished them luck, or when Robbie noticed Daniel's perfect posture and the spring in his walk, as if Daniel would always, always have enough resiliency not only for himself but for both of them if they needed it. In those fleeting moments Robbie wanted to seize Daniel and embrace him and never let him go. The hokey phrase *this is the moment you've been waiting for all your life* rang in his head and he ordered himself to do something, but he was paralyzed the way someone having a stroke is suddenly paralyzed. As the air cooled between them and the opportunity passed he felt relief that Daniel hadn't noticed, and he scolded himself for feeling relief, and he reassured himself that he'd have another chance and the next time he'd do better, or the next.

In the meantime he continued to do whatever work was put before him with a pack mule's determination. Just like he did now, setting down another box of castoffs outside his mother's wall, carefully, as if it mattered whether or not the contents got damaged.

◆ ◆

The following day, after Robbie and Daniel finished their morning tasks, Robbie's mother ordered them to take her charitable donations to "The Robbie and Maize Fund" to the garage and Robbie couldn't help wincing at her command.

When he'd informed his mother about the burglary a few weeks ago, he'd hardly expected her to react like normal mothers, with cooing concern, but neither did he expect her to be opportunistic—viewing it as a chance to get rid of her second-tier stuff. "Tough break," was all she said in sympathy. "But at least your timing's good. Now we won't have to put my extra furniture in storage. Consider it yours."

"Mom, thanks, really, I . . ." Robbie breathed into the receiver and paused. He didn't like her furniture, which tended toward the Victorian, but he was hardly in a position to refuse. He and Maize had no apartment insurance to cover getting cleaned out. Plus Maize apparently found Robbie's mother's taste less oppressive than he did. In the past few days, every time his mother pointed to something and said, "Could you kids use this?" Maize automatically chirped, "Sure!" and exchanged smiles of mutual gratitude with her, before Robbie had a chance to object. His mother and Maize agreed so often they felt like a tag team.

Robbie and Maize and Daniel spent hours going to the rooms his mother ordered them to, gathering like pawnbrokers the objects she could live without: cumbersome lamps, beveled mirrors that made everyone look sallow, Louis XIV–style dining chairs and spare earthenware plates and rugs unraveling at the fringes. His mother had even offered them the twin mattress from Robbie's bedroom—the one item Maize declined, to Robbie's relief.

While the three of them were hauling an old mahogany headboard into the garage Daniel said, "Please tell me you're not taking this to your apartment. It's butt ugly."

"I know," Robbie said. "But I don't have anything else right now."

"I kind of like it," Maize said.

"You like it because you're in desperate scavenger mode. It looks like something an old lady would take to assisted living." Daniel stared at Robbie and said, "Come on. Who needs an antique headboard, anyway? We could get you something better if you wanted it."

"I don't have a paying job," Robbie said, "if you'll remember."

"How could I forget," Daniel said. "Poor Robbie who's come down so far in the world."

Robbie pursed his lips. He'd rarely complained to Daniel about his housing or his lowly position at the newspaper, though he could monologue about his disappointing internship for days if he allowed himself to start. It was Daniel who beefed to Robbie—about his long shifts at NYU, his lack of disposable income, his surrender of his entire twenties to his professional training, and, lately, about Robbie's unwillingness to spend more nights with him. When Robbie had first met Daniel in a diner a few months ago, he'd noticed his critical streak and conflated it with analytical rigor. It excited him to be around a great-looking, affectionate guy who did serious work and had strong opinions. Daniel was nothing if not fervent, so Robbie figured this was a man who'd appreciate his ruminations the way Maize did. But as it turned out, Daniel was impatient with signs of ambivalence in Robbie—his cogitation and introspection and inner debates—which he seemed to view not only as dilatory but potentially dangerous, as if Robbie were a patient who'd expire pursuing a second opinion and a third and a fourth rather than committing to a course of treatment.

"Daniel," Maize said now. "We have an empty apartment, and no money for new furniture."

"So be spartan." Daniel addressed Robbie rather than her. "It's less to take care of, and you'd be surprised how well you can do without things you thought were essential, just because you're used to having them around. They're much easier to give up than you think."

"Sounds bleak," Robbie said. He resisted saying *Sounds Dickensian* because he knew that would make Daniel scoff. He pictured Daniel's medical student housing: one room with a mattress on the floor, a can opener, a tiny television, a tinier microwave, a sound system, and nothing else.

"It's not," Daniel said. "Trust me."

Robbie shrugged. He half wanted to take Daniel's advice but he probably shouldn't add furniture to the list of things he'd already been forced to relinquish since finishing college a year ago: his comfortable dorm room and his convenient meal plan; his nicely structured week of stimulating classes and library research and midnight snacks with Maize; the blanketing approval of professors and deans and his pride in his academic success, which looked increasingly petty as time passed; and maybe most important, the sense of his life as a series of discrete sections like classes—chapters of time that had little connection to one another if he didn't wish them to. It was as though the universe had given him permission to abandon whole populations of people continually, like a high school boy going away to college or a college graduate headed toward advanced study abroad. Because it was necessary for progress. How exhilarating that had seemed to Robbie—the cleansing prospect of shedding his past like a priest taking a vow, with fond memories or bad memories or no memories at all, with a stark demarcation between that stage and the new one just ahead.

No overlap. No bridges. No bleeding of one character into the body of another. And no one would trail him—not his parents or classmates or teachers or lovers—and he needn't be haunted, they'd reappear only in dreams and fleeting memories as he shifted from one place to the next. He could leave it all behind as easily as he and Daniel left heavy objects outside his mother's wall, for someone else to haul away later.

But it was getting harder to believe this now that he was out of college. It was like his special student visa had run out on him. The segments of experience weren't as isolated as he'd hoped. They turned out to be part of something larger that bounced off something else and reflected it: a diptych, a triptych, a polyptych, and so on. Each panel of time obliquely mirroring another panel in an ongoing series he didn't realize he was part of while it was unfolding, or that he sensed only dimly because he was distracted by the rigors and urgencies of the present.

He wasn't a student anymore, at least formally. He was nearly twenty-three and out of school for a year. Whether he liked it or not, many things had started to merge and coalesce in an unsortable tangle, enlarge and expand and grow complications like mold. And there wasn't much he could do to stop it from happening.

"Well then?" Daniel said now, knocking on the antique headboard as if testing its solidity. "Yes or no, Robbie? It's your call."

Even as Daniel challenged him Robbie noticed that Daniel had sexy *knuckles*, which made him feel like a maniac.

"I vote yes," Maize said.

Daniel was staring at him, still waiting for a decision, and so was Maize. Although it was a simple matter, he couldn't make a choice. He said, "I don't care either way," and he told them both to leave the headboard where it was. He'd figure it out later in the week.

◆ ◆

The following morning, as the three of them were sipping coffee and rubbing sleep out of their eyes at the kitchen table, Robbie felt a dull ache in several places he'd never felt before. Overnight he and Daniel had made love more strenuously than usual, with Robbie whispering, "Is that okay, Daniel? Is that good for you?" again and again as they went along. Afterward he'd twisted and turned in bed and observed his Daniel, whose looks changed subtly with each of his movements while he slumbered, as if he were housing several relatives of himself within the same body.

Robbie had noticed that about Daniel before. In a certain light Daniel's face was smoldering yet fine, with its bright, assessing eyes flicking up and down Robbie's body and its firm chin and high forehead like a Holbein. But then suddenly a coarseness would swarm his features; it appeared briefly depending on the angle of Daniel's head, brutishly intensifying his looks before receding. Whenever Robbie had noticed it, Daniel had turned left or right or got up and walked away, as if he'd caught Robbie observing and wanted to block his vision until the moment passed.

But last night Daniel had slept through it all so Robbie got a longer view.

Now Robbie's mother stormed into the kitchen brandishing

a mop. She said, "I need an upstairs maid." Etta had the day off to visit a hospitalized relative and there were a number of tasks his mother didn't want to do alone. One of her three minions should spend the day with her upstairs while the other two re-painted a few windowsills in compliance with the sale contract; the buyers' inspector had noticed a little rot and their persnick-ety lawyer had stipulated repainting as a condition of closing.

"I'll help you upstairs." Daniel stood and bowed in her direc-tion. "At your service, ma'am. Your wish is my command."

"Really? Oh." After a beat Robbie's mother said, "Thanks," and smiled. But her expression was tight and nervous and what followed was more silence, as if she was waiting for something else.

"Or, you know, I could," Maize said.

"Fine then, Maizie. You're on," his mother said. Her whole body slackened around the mop.

Daniel squinted and said, "I volunteered first. Is there some-thing wrong with me?"

"No. Not at all," Robbie's mother said. "I just figured you'd be better at the windowsills."

"Scraping paint isn't complicated," Daniel said. "I'm sure Maize could manage it."

Maize said, "Sure."

"Maybe another time," Robbie's mother said. "What I need help with today is sort of women's work, anyway. Girl stuff."

"How old-fashioned and sexist you are, Mom." Robbie smiled as he crunched on an English muffin, hoping to diffuse whatever was swirling around them like dry wind. But when he looked at Daniel, his face had choleric splotches. "Do you want me to vac-uum or dust if Etta's not around?"

"Robbie told me your buyers are investment bankers," Daniel

said. "I'm sure they won't give a damn about a little chipped paint on the windowsills."

Robbie's mother's posture straightened around the mop.

"Trust me, Daniel. They will," Maize said. "I worked with buyers like that all year. That's *exactly* who cares about a little chipped paint. You'd be surprised how petty people can be."

"No I wouldn't," Daniel said.

"Or I could make the beds," Robbie said.

"That's women's work, too." Daniel scoffed. "If not girl stuff. What—you a homo or something, Robbie?" Daniel said.

Maize laughed, but no one else made a sound. Robbie's mother's eyes narrowed at Daniel as if reacting to glare.

"Correct," Robbie said. "And I'm frighteningly good at making beds. Military corners and everything."

◆ ◆

"Quant'è bella giovinezza / Che si fugge tuttavia / Chi vuol esser lieto, sia: / Di doman non c'è certezza," Robbie recited later that day toward a bay window, with his breath clouding the glass. He and Daniel were standing on twin ladders, scraping paint. He informed Daniel that he'd first heard those lines of verse in Italian class at college and they'd reverberated in the years since like a song he couldn't get out of his head. They were by Lorenzo di Medici, the Renaissance patron of artists and thinkers, whom his teacher had called "Lorenzo Il Magnifico." *"How beautiful is youth / That is fast slipping away . . ."* Robbie began to translate, but before he could finish Daniel said, "Spare me, Professor. I'm trying to concentrate here."

Daniel hadn't said much else to Robbie in the past few

hours—not since asking him, "So why doesn't your mother like me?" and having Robbie pretend that he didn't know what Daniel was talking about, his mother was brusque with everyone, that was just her way, especially with men, including Robbie himself, particularly since his father left.

That was true enough. His mother wasn't the maternal type and she hadn't had so much as a lunch date with a man in a decade. But the explanation didn't satisfy Daniel. He stood silent on his ladder while Robbie filled the air with chatter like Nature rushing to fill a void, and when Robbie ran out of chatter he started quoting random facts and figures and lines of poetry without much of a segue, and when even that started to falter he went inside to check on Maize and his mother, who were having a lively conversation while they worked and looked contented even when they weren't occupying themselves.

The last time he'd escaped inside, his mother was wearing a head kerchief, humming to herself, and Maize was taking a break—sitting on the edge of her guest bed, writing in her journal. Over the past year Robbie had caught Maize doing that more and more often, scribbling intensely with her head bowed toward a blank page, grinning wispily and flushed with the ecstatic concentration of a zealot. He rarely knew what Maize was writing since she often snapped her journal closed at the sight of him, but occasionally he prodded her to read it aloud—uncanny descriptions of people and places and queerly acute conjurings of emotions or half-feelings, if half-feelings could be said to exist at all. Again and again he'd said, "You're a writer, Maizie, you are, you could do it professionally," but each time she'd merely chuckled at the outrageousness of it, as if he'd suggested she be a circus performer or a skydiver, and she changed the subject.

God only knew what Maize was recording in her journal this time around. Probably something wry about this oversized house and the oversized personalities inside it. When he'd told her he'd invited Daniel to join them up here she'd said, "Are you *sure* you want to throw the two of them together for a week? I mean, it's not like it'll be a relaxing situation to begin with and, um, I don't know about Daniel."

Robbie had willfully misinterpreted her by saying, "Yeah, I realize you hardly know Daniel. I have to get you two together more," and in her usual fashion Maize had tactfully let it drop. Robbie had done the same thing whenever Maize mentioned other men to him, most recently a guy from work she went out with about a month ago, whose name she either didn't specify (was it Leo? Max? Avi?) or that Robbie forgot within seconds of hearing it.

Now Robbie and Daniel finished the windowsills. They were sweaty and grimy, with their hair dandruffed by paint flecks and their T-shirts sticking to them like poultices. Robbie gave Daniel first crack at the shower and sat waiting for his turn while his mother rustled up dinner downstairs, with a clatter of pots and pans and curses. She'd never been good in the kitchen, unlike his father's girlfriend, who was not only tall and gorgeous and talented but a whiz of a cook. "Your typical blonde nightmare," his mother once described her.

Upon hitting the shower Robbie shampooed his hair three times, reveling in the hot water and directing the spray between his shoulder blades, lingering until his fingertips shriveled. Daniel was waiting for him when he returned to his old bedroom in nothing but a towel—not in plain sight but hiding in the corner like a mugger. He stole up silently from behind and touched Robbie's back, making him yelp.

"Don't say a word," Daniel murmured into Robbie's ear, reaching around to yank off Robbie's towel in one deft motion. "Just do what the doctor orders. This won't hurt a bit."

Then he was all over Robbie—rougher than he'd ever been and possibly more ardent for his roughness, which was comforting to Robbie after their earlier silence yet also a pity since he, Robbie, wasn't in the mood. Although you wouldn't have known it from the way his body reacted. He stood there and then lay there on the floor submitting to Daniel and putting up a good front, grabbing at Daniel each time he himself was grabbed, amazed at what a cheap reliable workhorse appliance his body was, running constantly at all hours and even at night like a refrigerator.

Robbie almost wished Daniel would be rougher still with him—slap him to dislodge whatever was holding him back at the moment. This glazed state was what he usually experienced after sex rather than during it. Whenever he separated from Daniel he examined himself for bruises and welts and blemishes but found only his unmarked flesh, maybe a bit swollen but otherwise completely unchanged.

Now while they were still in the throes of it Robbie's mother called to announce that they were expected downstairs.

"Robbie? Robbie?" she yelled. "Where are you? Dinner's ready!"

"We should stop," he said to Daniel.

"Not yet," Daniel said.

"Robbie? Daniel? Why aren't you answering me?"

He heard his mother say something he couldn't quite make out to Maize, then the muffled reply of Maize's voice.

"Really," he said to Daniel. "We should go."

"No." Daniel pushed Robbie back to the carpet, got up and checked to make sure the door was locked, and threw himself on Robbie when he came back. They were both so sweat-pebbled and smelly that Robbie wanted another shower already.

"Robbie?" his mother called again, but Robbie wasn't physically capable of replying.

It wasn't until he overheard his mother asking Maize to go upstairs and fetch them that Daniel stopped, and then only after there was the first creak on the long staircase.

Daniel bolted up, threw on the clothes he'd piled near the door like a quick-change artist, and left Robbie lying naked on the floor to fend for himself.

"There you are," Robbie heard Maize say to Daniel. "Robbie's mother's starting to bug out."

When Maize and Daniel returned to the dining room Robbie clearly heard his mother ask, "What's keeping my son?"

"I don't know what's keeping him, ma'am," Daniel said. "I think you'll have to ask your son that yourself."

◆ ◆

Later that night, Robbie caught Maize writing in her journal again. He was on his way back from brushing his teeth, having declined Daniel's invitation to visit him in his room because he was too exhausted for a second round. Once again he found Maize perched on the edge of the bed in the room next to his with her pen moving frantically.

"My, but we're prolific these days," he said. "A regular little Trollope."

"Who you calling a trollop?" Maize said. It was a joke of theirs ever since Robbie had helped her with a paper on the Palliser novels back at college.

"You," he said. "What are you writing?"

"Oh—this?" Maize looked back at her journal. "Just about

some of the guys I knew when I was a college slut." She sighed. "Goodbye to all that."

Robbie knew she was hardly exaggerating. In the eleven months since they'd moved to the city, Maize had had sex with only one man Robbie heard about: the hot young cop who'd responded to her emergency call after she'd found their apartment cleaned out. And that was merely a one-afternoon stand. She'd never been prettier and more alluring than in the past year—men leered at her and hit on her every time they were out together—but she met any sign of amorousness with a vacant stare. She acted a lot like Robbie in his early college days—as if sex would trivialize her life and degrade her passion for higher endeavors. The only time he'd detected a spark was the night she went out with her real estate coworker, and that might have been because she was drunk—teetering as she'd propped herself against their front door and shrugging when he'd asked how it had gone.

"Yeah, you haven't been getting much," Robbie said. He walked into her guest room and sat on the bed beside her. "What's up with that?" He couldn't stifle a yawn and he stretched out on the mattress.

"Well, there are a million guys out there, but how many of them are, you know, really worth it?" Maize said.

"You didn't worry about that in college," Robbie said. They lay next to each other now, their heads on adjacent pillows just a few inches apart.

"Well, I do now. Or maybe I'm just becoming a lesbian and I don't realize it."

"You should be so lucky," Robbie said, and Maize laughed. "No, I'm afraid we're both stuck with men." He smiled wistfully and touched her pretty hair and said, "You're gorgeous, you know," and went back to his room for the night.

◆◆

The next morning, before anyone else awoke, Robbie checked his cell phone. After three days away there were only four messages: a phone company solicitation, a hang-up from someone who'd put down the receiver too late, a junior editor at the newspaper wondering where Robbie had hidden the heavy-duty stapler, and a long-winded message from his father in Rome.

"Robertino!" his father's message began, in his usual chipper businessman's tone. "This is your papa and Clarissa sending our greetings to you from bell' Italia." Through the staticky connection Robbie could hear Clarissa shout, "Hi, Robbie! Miss you!" in the background. His father inquired how Robbie was doing, and what he was doing, and whether anything was new "on your Rialto" as he put it, and he asked how Robbie's internship was progressing at the newspaper, and how his roommate with the strange name was faring. Then he reported that he and Clarissa had recently gone to Paris on a trip that was half business and half pleasure, and that they'd had a great time despite his lousy French, and a charming suite at the Plaza Athénée, and that his work was busy as always, and that a gallery had recently expressed an interest in showing Clarissa's paintings although Clarissa wasn't sure whether she wanted to do it, you knew Clarissa, always modest and hiding her light under a bushel, but Clarissa was otherwise fine and getting a tremendous number of canvases finished, not to mention reading voraciously as usual . . .

His father was in the middle of telling Robbie something else—that he was thinking of joining what he called an "exercise club," which Robbie guessed was the same as a gym—but he got

cut off because the voice mail's time limit expired as he was saying the word *however*.

Robbie replayed his father's message twice as if it would yield
more with repetition. He imagined his father felt stung by the
interruption. He was a man used to holding forth and having his
audience listen as long as need be. His heartiness shrank every
room he entered, but there was a good side to that, too: he was
oblivious to negative signals. Possibly he hadn't noticed being
cut off and just kept talking until he got to his usual farewell of
Mille baci, a thousand kisses, putting Clarissa on the phone at
the last minute to say the same.

Still, the call made Robbie shudder. It wasn't like his father
to simulate an entire conversation into a machine. The international messages he'd left Robbie regularly, every few weeks or so,
weren't verbose. This was Robbie's fault. In the month since his
mother had summoned his help with her move, he hadn't returned his father's calls or even shot him a brief e-mail, as if this
would somehow protect them both from his mother's withering
resentment. When Robbie had returned from his Roman reunion
trip two years ago, he'd made the mistake of telling his mother
how welcoming and affectionate his father had been, followed
by the colossal error of saying that Clarissa was surprisingly interesting and talented and that her brother George was drop-
dead gorgeous.

How dim was that? Had Robbie expected his mother to be
delighted for him after his long estrangement from his father?
He'd been as unblinkingly critical of his father as she was up till
that point, so of course she took it as a betrayal.

"Spare me the heartwarming details," she'd said when Robbie continued describing his Roman trip to her. "I don't want to
hear about it—I don't want to know about it!" And she'd burst
into tears in front of him for the first time in his life, having

stayed dry-eyed during her whole divorce and even at the funer-
als of her own parents.

He'd taken his mother at her word since then. He didn't
mention his father or the fact that they had a relationship again
after years of silence. He didn't accuse her of demonizing his father over a failed marriage that was possibly half her fault. Nor
did he let on that his father occasionally wired him a little money
"to paint the town," although it might've given his mother satisfaction to know that part of her ex-husband's wealth wasn't being spent on himself and Clarissa. It was less complicated for
both of them if Robbie kept quiet. And in the rare moments
when his mother asked him—in a painstakingly casual tone—
whether he'd heard anything from his father lately, Robbie fidgeted and said, "No, I haven't," even if he'd spoken to his father
that day or the day before.

They studiously ignored the subject of his father, sort of the
way, he now realized, he'd focused on Daniel's statuesque physique and professional solidity and ignored other things before
coming up here. Robbie had disregarded the way Daniel took
his hand a little too firmly during their few restaurant dinners
with Maize, or badgered them both whenever they shared an
opinion about a play or a book or a movie ("You two liked that?
I can't believe you liked that"), or glared at Robbie whenever he
failed to back up Daniel's more questionable pronouncements
(beige was the best color for a living room sofa and most lawyers
were people who weren't smart enough to get into medical school
and Germans were obsessively clean because they had a dirty
history), which issued more frequently during their nights with
Maize than they otherwise did, as if her presence uncorked
Daniel's need for self-assertion.

There was rarely enough reassurance for either of them, Robbie was starting to discover; in that respect they were well or

terribly matched. Or there was sufficient assurance somewhere but Robbie couldn't access it. Daniel had endless appetite, he had vaunting ambition, he had ceaseless drive, he had boundless energy, and like Robbie lately he was practically a sex addict. Even on mornings after Robbie had spent the whole night with him and was dressing to leave Daniel's room in NYU housing for work, he would reach his long arms toward Robbie and say, "Where are you going so fast? Have you decided you don't like me anymore?" and Robbie—rolling his eyes yet flattered—would strip and jump into bed for a quickie before he was allowed to depart.

It mystified Robbie why Daniel clung to him. He wasn't nearly as handsome as Daniel, and he looked puffy-eyed in the mornings, and he was so high-strung that his hands sometimes shook for no reason at all, and he wasn't en route to an interesting career. In fact his work life so far was an utter flop.

He didn't tell Daniel much about his internship at the newspaper because it was too boring. Instead he reported the details to Maize, just as she'd relayed the special horrors of working for André Gilbert to him. They made a little sport of whose work life was worse, offering their humiliations for comic relief (*I restocked the office's toilet paper! I had the boss's shoes shined!*), but when they went too far with it they crossed into glumness and had to comfort each other by saying it would get better soon.

But his own job wouldn't ever get better because it wasn't even a job. It was an internship and not remotely as advertised. It was subsecretarial and exploitative. In seven months, the closest Robbie had come to the editorial experience promised was the emergency fact-checking of a book review on a day when two junior editors had called in sick. He'd been working at the Arts section of the newspaper about eight weeks—nearly as long as he'd known Daniel—for a California avocado heiress named

Jocelyn, who had bohemian airs and flowing skirts and a Yale degree and a trust fund. Before that he'd been the minion of a fifty-something man named Howie, who'd appointed himself the Czar of All Things Queer at the newspaper, and for months before that a "floater" from department to department, staying at each desk just long enough to feel completely alienated and superfluous.

Robbie thought that when he'd finally landed in the Arts section everything would improve, but it hadn't. If anything, it had gotten worse. It wasn't just that he had to answer the phones and change the toner in the printers and run the postage meter and pack up thousands of CDs and DVDs and review copies. It wasn't just the mouse droppings he found on his desk in the mornings or the fact that the office was musty and windowless. It wasn't even that Jocelyn stole Robbie's few ideas about layout and organization and passed them off as her own right in front of him, at the staff meetings where he took the minutes, or that he'd allowed her to string him along for weeks and months with false promises that his internship might someday turn into a real, paying job if he worked hard and waited, when by now it was clear that it wouldn't.

No, he could have put up with all that. What irked him most was that he'd been snubbed for his highbrow-mainstream taste (playwrights and directors and classical musicians whom Jocelyn called "the usual suspects," followed by snoring sounds) and re-buffed everywhere else at the newspaper, apparently, for his appearance. He didn't have tattoos like the other expensively educated assistants on the staff. He didn't have piercings. His hair was combed into the same neat side part he'd worn all his life rather than artfully mussed, and he didn't wear camouflage cargo pants or vintage rock tees or flip-flops to work either. He didn't even own clothes like that. He showed up each day in the fine shirts and elegant Milanese sports coats he'd gotten from his father, wearing high seriousness on his sharply pressed sleeves, and they treated him like a bourgeois square they could roll their eyes at, or an uptown spy to be viewed with suspicion, or simply as someone too dumb and too uncool to bother with even if he tried desperately to make conversation.

"Maybe I should show up naked," he'd said to Maize one night, to which she'd replied, "Not your style, Robbie. You don't even like to be naked in the shower."

"You're shallow! Talk to me!" he'd wanted to scream at his coworkers on particularly frustrating days. "I have a lot to offer! If you're not going to pay me a salary, the least you can do is make conversation!" But as the dreary months passed he felt more and more like a high school nerd sitting alone in the cafeteria, eating a sloppy joe that spilled onto his lap while the popular kids smirked at him from a distance.

It was all the more painful because the editors *were* friendly and chatty to some of the other assistants. They were downright effusive, for instance, with a plump and sassy Barnard girl in the production department named Shawniqua, who wore a uniform of sweat pants and Doc Martens and tight tees splattered with subversive phrases. On the day Shawniqua came to the office in a red tee with black lettering that read I GOT THE PUSSY, I MAKE THE RULES, no fewer than eight editors and writers had said, "Love your outfit!" as they passed her layout table before sweeping by Robbie as if he were untouchable. Robbie had counted her compliments, and was ashamed to have.

Now Robbie listened to his father's pathetically long voicemail message for a third time, saved it, and turned off his cell. He didn't want to worry about his father or think about the newspaper people while he was up here at his mother's, but he couldn't help himself. He stewed about all of it as he slipped into Daniel's guest room as quietly as a prowler, making no sound as he opened the door and closed it behind him.

How enticing Daniel could be when asleep. Robbie lay next to him gingerly and tried to breathe in sync with him again. But he couldn't quite manage it. Suddenly he was swamped by the implacable sense of solitude that sometimes overcame him— the loneliness that threatened to implode him and render him unreachable. He wished Daniel would roll on top of him, sealing his mouth with his own before either of them could say anything wrong, but he didn't. Daniel didn't know Robbie was beside him. Their bare arms brushed each other and Robbie lay there inhaling and exhaling and staring at the ceiling, waiting till daylight, when they all would rise for their next assignments.

◆ ◆

Maize had lied to Robbie. She hadn't been writing about college hookups in her journal when he'd caught her sitting on the bed during her work break. She'd been describing her fumbling encounters with her real estate coworker Eli, whom she hadn't spoken to until shortly before she got fired but on whom she had spied at his cubicle for several months beforehand.

For all she knew, other people in the office had glommed on to Eli, too, since he was impossible to block out even if you tried. Eli was extremely tall and rangy and redheaded. The strong features in his lean face made him look, Maize had thought immediately, like a slightly underfed Viking, and he turned himself out like nobody else in the office, in blunt defiance of the dress code, wearing scuffed boots, motorcycle jackets, ripped jeans, and brightly crocheted skullcaps on cold days. When Maize first overheard him speak from four desks away his voice was husky, with a gravelly rasp that somehow made it seem smoother and more lyrical than a regular voice: a Hells Angel reciting sonnets. Yet when he smiled his face blazed with a white boyish light and he looked, for a second, like a severely overgrown eight-year-old who'd gotten waylaid en route to the playground.

Maize couldn't resist darting her eyes in Eli's direction on the two or three afternoons a week that he loped into the office. Nor could she help wondering how he'd scored a part-time gig when all the other assistants like her were slaving six full days a week. Nor could she help marveling at his cheerful insubordination toward his boss. He slouched at his desk, rolling his wide shoulders forward—the apologetic posture that Maize had often observed in tall people—yet there was nothing else that was the least shrinking about him. He listened to his iPod constantly as he performed his clerical tasks, as though literally tuning out his brain-numbing duties, nodding almost imperceptibly to whatever he was listening to at the moment, and didn't remove his earpiece even when he answered his boss's phone, as if passively refusing to be distracted from what mattered to him.

"Yo, Empress," Eli called whenever his boss (a high-octane barracuda with the unlikely name of BeeZee) pranced into the office on her kitten heels. He'd visor his hand over his smooth forehead to give her a mock Scout salute that he ended with florid curlicues. If BeeZee stormed up to Eli's desk—long nails digging into her waist—demanding to know exactly when Eli intended to finish a work project she'd been waiting for, he would say, "It will get done when it gets done, BeeZee," and she'd let it drop. The one time Maize had witnessed her yelling, "That's simply not acceptable, Eli!" he'd lifted his pointer to signal a pause, slipped on a pair of thick Clark Kent–ish eyeglasses, and trained a flat stare on BeeZee as if wanting a sharper view of the ugliness before him. In response BeeZee scurried off to the bathroom like someone who'd just realized she'd been walking around all day with her zipper down.

O, to be that self-possessed! Maize had never been truly intimidating in her whole life—to a boss, no less—and she'd let out an involuntary chuckle at the sight of it, which made Eli turn her way and perhaps notice her for the first time in the nine months she'd been there. He beamed his boyish white smile at her and made a circling gesture around his ear to indicate his boss's craziness, and when he kept smiling her way Maize buried her head in her work again and blanched at having been caught staring.

A few days later Maize was in the office copy room, stymied in her efforts to make multiple sets of a co-op board package and cursing under her breath at the machine that kept jamming on her, when suddenly she heard Eli's deep voice behind her saying, "Allow me," and then he was in front of her, fixing it with a few deft strokes, and towering over her head-on. "All yours," he said.

"Thanks—thank you," Maize mumbled as she resumed her work, gaze averted. When he didn't answer she supposed she should say more. "You've saved my life. Really, André will disembowel me if I don't get this package out by five, and I'm a disaster with anything mechanical."

"André's a squirt," Eli said. "You could probably take him with one hand tied behind your back."

The image of Maize beating André to the ground popped into her head and made her laugh. "Well, I don't know about that," she said. "But thank god somebody here is competent with machines." She leaned toward him a bit and whispered, "I've noticed you're pretty good at handling your boss, too."

"She's another machine," Eli said. "Only a simpler and cruder apparatus than this one."

"How long have you worked for her?"

"About a year. But the market's tanking, so BeeZee won't be able to afford me anymore. I suspect it's coming to an end."

"You think?" Maize had been so consumed with her petty tasks that she hadn't looked up from them long enough to notice the condition of the market or anything else beyond her desk. The pulse in her neck jumped like a fish.

"That's my forecast." Eli predicted that BeeZee would probably invent a fake reason for getting rid of him in the down market, so that she wouldn't look like she was faltering as an agent, before she hired another assistant to do the same job at a much lower salary. He said he didn't care as long as she gave him severance, which would buy him a few months to rehearse with his band.

"Oh, you're a musician?" Maize asked, hearing her own dimness. What else would someone in a *band* be?

"I am." He smiled differently now—diffidently—and shifted his weight from one long leg to the other as though her interest in his nonoffice life required a chord change.

When she asked him what instrument he played he replied, "Bass, drums, piano, and violin," and when she said "Wow," he asked her what work she did when she wasn't stuck at André's desk.

"What do you mean?" she said.

"You're creative, right? You look like a painter." He narrowed his big gray eyes at her. "No. I take that back. You look like a writer. I'm guessing a writer."

"Me? No." She shook her head and looked at the floor. "I mean, sometimes I write in my journal, but it's not for anyone else."

Now she peered at her blouse and her skirt and her sensible shoes—the boring professional attire André required—and though she was flattered to be mistaken for an artist she couldn't fathom how anyone could look at her and come to that conclusion. She felt mortifyingly straight as she stood there dwarfed by a guy dressed like a road warrior and she decided to deflect the discomfort by playing it for laughs.

She smiled at Eli. "I wish I were an artist. But I'm just an average flat-footed girl from the suburbs. If I have any special talent, it's for shopping. I spent my formative years in malls."

Eli glanced at her from his sovereign height, grinning as though faintly amused, and he narrowed his eyes further still. "Somehow I doubt that's what you are," he said. "You don't seem average to me."

"Swear to god—that's it!" Maize spoke a little too loudly and emphatically, in her broad parody of herself. "And you know something? Now that I live in a city without malls, I do nothing but come here and go home and come here again. On weekends I dust my apartment." She made a cartoonish pout as she hefted her load of copies and prepared to retreat to her desk. "That's the sum of my stimulating life in the world's greatest city."

"Even tonight?" Eli said.

"Sure." She shrugged. "Every night's the same."

She was about to turn to him and say, *Thanks again for your help. I'm done here*, when he said, "I think I can fix that for you, too. Come out with me tonight."

◆ ◆

When Robbie had entered the guest bedroom and interrupted her journal writing the other day he'd broken her focus from Eli, which she supposed was just as well. It was far easier and less frightening to be describing André again, instead—everything she could register about him, from his Gucci loafers and custom suits to his obscenest turns of phrase.

She was ashamed to be dwelling on André a full month after being fired by him. If she was a stronger person she'd have moved on as ruthlessly as André himself did, dropping irresolute buyers from his phone contacts list, ordering Maize to lose the numbers of "poor people" who didn't have a net worth of $5 million minimum, informing parents from his adopted son's school that they were out of their gourds if they thought he'd be attending their fund-raisers, though he might order his underemployed stay-at-home partner to mail them a check if they asked him nicely.

Maize couldn't set the subject of André aside just yet, as if André were an unsolved puzzle or a towering figure among men although he stood only five feet six.

In fairness, André was nothing if not memorable—a veritable font of zingers Maize had quoted to Robbie from the start. He was as crudely fascinating as a horror movie you were appalled to find entertaining yet couldn't stop watching anyway. And he had a split personality. If Maize didn't know André, she'd never have guessed that the short, caustic, potty-mouthed man who criticized her work and brayed at other brokers and routinely denied them access to his listings was the same supple charmer who seduced sellers into giving him their property to handle and wheedled buyers into ponying up far more than they thought a place was worth. It was astonishing how deftly André could switch from one persona to another, between sips of the espresso he sent Maize out to get for him three times a day, and it was most impressive when he had multiple phone calls on hold and he pivoted from Mean Vulgar André to Smooth Cajoling André at the push of a button, into his headset, like a psychic channeling different voices during a séance.

Well, face it, Maize thought, as she sat on the edge of her bed with her journal again. She and André had had a sort of weirdly intense bond, with André as the harsh, reluctant mentor and Maize as the—what? She wasn't André's protégé by a long shot. Although she wasn't certain what she wanted to do with her life yet—she wasn't directed like Daniel or Eli or the legions of painfully bright young things in this city—she knew she didn't want a career in the shark tank of Manhattan real estate. Working for André was merely a phase en route to whatever came next. Yet whether or not he'd meant to, André had nonetheless hammered some knowledge of his industry and his world into Maize with an endless series of rules and regulations that issued from his mouth as frequently as barbs directed at his cobrokers.

Never cut your commission, he'd instructed Maize many times during the year she'd worked for him. *Fight against giving referral fees. Never let sellers be around during showings and don't be nice about it either, throw them out of their own damn homes if you have to. Never work with fashion types because all they want to do is shop, they're rarely satisfied, and they'll waste years of your life. Ditto with interior designers. Ditto with movie people unless they absolutely have to have an East Coast pied-à-terre pronto. A celebrity waste of time is the same as a nobody waste of time unless you get publicity from it. And never take a buyer out for the first time on a weekend— say you'll be in Paris or the Hamptons or your country home—or they'll never respect you. And never do after-hours showings because they'll always be late, and never do early mornings because if they're serious they'll make the time at lunch, and never ever take shit from anyone—sellers or buyers or brokers or lawyers or mortgage brokers or appraisers—and never forget the client isn't your friend, you're the hired help, but never signal you understand that or they'll walk all over you.*

And also, he'd said shortly before firing Maize, *always prefer single people to couples. Avoid couples like the plague so you have half the battle and don't get caught in their unbelievably tedious cross-fire of tastes.* A statement Maize came to take partly as André's comment on his own home life.

Maize gathered that André's longtime partner, Trevor, was at best a bore to him, though André had never said it in so many words. Whenever Trevor called from their Tribeca loft, where he doodled on computer drawings or did architectural renderings or some such, André rolled his eyes. Sometimes he grunted for good measure. Nearly always he had Maize take a message instead of listening to him (*Please tell André the dishwasher just broke down, please tell him the nanny's asked for two weeks off in November and we need to discuss it, please remind him it's Parent Night at Jordan's school and he can't skip it again*) or he ordered Maize to relay warnings that he, André, had important business meetings, sales pitches, client meals, and wouldn't be home for dinner, and Trevor should cook something for himself and their son or order it in from Bouley, but it had better be something nutritious and no desserts or he'd kill him, and he'd better make sure Jordan was in bed before ten because if he came home and found him awake he'd have to axe-murder both of them.

Maize knew it was snobbish of her to find André so coarse and scrappy. André might be successful and affluent but apparently he hadn't had her advantages. When Maize once idly asked what he'd majored in at college André had said, "Nothing. I didn't go. My family was broke and I never liked school anyway. I majored in life." And when Maize bowed her head in shame for having brought up the subject, André said, "Lookit, how adorable—you're *blushing* for me," and he'd drummed his manicured fingernails on Maize's desktop. "Don't worry your little head, Maize. Maybe I can't say *I don't have the rent* in three languages, but my life turned out fine anyway." And he'd leaned closer to laugh in Maize's face.

Over the months, increasingly, revoltingly, Maize heard herself picking up that homely cackle of André's—heard it coming from her own mouth—and she heard herself using André's dominator tone during her own business calls as well, barking "Cut to the chase" when another broker's assistant went on too long. She caught herself hanging up a few times when she was crazily busy and agents were asking about a property that had sold long ago or blurting, "Get that signed contract back to us today or we'll turn this deal around so fast your head will spin," shocking herself as much as the person she'd just threatened. Her aggression even thrust out at home occasionally, when she said things to Robbie like "Don't be a complete idiot" or "Get your head out of your ass," and saw the shock on his face before she could add something to cushion the blow.

In those moments she wasn't the overbearingly polite girl who said "Please" and "Thank you" and "Excuse me" even to people who didn't deserve it. She was André Gilbert or a cross-dressing variation on him. André Lite. Now that she'd been fired she could only loiter in the memory of it, like an audience refusing to leave after a final curtain.

Perhaps André had a hard time letting go of people, too, despite appearances to the contrary. Perhaps Maize would have understood that sooner if she'd been smarter or more observant before it was too late. Now she got up from the bed and walked to the other side of the house where she could see Robbie miserably scraping sills with Daniel, looking like a condemned man. Then she plodded back to the guest room to write about the moment when everything changed irrevocably between herself and André and she'd been too unsettled to realize what had happened.

She'd been sitting in André's office on a Monday morning, several months into her job and one day after an obligatory birthday visit with her mother in the suburbs. She was stuffing envelopes with promotional letters about André's latest record-breaking sale and stealing looks at Eli now and then and trying not to dwell on what had happened in Connecticut the day before. She'd been so stultified and sugar-glazed at her mother's place, after allowing herself two pieces of cake, that she'd picked the local newspaper off the coffee table and started leafing through it desultorily—astonished to find a wedding announcement for Bethany Campbell at the back of the second section. She'd flipped the page twice and then three times before reading it. Bethany was still blonde and smiling yet somehow faded, as if her beauty had gotten blurred by a little extra weight or experience of the world, and the groom standing behind her in the picture seemed unworthy—or at least unworthy of Maize's idea of Bethany. A blandly handsome Dartmouth graduate with prematurely thinning hair and a stiff smile to match his suit, he looked like a junior mascot version of the many investment bankers Maize had shown glitzy lofts to in the past year, and she supposed Bethany would be one of the women who accompanied those men.

Had she expected Bethany to be exceptional? To break out of the cage of her former identity and become someone completely unexpected? Not if Maize was being realistic. Bethany's whole life had announced *I Will Marry Well* from the moment she hit puberty. Yet a dazzling disappointment had swept over Maize at the sight of Bethany's photo, an aching homesickness so keen it was as though she'd discovered Bethany disfigured or bankrupt or as if the wedding announcement were an obituary. Inexplicable and irrational tears had come to Maize's eyes as she threw the newspaper away. There was absolutely no reason to take it personally but she did. It felt like—what?—the end of something. And that night she recorded everything she could remember about Bethany in her journal—the clothes Bethany wore in high school, the way she walked, the sound of her laughter, the pure sweet lemony smell that atomized around her like a disposable aura—until she was too fatigued to remember any more and she fell asleep.

She wrote in her journal all the time now—sometimes twice a day—as if saying *I Was Here Too* would make her life real to her when it was possibly just the opposite, a semifictional version of experience that made it more meaningful and bearable than it really was.

Probably there was no point in jotting about herself or Bethany or André or Eli or Robbie or his mother, but she couldn't stop. She supposed you couldn't leave everything behind but you should try to get rid of as much as you could, the way Robbie's mother was throwing out her knickknacks and mementoes. Only it was harder if you were like Maize—someone who saw a picture or heard a voice and suddenly felt weird mournful churnings in her current existence, like sediment at the bottom of a lake. It was amazing how even marginal presences could incite so much emotion in her, as if she were an overcharged magnet drawing all the stray filings within a radius of several miles.

Suddenly the office phone had rung, snapping her back to the present. Maize drew a deep breath and girded herself, suspecting it was a broker she'd overheard André eviscerating that morning before going out to do showings. Instead it was André himself.

"What the hell took you so long to pick up?" André said, though Maize had lifted the receiver on the second ring. He was panting lightly. He explained that he was in the East Seventies, outside his new townhouse listing, which he was supposed to show to a cowboyish CEO who'd just been profiled in *The Wall Street Journal*. Trouble was, he'd left the frigging keys to the townhouse in the office and he needed Maize to drop everything and deliver them to him immediately.

"You mean like, um, right now, André?" Maize had asked stupidly, flummoxed since she was in the middle of ten other tasks.

"What does *immediately* mean to you, Maize? To me it means five minutes ago," André said. "Move that little tush. I'm standing outside this house like a bagman and the hotshot is on his way. They're somewhere in my desk. The desk key's taped under my chair."

"Oh." André had never divulged where his desk key was before. (The one time Maize had asked about it he'd said, "Mind your own beeswax.") "Okay. Do you want to stay on the phone while I look?" Maize said.

"What I want is for you to *get here* ASAP. I'm pretty sure they're in the top middle drawer. Stupid stupid stupid!" André hissed into the receiver, and Maize flushed before she realized André was lambasting himself rather than her. Maize promised to be there right away.

There were plenty of things chocking André's middle drawer—business cards, address books, cuticle scissors and paper clips and a screwdriver—but no keys except for something so tiny it could only fit a post office box. Maize combed through the drawer a second time but still came up empty. "Please please," she said aloud to herself. She could picture André yelling at her on some fancy street corner, quivering with rage at her tardiness as he stood beside some customer who wore a perturbed expression along with a Bluetooth and a hundred-thousand-dollar wristwatch.

She'd looked over toward Eli's desk for a second reflexively, hoping his large solid presence might steady her, but it was one of Eli's days off so he wasn't there.

Maize told herself not to panic. She would find the keys. Of course she would find them. They were here somewhere. She'd hunt through every other drawer quickly yet carefully and find them and André wouldn't be angry at her. On the contrary, she'd be André's heroine.

But André's right top drawer had nothing.

And André's right middle drawer had no keys either.

Okay, she thought as she yanked open the bottom right drawer. Now I'm getting somewhere. Under a pile of manila folders there was a heavy steel box with a delicate clasp that rattled promisingly when she picked it up and placed it on her lap. She had some trouble getting the lid open—the clasp was stuck so hard she had to force it—so when she succeeded it popped violently and almost grazed her chin.

Her hands quivered when she saw what she was holding. Inside the fireproof box she found a pair of platinum cufflinks, a pearl-and-sapphire ring like the one André's client Betsy Talbot had worn at a pitch session, an invitation to a museum costume ball addressed to another of André's clients, a gold tie clip she'd never seen André wear in the office, six twenty-dollar bills and nine fifties and four singles, a key chain with a Bentley logo but no key, a French votive candle still in its wrapper and smelling of apricot, two Deco candlesticks she'd admired in the butler's pantry of a classic seven they'd recently sold in Carnegie Hill, five Tiffany silver swizzle sticks a seller had complained went missing after an open house ("Tell her we'll find them and shove them up her tight ass," André had said when Maize relayed the complaint), a dirty linen handkerchief with the monogram PCF, an Hermès belt buckle, and matchbooks from the Carlyle, the Hassler, the Quisisana, and the Savoy. There was also a lot of loose change that sullied Maize's fingers as she pawed through it looking for the keys.

She had absolutely no business poring over these objects. She was in far, far too much of a rush to be dillydallying, but she couldn't help herself. She closed the box and clamped it shut and shoved it exactly where it was before, under the files, then she proceeded frantically to the next drawer. She found four sets of keys in the middle left drawer, grabbed all of them, locked the desk again, threw on her coat, and sprinted out of the office.

It was only in a cab hurtling up Park Avenue—between reassuring calls to André that she was on her way and requests to the driver that he please go as fast as possible—that she allowed herself to muse about the significance of the artifacts she'd uncovered. They were mostly the kind of small things you wouldn't notice were missing until well after they disappeared, not for weeks or months or years, because you didn't use them every day. When you eventually realized they were gone you wouldn't have an inkling of where they were, although you were sure they must be somewhere just out of reach. And when you failed to locate them you'd blame yourself for losing them. When the truth was that you'd been robbed.

Her concentration broke as the cab screeched to a stop in front of the townhouse and she paid the driver, neglecting to ask for a receipt.

"There you are! Just in the nick!" André said as Maize scrambled to hand him the keys, but instead of thanking her he made a shooing gesture and ordered her to run along back to the office.

Maize had written about that incident right after Robbie interrupted her the other day. She had recounted plenty more about André in her journal over the past month but she didn't know why. To what end? It was like she was gathering evidence, like she could still be attacked by André tomorrow or the next day or the next, though André probably didn't give her a thought anymore and had moved on to the task of harrying his new assistant. When she considered the possibility that she'd already been forgotten, a sickly, anxious feeling of having been jilted—not merely by André but by that whole period of her life—reared inside her. However misplaced, that was how she'd felt when her stepfather had left her mother's house and, as far as she remembered, it was the way she'd felt when her father had died young and suddenly, though she herself had been so young at the time, it was a gauzy memory: pure inchoate hunger for something she needed to survive but had no words for, like a primitive.

It struck her as strange that she hadn't felt slighted when men in the city ignored or disregarded her, and that when they did pay attention her breath tightened and she envisioned all the problems they'd have together before she learned anything about them. Undoubtedly it was facile to claim that she'd been too sapped by slaving for André to care enough, or too burned out by the aftermath of her job to rejoin the game. But that's probably what she'd tell anyone who asked, for lack of a better answer. She was nearly as clueless as the high school Maize popping in and out of Hal Jamesley's office between classes, as tantalized by whatever happened there as she was protected by the knowledge that it had to end.

She'd successfully evaded Hal—Hal and all other men except Robbie—before they really knew her. Her lovers might have assumed otherwise because sex allegedly tapped something primal, but they were wrong. There were several different kinds of primal drumming inside any one person, thrusting for dominance and then receding, each with an independent life, and it was sort of ludicrous to peg one or the other as the most essential. Which was most important depended on the season and the day and the moment, didn't it? And perhaps a certain amount of confusion about it was necessary, not only so you could keep dreaming your life but so your life could keep dreaming you.

◆ ◆

Robbie decided that he and Daniel needed a break. Enough with laboring together like a pair of field hands, saying little to each other while around them his mother and Maize and Etta clucked and chattered endlessly, folding and packing and ironing and wrapping. The silence between Robbie and Daniel was growing as uncomfortable as watching a make-out scene in a movie with a lover you barely kissed anymore. Maybe if they both lay by his mother's pool or plunged into the deep end together it would refresh them. He told Daniel to get out his bathing suit.

They'd been sunning by the pool for an hour, rubbing lotion on each other's backs and passing a thermos of iced tea between them, when a shadow passed over their bare torsos like a cloud. Robbie heard Maize's voice saying, "Get out of those lounge chairs, you lazy bums. We've still got tons of chores to do. Starting with the attic."

She sounded pushy and directive as though she'd caught her tone from Robbie's mother. Or maybe she was still flipping the bird at her awful ex-boss, proving how productive she could be despite his firing her. (*You think you're efficient, you treacherous snake? I'll show you efficient.*)

In a sleepy voice Daniel said, "Piss off, Maize." He gave a leonine yawn and stretched his muscular arms and legs. "As it happens we *are* working now. On our tans."

"Excuse me?" Maize said. When Robbie opened his eyes she was standing over them with her hands cocked on her hips.

"You're a doctor, Daniel. You know UV rays are bad for you."
She waited for a reply but none came. "And we're being paid to
help out here, remember?"

"You're right, Maizie. Of course you're right. Just five or ten
more minutes," Robbie said. "Promise. Then we'll be good."

"Speak for yourself, Robbie." Daniel yawned again. He sat up
in his chair, blinked against the light, and looked first at Robbie,
then at Maize, and then between both of them. Back and forth
and back as though the glare had rendered them indistinguish-
able silhouettes.

Then he got off the chaise, stood at the edge of the pool, and
slipped out of his shorts. His bare buttocks were stunning—
smooth and firm and three shades lighter than the skin around
them—like a pair of small, succulent honeydews. Just before
Daniel crouched and jumped into the pool, he wagged his back-
side at Maize and Robbie in a mooning gesture. He was under-
water before either of them could comment.

When his head reemerged his straight hair was as slick and
glossy as a seal's.

Maize yelled, "Woo-hoo, Daniel! Great ass! Hubba!"

"Gee, thanks," he said. "But I knew that already." He swam
toward the deep end and then turned back toward them. "There's
more where that came from. Want to see my special water trick?"

At the same moment Robbie said, "Not really," Maize yelled,
"Yeah, baby!"

"Okay. Here goes." Daniel was just a few feet away from them
now. He took a deep breath, pinched his nose, and did multiple
somersaults in the water, using his free arm to propel the rota-
tions, flashing them again and again while Maize whooped in
delight and Robbie sat there waiting for it to end. After five spins
Daniel stood before them gulping air, his body bisected at the
waist by the water, listing woozily with a wild look in his eye.

Rivulets streamed down his abs and disappeared into the water. Maize clapped loudly in appreciation.

Daniel had never looked more beautiful to Robbie than in that moment, with his hair and everything below it glistening and his broad shoulders strong as a god's wings. But all Robbie could think to say was "That's enough."

"No it's not," Daniel said. "I have one more trick." And with that he lay on his back in the water, thrusting so that everything below his waist showed flagrantly, bobbing on the surface like a water snake for what seemed like forever.

Then with one sharp scissors kick he sprayed cold water onto Robbie and Maize and laughed, swimming away again.

It took a second before they knew what hit them. Maize sputtered as though the water had entered her mouth. Robbie smelled the chlorine and wiped his stinging eyes with his forearm. Daniel paddled away from them toward the diving board and hoisted himself onto it, jumping up and down before he cannonballed naked into the pool with a big splash.

From the periphery of his vision Robbie noticed another movement. He glanced up and saw his mother standing in her bedroom window upstairs, immobile and transfixed with a grimace, before she caught Robbie watching her and disappeared behind her sheer curtains like a phantom.

◆ ◆

"Why the heck does your mother have a clay tennis court in Connecticut?" Daniel said as he and Robbie swept it a few hours later, in the setting sun. The red dust coated his sneakers and Robbie's like powdery dried blood. "Were you parents pretending to be French or Spanish or something? Don't you find this a pain? Hard courts make more sense in this part of the world."

Robbie didn't know which question to answer first. He was distracted by how opinionated Daniel was for someone who didn't even play tennis. He had a doctor's spillover decisiveness to nearly everything he said now, Robbie had begun to notice, as if he were constantly in the emergency ward. But when Robbie had asked Daniel why he'd flashed and spritzed them earlier he'd merely shrugged and said, "I dunno. I just felt like it. Lighten up, Robbie."

"The clay court was here when my parents bought the house. They were stuck with what they had," Robbie said now. "And for the record, we *are* European on my father's side."

"Well, if you want to go back three or four generations," Daniel said.

"Italian Jews, to be specific," Robbie said. "My father lives in Rome right now."

"I know that already, Robbie," Daniel said.

Robbie pushed the roller brush over the sidelines. He said, "Have you ever even played on a clay court? It's great. Slower than hard courts, so it gives your points a chance to develop."

Robbie knew what he was talking about. The bounces on clay were higher so you could have long, elegant rallies even if you weren't very good and slide into your shots without stumbling, the way someone contemplative slid into a thought rather than pouncing on it.

"No, I've never played on clay. But I saw my parents do it once when we were on vacation in Portugal," Daniel said. He moved over the court with the wide brush yoked to his shoulders like an ox.

"Then please shut up about what you don't know," Robbie said.

That hadn't come out the way Robbie had intended. As he retreated to the nearby shed with a shovel, to get a scoop of fresh clay for the hollows near the baseline, his ears stung with his own words. But maybe he needed to be blunter with Daniel. He was getting fatigued from tiptoeing around, worrying about Daniel's reactions to everything, and subtlety didn't seem to work on him very well. He wanted to get off this court and take a nap.

Robbie spread the clay and smoothed it. He rather wished Maize had been blunter with him, too—shouted something like "Are you crazy, throwing two people like your mother and Daniel together for a whole week? What are you thinking?" He also wished he himself had been more forceful everywhere rather than playing the milquetoast. He should have confronted Jocelyn for stringing him along in the Arts section—demanded she tell him when his position there would become paying. Instead he'd let her get away with several flirtatious dodges, the last of which he'd not only saved on his voice mail for weeks but transcribed on a notepad like a court reporter: *Hi Robbie, it's Jocelyn. Ah, Robbie, I have a meeting at eight thirty tomorrow morning with the publisher—this is meeting <u>nine thousand</u> about expanding the staff—Jesus Christ! These people are driving me crazy—without spending any money—you know, the old story—and I <u>presume</u> that I'm going to be free to take you out for a nice lunch to gab about it but I don't know how long this is gonna go and I <u>want</u> to get an answer tomorrow—but who knows?—so I would suggest that you not count on going to the restaurant just in case I get bollixed up— I don't think I will; I think it'll be fine and it will be something for me to look <u>forward</u> to, but nevertheless, we'll see . . .*

But he hadn't challenged Jocelyn or anyone else in months and months. He was becoming a slacker who didn't even challenge himself anymore. He was surrounded by new books he didn't read—he merely read book reviews—and when he tried rereading his favorites he found their magic had diminished, temporarily he hoped, as if written in a dead lost language he no longer knew well enough to translate.

"Want to play a set when we're done here?" he said to Daniel now. He hardly felt like playing tennis, but he thought he should make a peace offering. He might even throw the match to Daniel to make him feel better.

"Nope," Daniel said.

"Come on. You'll probably kick my butt. I'm so rusty and out of shape," Robbie said.

Daniel smiled for a moment, shyly, as if imagining the pleasure of beating Robbie on his home court, and Robbie suddenly had the impulse to drag him into the storage shed and sodomize him amid the dirt and grit.

"Or I could get Maize out here and we could play a round robin with her," Robbie said.

Daniel's smile retracted and he said, "No."

Although Robbie sensed he'd misspoken, he assumed the only antidote was to keep talking. "Maize can hardly get her racquet on the ball, of course."

Daniel said, "No, Robbie." He shook his head and said, "No. It's getting late. No."

◆ ◆

Back at the house, Robbie's mother clucked and said, "Cripes, I thought I had enough," and she announced that she had to drive into town to buy more packing tape.

Maize went to the guest room and leafed through her journal while she waited for Robbie's mother to return. She wasn't up for writing a new entry but she allowed herself to think about her one night out with Eli as she shifted and fidgeted in an easy chair, unable to find a comfortable position.

After she'd finished sending out André's board package that night, Eli had led her to a succession of strange places—first to a gallery showing photos of luridly mutilated dolls waving their mangled limbs in resort locations like Malibu and the French Riviera and Dubai (the artist, Eli had informed her, was a neighbor of his in Fort Greene), and then to a divey club near Tompkins Square where a quartet played an indistinct music wavering between jazz and classical and heavy metal (Maize guessed you'd call it fusion), and finally to a restaurant with a sign that read QUEER TAPAS BAR a few blocks from her apartment, which she'd never noticed before and which was, judging from its empty tables, either failing or had a late-night clientele. Between locales Eli did most of the talking and Maize nodded or spoke in monosyllables.

"Elias—*qué pasa, bizcocho caliente?*" a cute Latino waiter yelled the second they'd entered the restaurant, clamping his hand on Eli's bare bicep and asking what a "big strapping boy" like him needed to keep up his studly energies. The waiter smirked at Maize more sharply with each new round of cocktails—once he even curled his lip—as though she were a fly that had landed on the food and couldn't be readily shooed away or swatted.

Eli had eaten ravenously that night—he did have a lot of body to nourish, Maize supposed—but she'd ordered only drinks, which she'd downed too fast. Although her stomach was growling, she declined Eli's repeated offers to share his tapas, since eating finger food in front of someone she hardly knew felt too personal.

From the moment she'd realized she'd trapped herself into going out with Eli, she'd resolved to keep everything pleasant yet distant. Something about Eli compelled and scared her equally, so if he questioned her about herself she'd answer succinctly and change the subject to the office instead—André's deals and his clients, and how bad the computers were and stingy the company was with supplies—even if she bored both of them brainless.

When he asked her what her parents were like she said, "Oh, the usual" and expounded on what an interesting character she found André—how mean and manipulative he could be, and what a demanding perfectionist he was, but how she tried not to hold it against him because she sensed a boiling current of self-loathing under his frosty veneer although she didn't know exactly where it came from.

Eli beamed at her as she spoke. What a blazing smile he had! Then he put on a hillbilly twang and said, "As my Appalachian grandmaw used to say to me, 'Darlin', with some folk, self-hatred's just good sense.'" And when Maize laughed he started telling her about himself unbidden. He informed her that he was from a holler in Kentucky where his parents were tobacco farmers. Every morning he'd walked a long red dirt road to his school—an institution so backward that when he asked a high school guidance counselor about taking the SAT, she said it didn't exist. The only reason he'd made it north six years ago was a scholarship to Juilliard, and that happened only because, at five, when he'd entered his kindergarten classroom and saw an upright piano, he went straight to it and tapped out an entire country music song he'd heard on his father's radio, dumbfounding everybody. Within six months he was sight-reading Chopin. The other boys used to call him "twinklefingers" and beat him up, hoping to hurt his hands, until he got too tall to pick on anymore, and more recently his ex-girlfriend had kicked him out of their apartment because he wanted to practice too much on his keyboard and she complained that he was more interested in his *instrument* than in her. That was when he'd taken his extra job at the real estate office, out of necessity. For the rest of his money he drove a cab on the graveyard shift.

"Interesting," Maize said, though she knew she was too distracted or tipsy to sound sincere. When Eli had mentioned his dangerously incompetent guidance counselor she'd immediately thought of Hal Jamesley and his incompetence—which was more charming than dangerous—and she wondered where Hal was right then as she sat there in a bar, the same as she'd wondered about him in other bars or bedrooms with other men she hardly knew, when she wasn't contemplating how she'd describe her dates to Robbie later that evening or the following morning.

"Interesting," she said to Eli again, and the hollowness of her voice echoed. "I mean, that all sounds hard."

"I'm not complaining," Eli said. "There are worse fates. I'm in New York City. I could be in the holler, strumming on my ol' banjo."

He smiled again—bashfully to himself this time—and he ordered another course of tapas from the cute snotty waiter. He raised his plate to her and said, "Sure you don't want some of this? It's fantastic," but she shook her head no and gulped more vodka. When he said, "What about your background?" the room throbbed and she drained the last of her drink before speaking. She felt unutterably banal after his Lincolnesque tale of rural hardship and prodigy.

"My life story. It's unbelievably scintillating, I can assure you," she said. She launched into roughly the same digest of her personal history that she'd given many other men—the basics of birth and puberty and schooling—yet midway though her recitation she made the mistake of staring into Eli's eyes as she talked, noticing there were pretty gold flecks in the gray (he had oversized eyes like a goldfish's), and then she made the error of looking at his long forearms and fingers and his narrow torso and his clean jawline as she continued, and soon enough she'd careened way off track. She heard herself making jokes and using fancy turns of phrase—turning herself into a skit as Eli laughed and nodded—elaborating on her mother and father and stepfather and her high school friend Lyla, and describing the geeks and preppies and artistes and society kids she'd met at college, and her crazy upstairs neighbor who took hallucinogens and wandered their tenement hallways naked, searching for his little dog, and the Indian baker down the block who slipped more muffins into her bag than she'd paid for, and the Serbian superintendent who didn't speak English and had to be told what needed fixing entirely through pantomime ("Woe betide those of us who suck at charades," she said), and the sexy old lady who slinked down her block in micro-minis and fuck-me pumps every day and looked so great that both she and Robbie wished they were older heterosexual men instead of recent college graduates.

Robbie, she thought. She'd completely forgotten to tell Robbie she wouldn't be coming home after work, and she'd turned off her cell phone, so he was probably wondering if she'd been killed on her way back to their cubbyhole of an apartment.

Clearly the alcohol had gotten to her, or something about Eli's mesmerized attention, or some combination of both. She'd hardly ever spoken this freely with anybody except Robbie, whom she'd hardly mentioned in her monologue except to say that he was a wonderfully tidy roommate and that she'd known him "for eons."

"So that's me—fascinating, right?" she said as the waiter reapproached their table and laid his hand on Eli's shoulder, whispering something in Eli's ear and shooting daggers at her again.

"Yes," Eli said, but she didn't know if he was answering her or their server. Then her mind went blank and she couldn't think of another sentence to say except, "Please bring us the bill."

She staggered once when she got up from the table. She willed herself to keep a steady gait as Eli escorted her to her apartment, saying what a great time he'd had and that he hoped they'd go out again soon. By the time they got to her building she was worn out from the effort of walking straight to prove she wasn't a lightweight. The drug dealer on her stoop eyed her suspiciously—like he didn't recognize her—as if she and Eli were a pair of narcs come to make a bust.

"Well well," Eli said, and then he stopped speaking, too. A clammy silence rose up between them as he loomed over her. He was standing a little too close, kicking the curb lightly with his boot like a restless little kid on summer vacation, waiting for something to happen. He said, "You look happy, Maize."

"I do?" She smiled as if cued to show it. "Thank you for the invitation. Thanks."

"Sure thing," he said. When he said nothing further she said, "Okay then," and realized she couldn't finish, and heat came to her face. She looked down at his boot hitting the curb.

When she peered up at him again a grave expression had overtaken him—a serious look he hadn't shown her before— which she recognized as something like grief, or passion, or grief at the sudden appearance of passion that might not be returned, and she was as perplexed as if looking in a small mirror he was holding up to her face and tilting at an angle she wouldn't have tilted it herself. She was sure that if she didn't get away fast something humiliating would happen.

"I better go now," she said.

He said, "Right." He leaned his head toward her, and then his shoulders, and then his torso, and to stop him more than anything she picked a spot on his left cheek and pecked him and said, "Bye! See you at the ranch!" as she clambered past the dealer up the steps to her apartment, where she double-locked the door behind her.

To her relief he wasn't at work the following day, or the next, and the day after that André ordered her to leave and never come back again.

Her stomach had growled that night when she reunited with Robbie and they'd pored over paint samples that looked like miniature color field paintings. Her stomach growled now as Robbie's mother returned through the front door with the packing tape and called upstairs to let Maize know she was back and ready to resume whatever they'd been doing.

◆ ◆

The next morning Maize had trouble dragging herself out of bed. She had promised to spend a day with her mother across town while she was up here and the time had come. She had no choice in the matter. It was her penance for the implied disloyalty of lodging at Robbie's mother's house for the week. Not that penance was justified, since her mother didn't have room for her. Practically from the moment Maize went away to college, her mother had downsized from the modest three-bedroom house where Maize had grown up to a condo at the edge of the village, in a gated community called Sylvan Estates. Although her mother repeatedly claimed, "Of course you're always welcome in my home, Maizie—you're my daughter," Maize felt otherwise.

Her mother's condo was clean and bright enough but it wasn't accommodating. Whenever Maize endured a stay on holidays or summer vacations, her bed was a pullout sofa in the living room with the double-height ceiling, which Maize would stare up at for hours because the sofa mattress was like a medieval rack. Her bathroom was a windowless powder room with no bath (she had to shower in her mother's bathroom, among her mother's little tubes and wands and pots of makeup), her furniture and old belongings were in storage units three towns away, and all her mother's new furniture was expensive and rigidly elegant, as if she were assuring herself and others that she'd moved here out of choice rather than financial necessity.

Aside from her mother's clothing, the only thing she'd retained from their old house was a Chippendale-style dining set she'd had since her first marriage, which she'd plopped into her gleaming eat-in kitchen and which always looked so strange there, so out of place, that Maize had to remind herself it was where they'd had countless meals together over the years, first with her father and then with her ex-stepfather and then alone together after Bruce left. The table where Bruce told corny knock-knock jokes, which Maize had always laughed at, and where he'd helped Maize with her algebra homework because her mother knew numbers but was no good at shapes, and where her mother told Bruce to tuck in his shirt and comb his hair, and where Bruce repeatedly asked Maize what she wanted to be when she grew up and told her it was okay that she didn't know yet, she had years and years to decide and she could be anything she wanted. Undoubtedly her mother would want them to have lunch at that same table today.

"Robbie's mother's got the wrong idea, just moving from one house to another," her mother said to Maize in her Audi the morning she picked her up for her visit. "She should buy herself a nice condo like mine where everything's taken care of by the staff. Maintaining a house is an endless headache." She stared at Maize directly for a moment and sighed as if remembering it before turning her eyes back to the road. "But I guess she has too much rich-lady pride to move to an apartment."

"She's not like that," Maize said automatically, though she wasn't sure that was true.

"Right, Maize. That's why she has to pay a maid and three kids to do what most people do by themselves."

"*Our* house was much smaller," Maize said, because she knew her mother as usual was talking about herself rather than other people. They'd been together two minutes and already her pulse was jabbering from irritation. "I don't know where you get these ideas, Mom. Robbie's family is comfortable, but they're not rich. Or—I don't know—maybe they were once and they aren't anymore. If you want to meet filthy rich people you should see the clients I had to work with at André's office."

She caught herself using the past tense—a mistake since she hadn't told her mother about being fired—so she covered quickly. "Their financial statements would make you throw up. Honestly."

That was true enough. Before she was let go, Maize had complained to André about how similar all their clients were—that it might be refreshing to sell an apartment to someone besides a finance person or a corporate lawyer or a trust fund baby or a twenty-four-year-old who had a decorator. Their buyers' profiles were nearly identical to their sellers'. Sometimes she felt like the organizer of an alumni mixer between Wharton and the Harvard Business School, with a few madcap Sarah Lawrence types thrown in to add color. But André had snapped back, "Get real, Maize. Who else do you think can afford this overpriced crap we're peddling?"

"You're naïve as usual," her mother said to her now, and she sighed again as they turned onto the road to her part of town. "You can't avoid rich people. That's who runs the world."

"Yes, yes," Maize said. "The rich are always with us." But her mother didn't get the biblical allusion and she didn't laugh.

With that one word—*naïve*—her mother dismissed not only the sophistication Maize had developed at college but everything she'd been exposed to for the past year in Manhattan, where her mother had never come close to living and which she rarely visited. Maize felt she should defend herself, but why bother? Her mother wouldn't listen. She bit the inside of her cheek as they drew closer to Sylvan Estates, and her mother engaged her blinker to make a sharp right turn.

Maize pulled out her cell phone to avoid saying anything else for the moment. She checked for e-mails and text messages (there were none) and sent a text to Robbie reading WITH MOM ON ROAD TO NOWHERE. Then she dialed into her voice mail and, after a long pause, she heard Eli saying, "Maize, it's me again. I'm starting to feel like a stalker so this is my last try. I'll leave you alone after this," followed by a whistling sound from his lips or a faulty connection. She nearly pressed DELETE before she decided to save his latest message, as she had all his others, though she hadn't returned any in the weeks since he'd started leaving them.

How unconscionably rude she'd been to Eli, whom she'd never given her e-mail address. It made no sense that she froze at the sound of his voice every time and that her hand trembled on the receiver whenever she saw his name on the caller ID screen. Perhaps she was too traumatized by anything or anyone she associated with André's office. If Robbie happened to be around when Eli called and he asked who was ringing she said either "Sales call" or "Wrong number."

At least this latest message promised an end to it all. Eli was undoubtedly getting sick of her by now. The voice mails he'd left after André fired her had grown increasingly heated and repetitious, like a song refrain: *"Hey Maize, what's up? I heard about what happened at the office. How's your new life of leisure going? . . . Maize? Hope you've been okay the past couple weeks. Just checking in again to see how you're doing . . . Maize? Hey. You all right? It's Eli from the gulag. Can I get you out for drinks or a movie sometime? . . . You alive, Maize? It's been almost a month and I'm concerned. Plus I miss you. Please give a call."*

Now her mother rolled down her car window and waved at the security guard as they approached the complex's front gate, which looked like a border crossing except that it had a huge wooden sign with carved gilt lettering and a ridiculous man-made waterfall that cascaded even in winter. The guard raised the gate and Maize shuddered as they drove under it, half convinced that it would fall on them and knowing that was as irrational as someone with a fear of crossing drawbridges. In five years she'd never gotten used to the gate or anything else about the complex (or "estate community," as it called itself). When she'd had to stay with her mother on vacations she didn't go to the communal pool or tennis courts or the glitzy clubhouse with its gas stone fireplace and wainscoted walls and coffered ceilings. So she was unfamiliar to the other residents, who always eyed her warily like an intruder when they passed her during power walks through the neighborhood down the perfectly straight sidewalks. More often than not, she felt like she should be wearing a guest pass even when she was in her own mother's apartment.

It felt to Maize as if her mother had gone out of her way to make her unwelcome despite her assertions of hospitality. Starting with the model of apartment she'd chosen to buy—not a two-bedroom or even a one-bedroom plus den but a jumbo one-bedroom—with the excuse that it was a corner unit and much better positioned in the complex than the larger lines, with a nicer layout and lower monthly carrying costs, although she'd made a bundle selling their house and could certainly have afforded a bigger place if she'd wanted it.

"Now that you're home," her mother said as she sat at the dining table across from Maize, spearing lunch salad, "there are some things of yours in the hall closet I want you to sort through. Otherwise I don't want to hear you whine if I throw them out. They're taking up too much room."

"What things?" As far as Maize knew, her mother had disposed of everything she hadn't rescued before her move, like someone fleeing a burning house in the middle of the night clutching mementos.

"Nothing important. They look like college notebooks and worthless stuff like that."

Her mother still hadn't forgiven Maize for quietly switching her major from pre-law to cultural studies—an interdisciplinary humanist mishmash of sociology, anthropology, semiotics, comp. lit., philosophy, and film—without informing her until it was too late. Her mother had considered it the same kind of willful hippie nonsense that inspired her first husband to come up with Maize's name, a name she remained sorry to have conceded to in some hormonal fog, though she'd apparently conceded almost nothing else to him before he'd dropped dead at thirty-eight.

Maize curled her toes at her mother calling her college notebooks *worthless stuff*. Even more she resented her mother saying *Now that you're home*. Her mother was pointedly ignoring the fact that Maize had her own home in the city now—even if it was comically squalid—with something like a life to go with it. She was skimming over the fact that she'd done nothing in the least to make this condo feel like Maize belonged here, and that she treated Maize like a slovenly houseguest when she was present, and that the house where Maize had grown up was now occupied by strangers. She ignored the fact that Maize's real family home was elsewhere and locked away from her, as Robbie's childhood home would soon be from him.

Maize took a deep cleansing breath to clear her irritation. She wondered what would happen at Robbie's mother's house today, now that she wasn't there to act as a buffer between Daniel and Robbie and his mother. She worried about it.

"What's the matter, Maize?" her mother said. "Why aren't you eating? Don't you like the salad?"

"No, it's good. I'm not very hungry."

"I made it just for you, with shrimp, because I know you like shrimp," her mother said.

"Thanks." Maize picked at it and ate one shrimp, slowly, to show her gratitude. She breathed deeply again, but it wasn't enough. She needed more air.

"Do you think we could finish this outside on the deck?" Maize said. "It would be nice to look at the lake while we eat."

"It's hot and buggy out there," her mother said. "The lake's not moving right, or moving enough—something like that—so there are millions of mosquitoes. We'd be eaten alive. Let's stay here."

"Oh. Okay."

"So how are things at the apartment?" her mother said. "Did you and Robbie repaint your bathroom yet?"

"Yes," Maize said, though they hadn't. "It looks a lot better."

"What color did you pick?"

"Oh," Maize said. "Something neutral." She heard her own vagueness. "A shade of blue."

"Blue isn't neutral," her mother said.

"Light blue," Maize said. "It was Robbie's idea—actually, Robbie's boyfriend's."

"Isn't he a medical student? What on earth does *he* know about interior decorating?" her mother said.

Maize shrugged. Even with lies she couldn't avoid her mother's contentiousness; that was her mother's animating force, much more than any other quality. Her mother had scraped her way into the middle class, putting herself through community colleges and state universities and getting a C.P.A., and she'd bought all the accessories of a bourgeois matron years before she was one, defining herself piece by piece like an actor assembling a costume, starting from the outside in until she had the role down pat. But she hadn't quite escaped her background, Maize thought. She still had the poor person's habit of luxuriating in her bad luck and the injustices she'd suffered, trundling out resentments and displaying them proudly, the way a different kind of nouveau riche displayed jewels and cars and furs and the fake heirlooms they'd bought from somebody else's family. Perhaps nobody truly got away from her history, remaking herself from the ground up, but Maize supposed the illusion of it was essential: if you didn't have that you could hardly get out of bed.

She rose and walked through the living room to the sliding glass door. If she couldn't dine on the deck she could at least look at the lake. That was something. She thought about Robbie and then about Eli, finding it hard to consider them next to each other in the same room—as though they were opposed ideas—but forcing herself. She imagined introducing them at her empty apartment before she relocated the meeting to a more neutral venue—a street corner or a theater or a restaurant—just the way Robbie had with her and Daniel before this trip.

"Sit down again, Maize," her mother called. "We haven't finished. And I need to talk to you about something."

Maize went back to the table. Her mother was staring at the grain of the mahogany tabletop, which was remarkably free of scratches and dents, as if she were counting the striations. It was unlike her not to be looking Maize straight in the face, and when she spoke her voice had gone flannelly.

"I've always wondered . . ." She broke off in midsentence, as if she had to swallow something large though her mouth was empty. She splayed her hands on the tabletop. "I've always wondered . . . Well, I might as well spit it out." She exhaled.

"All right," Maize said.

"I've always wondered if Bruce was inappropriate," she said.

Why was her mother rehashing this now, a decade after their divorce? Of course Bruce had been inappropriate. Their marriage was an unsolved mystery to Maize. Bruce was shambling and sloppy and her mother was anal-retentive. He was upper-crust and paunchy and preppy and her trim, aerobicized mother was from a family of construction workers. She and Bruce had done nothing but bicker until her mother kicked him out— Bruce relocating first to a garden apartment nearby, then to Key West, then to Santa Fe and San Francisco, and finally to an address in Marin County that Maize had scoped out repeatedly on Google Earth: what looked like a small bungalow with trees that Maize imagined were fragrant eucalyptus and an aquamarine rectangle that might or might not be a swimming pool. Although she'd gotten birthday cards from Bruce they didn't speak anymore. But all that was a long time ago, Maize thought. Move on.

There was silence over the table, and her mother was looking directly at Maize now. "Sure. I guess Bruce was inappropriate," Maize said. "To use your word. But you'd know better than me."

"No, Maizie. What I'm asking is whether Bruce was inappropriate with you."

"What?" For a second she didn't grasp what her mother meant, but then she did. "What?"

"It's okay to tell me if he was," her mother mumbled.

"No," Maize said. "He never did anything sketchy. He didn't do anything, Mom. Ever."

"Are you sure?"

"Of *course* I'm sure."

"Maybe a little something?" her mother said, as if she were bargaining for a discount.

"Absolutely nothing," Maize said.

"Don't be afraid."

"I am not afraid," Maize said, and she wasn't. If anything she was livid. It was her mother who was behaving inappropriately with her, trying to caricature Bruce and foist the damage he'd done to her onto her daughter—sealing away the fact of Bruce's existence by tarnishing whatever pleasant memories Maize might still have of him. It constituted a kind of theft. But it had the opposite effect of making Maize recall Bruce all the more fondly: Bruce saying "Upsy-daisy" and carrying Maize into the house at night when she'd fallen asleep in the car and couldn't be roused by her mother's prodding; Bruce buying noisemakers and fezlike party hats on New Year's Eve when Maize was little; Bruce bringing her ginger ale and toast and magazines when she got sick; Bruce crooning loudly and badly along with Bono as he drove them in his car—the Subaru he gave Maize when he left—knowing his voice was awful and making a joke of it by saying, "I coulda been a star!"; Bruce making hilarious simian faces behind her mother's back toward the end, whenever she nagged them both about how sloppy they were and how low-rent their manners, while her mother demanded to know why Maize was laughing at her when she was addressing serious matters.

Maize missed Bruce more than she'd admitted to herself, and far more than she'd ever let on to her mother.

That was like so much of her adolescence with her mother: Maize had never told. A million secrets large and small she'd kept from her mother since turning twelve. She assumed that was natural unless you were one of those dippy girls who said things like *My mom is my best friend.* But sometimes she wondered why puberty marked the growth of secrets along with breasts and strange hair, multiplying secrets and more secrets like mutant cells, and the desire to hibernate from the same adults you'd been so close to and once believed you couldn't live without. As if adolescence were a cult you got initiated into overnight that forbade contact with old intimates lest you backslide.

Her father had died when she was four. Bruce was as close to a father as Maize had ever come, and then he was gone, and now her mother wanted to destroy whatever remained of him, the way certain people weren't content to throw away their trash, they had to have the satisfaction of burning it.

Maize looked to the right, past the sliding glass doors, past the deck to the man-made pond lined with benches no one ever used. Her mother didn't have a lawn to speak of or care for anymore and that was a relief to her, she'd told Maize repeatedly since moving here. That was the way she liked it.

Then Maize looked across the room at her mother, who was staring at the tabletop again. Her mother had once been beautiful; Maize had pictures to prove it. With effort she could be beautiful again. She was still attractive. But her features had tightened and drawn in on themselves over the years as she'd gradually closed down her life, going from friendships to periodic phone chats with her daughter and her sister in Illinois, from a real house to an impeccably dusted one-bedroom apartment with a double mattress that groaned under her in mockery every time she turned to face no one in the dark, from two marriages to sporadic dates (arranged by a paid service) with men whose age, height, weight, coloring, education, and interests were listed in printouts like items on a delivery menu.

Her mother had something approximating boyfriends—men she went out to dinner with occasionally, or to a movie, or whom she met after work for coffee dates—and for all Maize knew she had sex with them. But apparently none of them lasted, since there was no evidence of them in her condo. When she mentioned them glancingly to Maize, it was in the same tone as saying that she'd just had her cabinets repainted or her carpeting steam-cleaned or that a plumber had come to clear a clogged pipe. It sounded like a necessary bit of maintenance work she'd had to undertake before sending contractors back through the security gate, into the unguarded world outside her complex.

Her mother was becoming a member of the vast, unaffiliated tribe of the lonely. Maize saw them everywhere, sitting in restaurants with their books, or feeding themselves popcorn in movie theaters where they sat trying not to make noise as they sipped their sodas, ready to make way for couples who asked if neighboring seats were saved for anybody, or staring out bus windows or at overhead advertisements in subway cars, feigning rapt engrossment, or at parties nursing their drinks and gazing into the middle distance, searching for something that never quite came into focus, or outside walking the dogs they loved a little too much or a lot too much, or inside on the phone bending someone's ear with all the petty details, all the subordinate clauses, all the minutiae of their lives, all the redundant statements they couldn't resist repeating now that they had a real live audience.

If Maize wasn't careful she might join that tribe herself. She'd been a flank member in the last two years of high school, when Robbie had suddenly disappeared and they'd stopped speaking, only to have him accidentally show up at college freshman year. And she could have been mistaken for one in the past year as she labored at her office desk, speaking to few people except André or his clients, venturing furtive glances toward Eli's desk yet never getting up the nerve to cross the little space between them and say something.

Now she kept staring at her mother. She wished—she had wished for years—that her mother would look across the table and see her for who she truly was. Wasn't that the myth of what mothers were able to do—have an X-ray vision of their children, even if exposure to too many X-rays was well known to be damaging? But really, who was it her mother would see at the moment? Maize's focus was blurry and her ambitions were scattered. She'd thought it might toughen her up to survive in a cutthroat business like real estate, or that it would be stimulating to work at a newspaper like Robbie, or that it would be kicky to work with fashion houses like Robbie's father, or fulfilling to work as a watercolorist like Hal Jamesley or a musician like Eli, or heady as a drug to wrest people from sickness and death like Daniel, or soothing to work with numbers that added up neatly like her mother, or liberating to try all those jobs for a while and see which one suited her, the way she had with hair colors and styles and the way she'd once been with her lovers.

Yet no matter what she imagined for herself it was temporary and tentative. There was always another color shade, there was always another lover, there was always a different and potentially more arresting Maize beckoning from the sidelines or the periphery, warning her that if she dallied where she was too long she'd miss out on other options, another Maize luring her elsewhere and nowhere. At present her hair was its original color and usual length after countless experiments. She had no lover after hooking up through four college years, nor did she particularly want one. She had no job except for the terminal work Robbie's mother had offered her for the week. She was in roughly the same position she'd been in high school and looked pretty much the same, too. If she ran into one of her old classmates on the trip between her mother's condo and Robbie's mother's house, none of them would have the slightest inkling of the changes she'd been through since she was mousy little Maize hiding in the back row of social studies. Only Robbie would know.

"If Bruce really didn't do anything inappropriate, then why are you crying?" her mother said now.

"What?" When she fingered her cheeks there were indeed tears streaming down her face. She swiped at them brusquely.

"Maize?" her mother said.

"I'm not crying," Maize said. "My eyes are watering. I think I might be having an allergic reaction. Maybe to the shrimp."

◆ ◆

Back at the house that afternoon, while he and Daniel were in the sweaty attic that had basically become a junk room, Robbie checked his e-mail and found another urgent message from one of his coworkers. Again asking Robbie if he knew where the heavy-duty stapler was.

He didn't write back, although it was against his diligent nature not to. He'd left the stapler in the copy room file cabinet but they could figure that out for themselves. He was on vacation after all—if you could call this a vacation—and he wanted them to leave him alone so he could forget about his depressing job for a few days.

"Whoa," Daniel yelled from the other side of the attic. "Come over here, Robbie. Take a look at this."

Robbie was grateful to be called; he and Daniel hadn't been speaking much all day. When he joined Daniel he found him hovering over a long, rectangular white cardboard box lined with pink satin—a bit like a white coffin—with matching pink wisps of silk tissue paper scattered near the lid Daniel had removed. Inside was a white silk dress with ivory beads at the bodice and sleeves.

Could those be real seed pearls? In any case it was clearly a wedding gown. Robbie could tell that even before Daniel lifted it out of the box, releasing the smell of mothballs, its hem scraping the floor.

"What are we supposed to do with this?" Daniel said, holding it up.

"I wouldn't know. I wish Maize were here. She'd know what to do." Robbie touched it carefully—lightly and tentatively as he would a relic. Then he said, "Let's just shove it back in the box."

"And then what?" Daniel said.

"Forget we ever saw it and leave it here."

"We can't do that," Daniel said. "This house is supposed to be completely empty by the closing. It would weird out the new owners."

Before Robbie could stop him Daniel was at the top of the attic stairs, calling down to Robbie's mother. "Hi down there!" he shouted twice, more loudly the second time. "Advice needed!"

"What?" his mother called back. "What's so important? Etta and I are in the middle of something."

"Could you come up for a second?"

"What? What?" she said as she climbed the attic stairs. When she reached the top and saw Daniel holding up the dress she said, "Oh, please. Throw that out."

Robbie said, "You sure? Maybe you want to think it over a little."

"Of course I'm sure," she said. "It's useless."

"But I mean," Robbie said. "You know." He took a moment. "You could, at least, maybe, donate it somewhere."

"Where—a knocked-up-girl's society?" she said. "Look at it. It's yellowed at the edges. And nobody wants a used wedding gown anyway. That's bad luck unless it's the bride's mother's or grandmother's." She glared at Robbie and laughed a laugh that was more like a scoff. "I assume *you* have no use for it."

"Of course not," Daniel said. "But that's hardly the point."

"Huh? Pardon?" She turned her glare on Daniel. It was the first time since she'd looked at him since the pool incident the day before, Robbie noticed, as if she were too repulsed to hazard so much as a glance in his direction. "Excuse me, bub, but I hardly need to be told what the point of my wedding dress is by you, thanks. So get rid of it. Or here. Better still—" She grabbed the gown from Daniel's hands and laid it roughly over her forearm, where a bride would carry a bouquet. "I'll take care of it." And with that she turned her back on them both and stomped down the stairs, some of the voluminous silk catching on the steps as if it were a train she still hadn't learned how to walk with correctly.

"Charming," Daniel said to Robbie when she was gone. "Now I see where you get your warmth."

Robbie took his cell phone out of his pocket and glanced at the time. He read Maize's wry text message from the road. He calculated that it would be at least three more hours before Maize returned from visiting her mother, acting as she always did like Persephone freed from hell, though Robbie had always found Maize's mother pleasant enough. One hundred eighty minutes and at least ten thousand eight hundred seconds. It seemed like forever. He could hardly wait for her to get back.

◆ ◆

"Let's get out of here," Robbie said that night, after Maize had returned and the three of them were facing down another dinner at his mother's table. "Let's borrow the car and go somewhere fun."

"I'm game," Maize said. "Where?"

"Anywhere. I don't care. Anywhere," he said.

"We have to have a plan," Daniel said, "or we'll just be driving around aimlessly like suburban mall rats."

"Well, I don't have a plan—okay? My plan right now is to avoid going crazy from being cooped up in the same house for five days on end. Is that good enough?"

Maize felt like she should say something fast. Since she'd come back from her mother's, Robbie had been unusually snappish. Daniel wasn't responding much but Maize doubted that would last. She wondered what had happened while she was gone. When she'd returned and asked Robbie how his day went he'd only said, "I survived."

"I guess we could go to Playland," Maize said. A lame suggestion, but she was desperate to offer something. She turned to Daniel. "It's an amusement park."

"Oh goody-goody," Daniel said. "The three of us can buy cotton candy and pretend to be ten-year-olds. Sounds intelligent."

"I'll go get the car keys from my mother while you two figure it out," Robbie said.

But when he left Maize and Daniel just sat there in her guest room, avoiding each other's eyes and waiting for Robbie to return, until the silence between them was so embarrassing she had to break it by saying, "I wonder what's taking Robbie so long."

"His mother's probably hassling him about taking the car," Daniel said. "Sour old bitch."

"You shouldn't say that." Maize studied the knobs on the dresser. "You don't know her."

"I don't want to know her any better," Daniel said. "I've seen enough."

Maize pretended she needed a bathroom break just to get away from him—or if not from Daniel, from her disappointment for him. She felt sorry for him since he'd come up here so eager to win over Robbie's mother and impress Robbie with his usefulness, unaware of how skittish they both could be before they'd known someone a long time. She guessed it must be hard for someone like Daniel—someone used to succeeding—to understand why he couldn't. Perhaps he'd sat around trying to figure out how to crack the code to them. But it wasn't that simple with Robbie and his mother. They were a confusing pair—magnetic yet standoffish, passionate yet aloof—and Maize guessed they confused themselves as much as anyone else. Under their chill exteriors hot currents blew into the sealed chambers of their personalities, clouding up the perspective the way a driver's breath fogged a windshield on a winter day and made it difficult to see forward, so that the only solution seemed another blast of cold air. It made her shiver to notice it.

Not that she was one to judge, given the way she'd acted around anyone eligible or interested in her for the past five years.

Once Robbie got the car keys and they buckled themselves into his mother's Mercedes, it all felt better: like an improved version of countless nights from Maize's teen years. Driving and driving with no place to go, only this time around it wasn't frustrating. In fact it was sort of delicious, knowing she wouldn't have to return to her mother's, resting against the cushy leather seats of a fancy car, gliding down winding roads. They passed posh houses where the sprinkler systems had snapped on, sending up misty sprays that made the properties look like dreams of themselves. Suddenly it was easy to see how people could get seduced into living here forever: everything was lush yet tidy and manicured, with the borderlines clearly marked and irises flaring in the dusk light. Every place looked like a haven and every lighted lampshade glowed in the windows against the encroaching dark.

"This is tedious," Daniel said from the backseat. "Do we have any *idea* where we're going?"

"Sort of, sort of not," Robbie said as they turned a corner and passed the public high school. "Look, Maizie, your alma mater."

"Oh god, don't remind me," she said. "Drive faster."

"You know who I saw at the hardware store yesterday, when I had to get paintbrushes? Old Mrs. Franc, looking as certifiable as ever. She was screaming at the cashier about expired coupons or something."

"Yikes." Maize turned back to Daniel and said, "A seriously wacko guidance counselor," hoping she could change the subject by including him in the conversation if Robbie wouldn't.

"Was she your senior-year counselor?" Robbie said.

"No."

"Who was?"

"Not her. Someone else. It doesn't matter," she said. "Could we maybe stop at a diner or something? I'm getting thirsty all of a sudden."

She wanted to detour around the subject of Hal Jamesley— yet even if she didn't, what would there be to report? A minor flirtation in a college counselor's office, with someone who'd once shared his cigarette with her and accidentally touched her hand? Even after she'd abruptly stopped visiting Hal he didn't have the nerve to say anything to her—nothing beyond an over-zealous "Hi! Hi!" whenever they passed each other in the school hallways and a stabbed look when she smiled without stopping to talk to him. The most he'd done was slip a handmade card with one of his watercolors into her locker with the question *How Are You Doing These Days?* But she hadn't replied. If she told Robbie, he might think she was making the whole thing up.

And it would be the same thing if she told Robbie more about Eli. They'd had a makeshift date and she'd pecked him chastely on the cheek at the end of the evening. It was next to nothing.

Yet even after dozens of dates and hookups she'd never stopped thinking about Hal, really. She had to admit that to herself. Perhaps it wasn't Hal she pined for but the thrilled anticipation she'd felt in his office, the mystique of sex rather than the overripe smell of it. Was that how it had been for Robbie in the run-up to his affair with Professor J., before it went wrong between them?

She'd never again experienced what she'd had with Hal. Not quite. She'd kissed and danced and fucked and had volcanic orgasms but it—whatever *it* was—hadn't begun to happen except for the brief and distant thrummings she'd felt around Eli. The last sex she'd had was with the cop who'd answered her emergency call after their apartment was cleaned out, who'd invited her on a date and said, "I could really get into a girl like you" while they were doing it, pulling his torso away from hers for a second and staring at her with his slightly beady eyes, smiling nervously—both wicked and boyish—so that his amber-colored mustache furrowed and lifted like an alert. They'd been hump-ing against a wall in his apartment in Kew Gardens, so horny they hadn't gotten past his foyer to the bedroom, and he was still wearing his uniform shirt as they rutted and thrust together. She realized at that moment that she could make him fall in love with her if she wanted to and, just maybe, let herself fall in love with him. But instead she'd turned it into a joke. "What do you mean you *could* get into me?" she'd said, looking down toward their crotches. "You already *are* into me, last I checked." And they both laughed at how she'd deftly restaged a moment of true feeling into a fleeting farcical bit of craziness, saving them both. She knew she'd never see him again.

Despite that tryst she'd been sort of a eunuch the past year— for several years, really—dwelling on a guy she'd met at seventeen because it was easy. Or at least easier than sticking around to have her conversations with Hal go soggy or to discover that he was a second-rate artist and she wasn't nearly as special as he'd thought.

If she'd been a cleverer girl—more manipulative or more spiteful—she would have stayed with the cop long enough to get André into legal trouble. She could have told him everything that had happened with André, the same as she'd told Robbie, and had him or one of his fellow cops pay André a little visit.

On Maize's last full day at the office, André had Maize call his home machine and leave a voice mail saying that André would be working late again and not to expect him. Fifteen minutes later Trevor called back, screaming. Had André forgotten that it was their son's birthday party that night? What the hell was wrong with him? He insisted that he speak with André directly, but when Maize put him on hold André said, "No dice, tell the douche bag I'm out or in the middle of a phone conference."

When Maize did as ordered, haltingly, Trevor said, "Uh-huh. You wouldn't lie to me, would you?" and when Maize murmured that she wouldn't he said, "And you wouldn't lie to an eight-year-old on his birthday, right?" She heard him calling, "Jordan! Jordan! Get over here, please!"

Maize clamped her palm over the receiver and called across the office in a fierce stage whisper: "André! He's putting your *son* on the phone!" But André's only response was to snarl and say, "I'm not here." He slashed his finger across his own throat—a gesture he'd used many times before, whenever he wanted someone to stop talking immediately. Maize said "Help!" but André merely slashed his finger again.

"Hi. Who are you?" André's little boy was now saying into the receiver.

"Oh—hi. Hi there," Maize said. "Is this Jordan? Hi. I'm— this is your dad's assistant. His helper. I mean, I work with your dad." She had nearly said her name, but she was too abashed; she didn't want to be specifically identified with this appalling little interlude. "Happy birthday, Jordan!" she said brightly. "How old are you today?"

"Eight," he said. "I want my dad."

Maize looked up and saw that André had closed his office door behind him. "He's away," Maize said. "Away right now."

"What?" Jordan said. She thought he wanted her to repeat what she'd said, but that wasn't it. He was listening to something his other father was saying in the background, something Maize could overhear only in wisps, and when he said, "What? Okay," she knew that André's partner was feeding his son lines even before Jordan spoke them.

"Promise me my father isn't there," the little boy said. "It's my birthday. Swear it."

That was the limit. Maize said, "Um, Jordan? Would you hold on just a second, please?" She got up and went to André's office, a horrified look on her face, but when she knocked on the glass door André was talking into his headset and waved Maize away.

She had no choice but to go back to the phone. She had lied to an eight-year-old and left him waiting. On his birthday, no less. She prayed that when she hit the HOLD button again he'd be miraculously gone, but he wasn't.

"Well?" Jordan said. "Swear it."

"No. I'm afraid I can't do that, Jordan."

"Can too."

"No, I can't."

"Can too! Can too! Can too! Swear!"

"Okay," Maize said with a long exhalation like a moribund person feeling the last gasp of life drain from her. She could hear André's partner still whispering something in the background. For a moment it felt like she was at a clandestine initiation rite. She said, "I swear, Jordan. I promise. Okay?"

She got an instant headache the second she pushed the END button. She felt queasy and her head was still spinning when André came up to her desk a few minutes later. "What—what already?" André said when he saw Maize's expression.

"He sounded really upset," Maize said.

"I'll call him later. He's always upset. This time it's because I don't feel like taking fifteen obnoxious third-graders to dinner at Chanterelle. I'm the big villain. It's not like I forgot my son's birthday. My boyfriend conveniently forgets that I gave Jordan a new laptop this morning and three thousand dollars' worth of new games to play on it, not to mention a fabulous little suit from Marc Jacobs. But it's never enough. Never."

"I meant Jordan," Maize said, hanging her head. "Jordan is upset." Then she lifted her head and said, "Excuse me. You're having an eight-year-old's birthday party at Chanterelle?"

"My boyfriend's bright idea. To introduce them to fine dining experiences. Don't ask. Don't get me started. Okay," André said, waving his arm and turning his back. "I'm out of here."

Maize checked André's electronic appointment calendar. It said he was due on Mercer Street—at the loft of a pharmaceutical heiress named Vicky Heidegger, who lived with a much younger Caribbean woman named Edris, who had a totally shaved head. Vicky's loft was in contract and she and her girlfriend were in Anguilla at the moment, but André was supposed to meet with an art dealer for them so the dealer could take a look at their collection of Nan Goldins. Vicky had decided the Nan Goldins wouldn't go with the townhouse she was buying on Gramercy Park.

Maize knew she shouldn't stalk André to Vicky's loft—she should cool down—but she couldn't help herself. Enough! She'd taken enough! Lying to a little boy about the whereabouts of his father on his birthday! On top of fetching André's macchiatos and dropping off his dry cleaning and filling out his family's health insurance forms and asking *permission* to leave her desk when she had to use the bathroom. She'd been letting André treat her shabbily for months and it was time to take a stand. She feared that if she didn't do it right now she'd lose her ember of outrage.

So the next thing she knew she was in the lobby at Mercer Street, speaking to a doorman who informed her André had gone upstairs and who waved Maize toward the elevator that opened directly into Vicky's loft. She stomped her foot like a racehorse as the elevator rose, steeling herself for a showdown, but she told herself not to say anything in front of the art dealer. She didn't want André to accuse her of being unprofessional.

When she stepped off the elevator there was no one in the vast living room looking at the Nan Goldins. There was no one in the enormous open kitchen nor in the media room, which also had a billiard table. "Hello?" Maize said, but no sound came back except her shoes on the inlaid bamboo floor.

She headed deeper into the loft, toward the many bedrooms at the rear end. One after another was empty except for furnishings and art and sporting equipment—tennis rackets and skis and basketballs and a Ping-Pong table and ice hockey sticks—as if she were in a posh private recreation center. It reminded Maize of the time she'd said to André, "Manhattan's sort of become a playground for rich people, hasn't it?" and André had snapped, "Correction: a playground for rich people *and* their children."

In the master bedroom there were several photos of naked women on the walls—gorgeous and exquisitely framed pictures—but no real people. Maize chortled. It figured that she would finally rev up the courage to take a stand with André and her boss would evade her.

She was turning to leave when she heard a faint scrabbling sound in the corner of Vicky's bedroom. She looked in the sound's direction and noticed that the light was on in one of Vicky's huge walk-in closets. She felt obliged to turn it off before she left, but she prayed the scrabbling she'd heard wasn't a mouse or a neglected cat wanting to be petted for several minutes because its mistress was in the tropics. Although she liked cats well enough she wanted to get out of there as soon as possible. She approached the closet quietly, almost tiptoeing, so she could douse the light and scram.

When she got closer she did see a small animal—or what looked like a small animal with shiny chestnut fur. André was crouched on the floor of Vicky's closet on all fours in his suit, with his back to Maize and his soles exposed, trying to shove a small animal into his briefcase and having trouble with it.

What on earth was he doing? And why wasn't the creature in André's grip screaming in protest—hissing or yapping or whatever was appropriate to its species? Had André killed Vicky's cat and was he trying to dispose of the evidence?

It wasn't until Maize heard André say, "Goddamnit, get *in* there already," and saw André pull out the fur and stuff it in again, that she realized he wasn't holding an animal at all. It was a small fur piece—a fur muff, it looked like—that was giving André so much resistance as he rearranged the files in his briefcase to accommodate it. A fur muff made of sable.

As Maize stood there watching André struggling on the floor, all she could think was how ludicrous it was that Vicky or any other adult had a sable muff these days, like a character in a Russian novel. A sable muff was—what?—as outdated as wearing a monocle or an ascot or carrying a walking stick to look jaunty.

She was so focused on that thought that she barely noticed André had turned around on all fours and was facing her. But when André yelled, "Hey—hey! What the fuck are you—" his voice bulleted through whatever haze was shrouding Maize and she reflexively shot off toward the loft's front door.

"Hey! Wait!" André yelled as Maize raced over the bare floor and threw herself into the elevator—which was still, thank god, on Vicky's floor—pushing the lobby button immediately and repeatedly like someone fleeing a serial killer.

When she got outside the building she raced to the end of the block and turned the corner and waved for a taxi she could ill afford. She asked the driver to take her back to the office, but when she looked at her watch and saw it was nearly quitting time she tapped the lucite barrier between them and said, "Sorry, excuse me, sorry sorry," and asked him to take her home instead. By the time she arrived in Chelsea she'd already resolved to go to work the next day and pretend none of it had happened, except for reporting it all to Robbie. She prayed André would do the same.

So much for that bright idea.

"For the record, I'm not a trannie," André said to Maize first thing the following morning, in lieu of hello.

Maize squinted in wonderment—what was André talking about?—but when she grasped the cracked logic behind André's statement she couldn't help grinning. Swiping a fur muff from a lesbian's closet didn't make someone a transsexual—or trannie, as André put it—any more than licking a fat person's ice-cream cone automatically made someone obese. The notion was practically superstitious.

She glanced over André's shoulder toward Eli's desk but Eli wasn't there; it was one of his many days off.

"I'm not a trannie and I am not a thief," André said.

"I don't care, André," Maize said, sighing with an air of forbearance she'd never been allowed to use around André before. She realized that what she said was true enough. But exactly why *hadn't* she cared about André stealing from his clients? Did she secretly believe that overprivileged people like Vicky deserved to be rooked now and then, to redress some socioeconomic balance? It seemed curious to Maize now—curious and possibly amoral— that when she'd opened the steel box in André's desk and discovered his cache of stolen trinkets, her reaction had been curiosity rather than repulsion, even hours and days after her surprise and fear abated. In recounting the moment to Robbie she'd even played it as something of a joke, which possibly meant she'd been rubbing up against André's ruthlessness so long it'd become a part of her.

"I don't really care about your—your quirks, André. Your peccadilloes," Maize said primly. "I met all sorts of people at school, you know, so I'm quite open-minded."

"Open-minded. How big of you. All sorts of people, natch," André said. "People of color. People from ghettos. Freakoids and dykes with crew cuts in flannel shirts. I'm sure the Ivy League is very *diverse*, Maize, just like my kid's private school, so long as everybody gets that they're elitists who socialize only with themselves after they graduate."

Maize took a step back from André. There was a lot to object to suddenly—a lot to judge—but the thing that flared brightest was André's bigoted way of describing transsexuals and gay people. André was a homophobe, on top of his other vices! Which was flagrantly hypocritical, since André had a live-in partner, and a child he'd adopted with that same partner, and he'd been deep inside a lesbian's closet stealing something rather pudendum-like only fifteen hours ago. Who was André to be intolerant?

"In fact my transsexual acquaintances look a lot like you, André," she said, "and the lesbians look a lot like Vicky. Only they're much younger and more attractive than both of you."

"Is that so," André said.

"Yes it is," Maize said. "Not that I care either way."

"So you've said, Maize," André said. "Three times already."

"Well I don't," Maize said. "I couldn't care less. I don't care what you or anyone does with his or her body. I don't care that you have that little treasure chest of yours, or whatever you want to call it, at the bottom of your desk drawer. What I *care* about is that you turned me into your accomplice by making me lie to your partner and child about your whereabouts while you were"—she couldn't bring herself to say the word *stealing* for some reason—"out taking things."

Who knew how many times André had duped her into doing that?

"Granted. Out of bounds," André said.

The words that came to Maize's mind were *sleazy* and *disgusting*, but she didn't say them. Instead she said, "I don't care about

out of bounds. Please—you're talking to someone who screwed one of her college interviewers when she was seventeen."

Maize grimaced. She couldn't believe that had slipped out when she'd never told anyone else about it except Robbie. What did she think she was doing—flaunting a badge of brazenness to show André she could keep up with him? How was it that the Andrés of the world managed to extract things from people and give so little back in return? No wonder he was a terrific businessman!

André had bitten his top lip at Maize's mention of his treasure chest, so hard that he left tooth marks on it. Now he paused for a moment and bit his top lip again, longer, narrowing his eyes. "So let me get this straight," he finally said. "You're telling me you would've felt better if you'd *known* you were lying to my family?"

"Huh?" Maize said. "What?"

"So lying or cheating is fine as long as you know you're doing it and your ego doesn't get bruised? I'll try to remember that."

"Excuse me?" Suddenly the conversation had gone off track, and Maize had a strong feeling she didn't like at all where it was headed. In an effort to put on the brakes or reverse it a few yards she reverted to her earlier proclamation. "I don't care what you do, André. Just leave me out of it. You don't have to explain yourself to me. Could we please just drop it now?"

"Right," André said. "You're right. What the hell am I doing? I don't have to explain myself to you. I'm the boss and you're the employee, in case you've forgotten. It's supposed to go the other way around." He stood more erect. "Like, for instance, why don't you explain what you were doing sneaking around Vicky's apartment like a burglar when you were supposed to be here answering phones?"

"What?" Maize was surprised at how quickly André had switched gears, if not astonished.

"Like, while you're at it, why don't you explain why Vicky's Cartier bracelet was missing when she checked her apartment two weeks ago."

"Excuse me—what? Pardon me?" Maize sputtered.

"Excuse me? Pardon moi?" André said in a falsetto. "You heard me, Maize. Stop pretending you didn't." He cocked his hand on his hip and waited a few long seconds. Then a thin smile nestled on his lips and he said, "You're fired. Get out of this office immediately."

◆ ◆

"What a joke. Look at that," Maize said now, two hours into the drive with Robbie and Daniel. They had stopped at a diner for Cokes and French fries but mistimed any local movies and still couldn't decide on what else to do. "We're practically back where we started. Like we're homing pigeons." They were in their town again.

"So we are," Robbie said. He turned onto his mother's street.

"Such a wild evening," Daniel said. "I may die from all the excitement."

"Aww," Robbie said. He glanced toward the backseat. "We're not adventurous enough for you, Dr. Daniel? We haven't done enough exploring? Okay then." And with that he swerved the car suddenly to the narrow shoulder of the road and dashed the headlights and shifted into park. They were idling fifty yards from his mother's new house, which was so brightly lit from within—as if hoarding the neighborhood's electricity—it made the landscape surrounding it look all the more pitch dark. "Let's get out," Robbie said to them. "Let's do a spy mission." He turned off the ignition.

"Are you crazy?" Daniel said. "What if they have a dog?"

"I don't think they have a dog," Robbie said.

"It's trespassing," Daniel said. "Keep driving."

"It's practically my mother's house, anyway," Robbie said.

"Not for another week. Knock it off," Daniel said.

"Maize?" Robbie's door was already open and he got out to stand on the side of the road. "Shall we?"

"Get back in the goddamned car," Daniel said.

"Okay, I guess." Maize shrugged, then turned to Daniel. "You sure you don't want to join us? It should be all right."

"Absolutely not," Daniel said.

"We'll be back in a minute, then," Maize said. "Promise. Guard the car for us. You might want to get in the driver's seat just in case, you know, we have to make a quick getaway."

"You're a pair of fools," Daniel said as she closed the door behind her as quietly as she could.

Maize and Robbie scrambled over the low fence separating the property from the road. The sky was so starless that Maize could barely see Robbie a few feet in front of her. Robbie headed straight for the backyard, where no one from the road would notice them, moving swiftly as if he already knew this property as well as his own, yet making sure to stay beyond the light from the interior.

Maize wondered if this was what the burglars had done when they'd cased their apartment some weeks ago. But of course not. The burglary had happened in broad daylight and there was no lawn. Just a scuzzy alleyway too narrow for anybody to fit through except a child or an emaciated crackhead.

Robbie sat on the grass outside the house now, as if taking in a show, but Maize kept standing. Inside she counted four—no, five—people moving about from room to room. A young couple and their three small children, two boys and one girl. From a distance the parents looked tall to her, the man a redhead in an untucked blue dress shirt, the dark-haired woman wearing a short white dress and white sneakers, as if she hadn't bothered to change after a tennis match. Was that a terry-cloth wristband on her arm? No, maybe it was a piece of silver jewelry.

Maize found herself fixated on the father before she realized he had Eli's coloring.

The two boys clearly favored him—both of them fair and one of them also a redhead—and they raced in and out of the kitchen where their parents were stationed. At one point the older boy stood before the two adults announcing something and they both nodded at him as if paying serious attention before they spoke. First the father and then the mother. The woman touched the father on his arm when she answered as if in a show of solidarity. Then suddenly she left the room and the father and son kept talking. She came back a few moments later with the younger boy in her arms, stroking his head as though soothing him, drawing so close to the father as she cradled the boy that he could have been held by either of them. From the distance it looked like he was half supported against one parent and half against the other.

"Nice," Maize heard herself saying. They were a perfect nuclear family or at least the picture of it. "What do you suppose they're saying to each other?"

"Sorry, honey, I want a divorce." Robbie chuckled. Then he said, "I wonder where the little girl's gotten to."

She had been wondering that herself. Suddenly she imagined that the dark-haired little girl was locked in her room upstairs, writing in a pink diary with red hearts on its cover. Then she imagined the girl outside her room on the stair landing, looking down at her parents and her brothers from a distance. She imagined the girl did this frequently, often the outsider, always the observer, waves of attention rolling unnoticed from her toward the others, and that it'd be the same in whatever new house they were moving to, as it had been for Maize when she'd shown all those properties for André. She would look at the furniture and the art and the mail lying on the tables and she'd fantasize about the life that took place in those apartments and lofts and penthouses and townhouses and, fleetingly, about the life she'd have there too if it magically became hers. In that alternative universe she'd possess many things she didn't yet have (furniture that wasn't secondhand, great clothes, shiny gadgets), and more important, the career that went with those accoutrements. On certain days she was an advertising executive in a nip-waisted suit coming home after giving a dazzling presentation, laying her expensive kid gloves and briefcase on the console table and plopping onto a down sofa. On other days she was an actress between location shoots, subletting a furnished loft for an astronomical price, pouring herself a glass of pinot and admiring the skyline view before going to bed because she had an early call the next morning. On others still, more and more frequently, she was a writer with intelligent-looking eyewear come home late at night from a newsroom where she'd filed a column or an article or from a magazine where she'd done a strenuous edit on a short story, with a kindly editor who prodded her gently and gave her brilliant ideas for revision.

And then a buyer or a broker would ask her a question about maintenance charges or the building's pet policy and it would all evaporate. She was just herself again: a flunky who had to remember to turn off all the lights before leaving and make sure the door was locked behind her.

"What do you bet they give the older boy the biggest bedroom in the house," Robbie said. But Maize didn't answer.

It occurred to her that even in her most elaborate fantasies there was rarely a man there with her in those apartments, reaching for her hand or sitting across the breakfast table, waiting on the sofa or in the bedroom. And that the few times she'd tried to picture it the most she could conjure was a male body without a face, like a store mannequin or a criminal informant whose identity needed to be digitally censored on a TV news show, en route to a fake new witness-protection identity. Otherwise she was always solo in those fantasy homes—nothing except for cameo appearances by Robbie. Nothing but stirrings from an adjacent room, someone pacing or opening drawers or playing music so faint it was like a weak radio signal from another country. Surely there was something wrong with that.

"My mother's house," Robbie said now. He continued to stare ahead at the lighted tableau. "You know something? You know?" he said, but he didn't elaborate and she didn't ask him to.

Maize said, "Yes."

"I think we'd better get going," Robbie said. His voice had gone a bit phlegmy while he'd sat there looking at the couple and their children, but he didn't bother to clear it. She followed his steps the same way they came. If anything Robbie was even more careful to stay far outside the light where they'd cast no scary shadows, as if he suddenly recognized the extent of the danger he'd put them in and was eager to sneak back to the car as soon as possible. But when they hopped over the fence together both Daniel and the car were missing.

◆◆◆

Robbie didn't talk to Daniel again that night. At first he'd had the crazy thought that the car had been hijacked before he realized that Daniel simply must have gotten impatient waiting for

them. After he and Maize walked home he'd discovered Daniel
upstairs in his guest room with the door ajar, asleep in the dark or
pretending to be asleep, very quiet and still, his breathing shallow as he lay there with his eyes closed.

Robbie couldn't fathom how Daniel had gotten into the
house by himself without a set of keys. Had he broken in—
jimmied a door with a credit card or crawled through an open
window on the first floor? But Robbie's mother never left the
windows open even in daytime. They were always locked and
sealed shut. How Daniel had entered his house was a mystery.

He'd backed away from Daniel's room and headed toward
his own for the night. Maize's door was shut, too, and he resisted
knocking on it at first. But then he couldn't stop himself. Sometimes it ambushed him without warning, the desolate feeling of
aloneness, the fear that his life would vanish as if it had never
been there, whatever spark or brightness he'd had gone the way
the night sky swallowed a dead star. The panic that he could be
attacked at any moment with no one to hear him scream.

His heart was pounding. Through the door he whispered,
"Maize? Maizie? Are you asleep? May I come in?" and he heard
or thought he heard her say, "Of course."

His mother woke them early the next morning. Robbie was
lying next to Maize when he heard three raps on the closed door,
then her calling, "Up and at 'em." In the ebb state between sleep
and waking he forgot where he was for a moment, and exactly
when it was.

"Breakfast time," his mother said through the door. "I'm
making pancakes from scratch, you lucky dogs." He heard her
knock on his empty room next door.

"Oh god, no," Robbie whispered as Maize opened her eyes.
He'd meant to head back to his own bed overnight, after they'd
talked, and he nearly did at 3:30 a.m. but he hadn't managed it.

"Her pancakes are leaden," he whispered. "I've never had the heart to tell her. She's so proud of them."

"Don't worry." Maize yawned. "Daniel will probably do that for you."

Robbie shot up in bed. He'd better stop his mother before she got to Daniel's room. Daniel was grumpy enough already and, like any med student who fetishized his sleep, he could be truly surly if anybody woke him by surprise.

Robbie hopped off the mattress in his rumpled T-shirt and boxer shorts, shouting "Ow!" when he stepped on a pen lying near Maize's bedside journal. He hopped on one foot to the door and opened it and called, "Mom, don't!" but it was too late. His mother turned around to take in Robbie—his bleary eyes, his bed head, his disarranged underwear—while beside her Daniel stood propped against the doorframe, vectoring his gaze down the hallway toward Maize's room and bull's-eyeing on Robbie as he stood there barefoot and half-clothed.

"Hi," Robbie called. "Good morning."

Daniel merely blinked as if at excessive sunlight.

"Pancakes," his mother said again.

Robbie said, "Be right down."

◆ ◆

Later that morning, in Robbie's mother's bedroom, Maize couldn't suppress a frown. The first thing she noticed upon entering was a handbag lying next to a heavy dresser. It was a designer bag she'd seen a lot in the city; half the fashionable women in Manhattan seemed to carry it, though it wasn't particularly attractive or well constructed. A lumpen duffel in a sort of rubbery, fake-looking leather (if it was leather at all) with the designer's name emblazoned over it and superfluously bulky hardware that seemed better suited to a saddle horse than a woman. Maize had read online that it was the It bag for summer. She'd have assumed Robbie's mother was above caring about such things but she guessed that was unrealistic. Perhaps nobody escaped the affliction of wanting what everybody else wanted— handbags or cars or appliances or other status symbols—unless she was hopelessly out of it. Everybody got brainwashed about the goods of the Good Life. And even if you somehow escaped getting duped into wanting them, you couldn't help knowing what they were and noticing who had them and who didn't.

The apartments André had made Maize show were inter- changeable in that way. They all had the same stainless steel re- frigerators, the same stone countertops, the same silent German dishwashers and "professional" stoves nobody seemed to use, the same limestone or marble or subway tile baths, the same vintage- reproduction hardware and gooseneck faucets, the same cus- tomized closets and Italian bed linens, with only the slightest variations in color and style. If a property didn't have all those features it would "need work on the finishes" until it looked like every other apartment the buyer had seen or might see, in person or in an ad or in a movie. Apparently people didn't look at pic- tures anymore and ask if they were lifelike. They looked at their lives and compared them to images they'd seen somewhere.

Or at least André's clients did when they said things like *The finishes aren't what I'd hoped*, meaning not as expensive-looking or as precious as they required.

But really, who was Maize to judge? She herself felt attracted to certain objects not because they were beautiful but merely be- cause she'd been overexposed to them and couldn't afford them. Like the duffel sitting before her now. It was ugly yet enviable.

"Oh, *that*," Robbie's mother said, when she noticed Maize staring at it. "I hate that pocketbook. It weighs two tons and it has no inside compartments to store anything. My shopaholic sister-in-law gave it to me for my birthday—I think she got it at Neiman Marcus—even though I have pocketbooks coming out of my ears. It's my sister-in-law's personal mission to make me over into a fellow princess like herself. God only knows how much it set her back."

"It costs thirty-nine hundred fifty dollars," Maize said, embarrassed to know the price off the top of her head.

"You're joking," Robbie's mother said. When Maize shook her head she said, "My poor brother. That sap is going to end up in the gutter. Mind you, he'll have cashmere blankets to keep him warm in the gutter, but no food."

She and Maize went to work on her walk-in closet, a wide airless chamber where there were two walls of dresses and jackets and pants and blouses hanging in no particular order and a third wall piled high with boxes and shoes and smashed purses. How disorganized it was compared to Robbie's closet, where everything was meticulously arranged and there were shoe trees, and where his least favorite items were tucked in the back so he wouldn't be reminded of his lapses in judgment. Yet Robbie's closet was too orderly, like one of those boutiques where the clothes are so artfully displayed you're afraid to touch them, much less try them on. Robbie still needed to let loose—to open his arms wider and embrace the unruliness of existence. He'd been trying to do that since their senior year of college, but when you opened his closet door you could see how far he still had to go.

It took Maize and Robbie's mother three hours just to pluck out all the jackets and blouses and determine which were keepers. In the early afternoon, when they got around to cleaning out the two bureaus in the master bedroom, Maize opened the bottom drawer and found a large white leather book—what looked like a photo album, hidden under a frilly cream nightgown with a matching jacket that had embroidery at the shoulders. It was the only ultrafeminine garment in his mother's wardrobe, so its placement seemed intentional, as if it were put there to distract people from what lay beneath it.

"Yikes, my fairy queen outfit," Robbie's mother said when Maize took out the garment along with its matching satin-and-lace robe. "You're probably too young to know this, Maizie, but they used to call these 'peignoirs.' Unless you were a sissy, you were only supposed to wear them on special occasions."

"You mean like Christmas?"

"No. Like your honeymoon. What else did you dig out there?"

Maize plucked the album from the bottom drawer and brought it over to Robbie's mother. She wanted to explain that she wasn't snooping around but she didn't. Robbie's mother sat on her bed and opened it. As she turned through the first few pages she said nothing but "Yow" and "Yeesh" and gave a wistful smile, which Maize took as a cue to sit next to her as she looked.

What Maize saw was shocking—shockingly lovely: Robbie's parents young and beaming and almost unbearably vivid in picture after picture, before their bodies and senses had gotten run down by middle age, and Robbie as a bald and cheerful baby held like a prize by one or the other of them before the camera. His father in his twenties was even handsomer than Robbie, who himself was handsomer than he realized, with his mother's eyes and his father's nose but also a nervousness to his looks that neither of his parents had. Robbie's nervousness was like a recessive gene that had skipped generations.

"You were a knockout," Maize said as his mother flipped the pages. "You looked happy." As she spoke she recalled Eli saying the same thing to her on her front stoop—*You look happy*—and she realized that she had been despite her fear and stiltedness.

"Maybe yes, maybe no. I don't remember. People look that way in snapshots because they're always told to smile," Robbie's mother said. "But who knows."

She grinned to herself, then looked at Maize for a long moment and splayed her hand over the next page so that Maize couldn't see it. "My husband was a looker. I'll give him that. Funny thing," she said and turned the page. "You know when I *got* that it was curtains for us? Everybody thinks it was when he left with what's-her-name. But it hit me when he didn't like my roast chicken anymore. I had my own recipe and he'd always scarfed it down. Second and third helpings. Toward the end he'd complain it was too salty or tough although I made it exactly the same. He just pushed it around his plate." She looked at Maize and laughed. "That must make me sound nuts."

"No, it doesn't. Really." Maize herself had been starting to notice, more and more, that meaningful changes didn't happen when you expected and that you didn't graduate when everybody else claimed you did, with ceremonies and celebrations and moving vans, with diplomas and severed ribbons cut to applause. Those turned out to be nothing more than suggestions. The big changes came mostly at odd, unexpected moments and often in private, delayed or speeded up or beyond the last minute, during ordinary conversations instead of speeches, half hidden like a mole on the back of someone you mistakenly thought you loved but in fact didn't, or in sentences you might tune out on another day in another mood in another light, or in all variety of unplanned meetings. And while you were waiting for them to occur things got taken—not just from you but by you, though you hardly noticed until it was over.

She had to admit to herself that André wasn't the only thief in the office. She could see that now. She'd taken things from André, too—not only his abrasive phone manner but his deep cynicism about people in general and about men in particular, as if she'd had André's life experiences when she hadn't. She'd been borrowing from André out of sheer ignorance of the world, and before that she'd been taking whatever she could from other people—her peers and her teachers and more distant figures—from fear that if left to herself there'd be nothing of great interest or almost nothing, because she was young.

"No," she said again to Robbie's mother. "It's not insane. I understand."

She leaned toward his mother. She wanted to put her arm around her shoulder but was afraid she would recoil.

"Honestly? You're not just humoring an old bat? You were always a smart kid," his mother said. Then she shook her head briskly as though clearing space for another topic. "Enough about me already. What about you?"

Maize blinked at her. "Me?"

"Yeah you, toots. For instance, any boys these days besides my son?"

"No. Not really." Maize leaned back a bit as if shrinking from inadequacy. She felt herself blush. Much as she liked Robbie's mother, she wasn't going to talk about hookups—not to a woman who probably hadn't had sex in years—and the thought of addressing anything else made her cringe.

"A gorgeous chickie like you?" his mother said. "I don't buy that. You're holding out on me." She raked her hand through her hair. "Unless what I hear is true and boys are even worse dogs than they were in my day."

"No, not all of them," Maize said. "There was a guy from work who was . . . nice," she said, although *nice* seemed a pallid way to describe Eli. "But we stopped talking after I got fired."

She didn't know what shocked her more—her impulse to defend heterosexual men or to invoke Eli after a month of denying his existence. She'd mentioned him fleetingly to Robbie the same night they'd gone out—not revealing their awkward kiss on the stoop—but she hadn't spoken another word about him since.

"How long were you dating this boy?" Robbie's mother said.

"Dating?" That sounded so old-fashioned. "No, it was just one night."

"Got it. Nice guy, but dull."

"No. Really. He was smart and talented. And he was attractive."

"Then why aren't you in touch with him?" Robbie's mother stood and stretched herself and looked down at Maize. "Obviously I'm missing something here."

Maize shrugged. "I don't know. He's called but I haven't gotten back to him."

"Why?"

Maize shrugged again and looked at the scalloped bedroom carpet. She was tempted to say something innocuous like "I've been busy" but she realized how dysfunctional that would sound coming from an unemployed person.

"I guess I've been sort of rude," she said.

"Get back to him."

"Maybe I should."

"Not maybe, Maize. If he's a good egg get back to him. Call him. Or e-mail him or text-message him or send a smoke signal or whatever you kids do these days." When Maize looked up at her wide-eyed, Robbie's mother said, "What—you want to end up like me?"

There was no right way to answer that question; either a yes or a no would cause equal offense, so Maize said nothing. She'd always considered Robbie's mother unassailable—armored against the doubts and regrets that plagued Maize on a daily basis—yet perhaps that shallow admiration was a kind of disrespect. In the muggy closeness of this woman's bedroom she could see, for a moment, that they were more alike than they seemed and she could let her question reverberate in the silence.

Why hadn't she called Eli? Why had she dragged the figment of Hal along on her dates and her hookups like an invisible chaperone who'd prevent her from doing anything rash, or anything much at all? She had no idea. She could be insightful about other people, but she was pretty much an idiot about herself.

"I've squawked enough," Robbie's mother said. "You'll do whatever's best. You've always understood things." She sighed. "I wish I could say the same for my son."

"What do you mean?" Maize said. "Robbie's very smart."

"I don't think Robbie gets it. He thinks I wanted it to turn out this way."

"What way?"

"This way. All of this." His mother took her hand off the album and made a sweeping gesture that encompassed the room and perhaps her entire emptying house. "Me, my husband, Robbie—the whole mess. Honestly." Her voice caught on the last word, but she recovered by clearing her throat. "It's not like I planned it." Then she improved her posture, looked in Maize's eyes, and said, "Tell me something. Is Robbie all right?"

"Yes," Maize said.

"You'd know a heck of a lot better than me these days."

"Yes, he's fine," Maize said, though she wasn't sure of it.

"He seems confused to me. He was such a clearheaded little boy that my husband and I used to call him 'the junior executive.' But when we split up he changed. He covers it, but he seems— Well," his mother said. "I worry about him."

"You shouldn't."

"I worry about him all the time. Don't tell him. All the time."

"He's fine," Maize said loudly.

But as if to contradict her Robbie suddenly appeared in the open doorway to the bedroom, looking quite the opposite. His hair was frowzy and sweat-plastered, his clothes were disheveled, and he looked as stricken as someone who'd just been mugged. "Who's fine?" he said.

His mother snapped the photo album shut.

"Nobody," Maize said. "Where's Daniel?"

"What's that you've got there on your lap?" Robbie said.

"Nothing." His mother tightened her grip on the album.

"Where's Daniel?" Maize said. An alarm buzzed through her suddenly.

"Gone," Robbie said. "Elsewhere. Daniel is gone."

◆ ◆

He and Daniel had been back in the basement that morning after breakfast, hauling boxes into various rooms upstairs and working in silence, which was a relief given the nasty things he supposed Daniel had wanted to say to him the night before. But after an hour in the heat Robbie couldn't take it anymore. He said, "Would you like to explain the stunt you pulled last night, abandoning us?"

"Abandoning you. That's rich," Daniel said.

"Come again?" Robbie said.

"Let's not get into it. You don't want me to." Daniel picked up a few unboxed, wrapped objects on the basement floor and headed toward the stairs. "I was tired," he said.

"We're all tired. We've all been working hard."

"No, Robbie. You don't understand me. As usual." Daniel turned to face him. "I'm sick and tired of this situation."

"What are you talking about?" Robbie said. "It'll all be over in two days."

"No it won't," Daniel said. He laid the wrapped objects on the floor between them. "Not my having to arm wrestle with Maize for your attention. Not your playing me off against the high school girlfriend you go to bed with whenever the mood strikes you. I mean, Jesus Christ," Daniel said. "You don't want anything to be different in the least, though you think you do. Maybe you should move up here with your mother. Or go to graduate school so you can bury your head in books again and never have a personal life. It's kind of the same thing."

"That's absurd," Robbie said. He looked at the objects on the floor and had to take a breath. There were a number of wrapped things on the floor, he thought, and even more things he could say in reply to Daniel, but what came out was "I don't *go to bed* with Maize. We sleep together, literally, sometimes. And as for not wanting anything different: I've never even introduced one of my boyfriends to my mother before, much less invited him to stay in her house for a week."

"Window dressing," Daniel said.

"Fine," Robbie said. "I don't get what you want."

"You know something, Robbie?" Daniel said. "Even if you don't care about me, which you clearly don't, you might think about how you're holding that poor girl back. It's selfish." When Robbie didn't answer he said, "And you're an idiot, for the record. I could have been good to you."

Daniel drew in a sharp breath, as if as surprised by what he'd said as Robbie was, and his eyes darted to a square wrapped box beside Robbie in a clear effort not to look him in the face. "I could have been good for you," he said.

Daniel didn't say it tenderly, as Robbie might have expected or read about somewhere. He spoke in the sternest tone possible, which only moved Robbie more. Robbie had the urge to step closer to Daniel, but he resisted it—why?—the same way he resisted the polite impulse to say, *I could have been good to you, too*, because it would sound pat, or he didn't know how to say it, or he simply didn't believe it.

His confusion took only a moment to solidify into something else. It hardened into anger and he indulged himself, because anger seemed stronger and clearer to him than whatever else was clouding up in him.

"All right then," he said. "I suppose I should thank Dr. Daniel for illuminating the dark and deeply unexplored nooks of my massively fucked-up psyche. I guess I'm a latent heterosexual and poor Maize hasn't figured out that I'm waiting to put the moves on her. Unless I can put the moves on my mother first. Which would be even hotter."

He went on from there, spraying buckshot, but he hardly listened to what he was saying. It was like he was two people simultaneously, the one who raised his voice at Daniel and the one who interrogated himself even as he spoke. What *was* Daniel doing up here, anyway? Why *had* he led him here under false pretenses? Why *hadn't* Robbie considered it more carefully before he'd invited him to do a job and thwarted him? Yet he didn't say any of that aloud at the moment.

Instead he heard himself say, "You're right, Daniel. I'm sorry for everything. Please. I need your help."

He hardly believed what he was hearing although it was his own voice doing the talking. They were simple enough words—sentiments he could've expressed to Daniel or J. or other men over the years yet never managed to get out, like someone with a horrible stammer. Maybe he could still back away from them if he chose—pretend that he was still merely asking for help with his mother's belongings—but he didn't want to anymore.

He said, "I'm scared, Daniel. Okay? I've been scared all my life. I don't even know why. I need you to help me." When Daniel didn't respond his voice trembled. "Maize is one of the few people who doesn't scare me. I don't know what I'd do without her."

That was the truth. It was only in Maize's company and in his small, silent, private world of reading that he'd ever felt safe—free from the sense of estrangement that had clung to him everywhere, all his life and unavoidably, like his own shadow. Now he said, "Please help me."

"I wanted to, but I can't." Daniel sighed. "So are we done here, Robbie? Are you finished?"

Robbie wasn't sure he was yet. He was rattled by everything he'd just said and—among other things—the thought that from now on, every time he snuggled with Maize for a second, he'd have to push Daniel's accusation out of whatever embrace they might be sharing. *You're holding that poor girl back.* He flashed forward to the necessity of having to make that effort hundreds and perhaps thousands of times in the future and another bolt of anger shot through him.

He'd never gotten in the way of Maize sleeping with anybody. He'd listened to her entertaining accounts afterward and he'd encouraged her flirtations and crushes—only lightly, maybe, but he'd thought he was giving her what she wanted, which was to avoid sappiness. Maybe he could've wheedled more out of her whenever she mentioned her encounters with men ("That's nice," "Sounds fun," "Good for you" was mostly what he'd said) yet he'd taken his cues from her, hadn't he? She'd made her interest in them sound like a hobby.

The last time she had gone out with anyone—that guy from her office whose name Robbie still couldn't remember—she'd pressed herself against their front door upon returning, dizzy and panting as if after a sprint, and he'd done nothing but offer her paint chips to look at. Yet he'd never believed he could hold her back even if he wanted to. He considered Maize more advanced than him in countless ways. It was true that she hadn't been romantically involved with anyone for a while but, as it turned out, he hadn't been as involved as he'd thought he was, either. He hadn't moved as far away from the old Robbie as he'd hoped and assumed.

"You didn't answer me," Daniel was saying now. "Are you finished?"

"All right," Robbie said. "Yes."

He turned his back and walked upstairs. In the locked bathroom he ran cold water over his wrists and the crooks of his arms, to cool himself down at the pulse points, and wiped the sweat off his forehead with toilet tissue. Then he sat on the edge of the tub and read whatever was lying around—a house-and-garden magazine with an article about brightening perennial beds with zinnias—as if nothing had happened and he wasn't expected anywhere. It wasn't until he found himself reading the photo credits on the back pages that he reminded himself he wasn't finished. He had to do something.

Daniel had come upstairs by now. His door was ajar and there was noise coming from the guest room. When Robbie went down the hall to say one more thing—he wasn't sure what yet—he was stopped by what he saw. Daniel was frantically packing his suitcase with one hand and using the other to phone the taxi company for a ride to the train station. He was shoving clothes and toiletries and whatever else was lying about into his bag frantically and indiscriminately, not bothering to fold or arrange them the way Robbie would, as if the cab were already honking in the driveway or he were a convict making a prison break. Then he threw his cell phone into the bag and tried to zip it shut. He had to try the zipper again and again, jostling things around since the suitcase was overstuffed, but he couldn't close it. He didn't notice Robbie standing there.

Robbie was thinking he should at least drive Daniel to the station—if his mother would give him the car and Daniel would allow it—at the same moment he saw a small wrapped object in the center of Daniel's suitcase, nestled next to a peanut butter jar and half swaddled by disheveled clothes. He heard the paper crinkle faintly as Daniel tried the zipper again.

Together they'd wrapped hundreds of objects like that over the past week. They'd carried dozens and dozens of them to various rooms for safekeeping, so it could be any one of them. But when Robbie noticed the elegant cross-stitch of masking tape over newspaper he immediately knew it was his mother's Murano vase in the suitcase. The same vase he'd had to convince Daniel not to throw onto the discard pile because it was more beautiful and valuable than Daniel understood, and which he'd wrapped with such grudging care.

He could have stepped forward and asked Daniel what he was doing. He could have pointed out that he was taking something that wasn't his, intentionally or by mistake, and he could've protected his mother's valuables better than he'd protected his own back in the city.

Yet he didn't do that. Instead he found himself backing away from the guest room quietly, as if he were the one who'd packed away something that didn't belong to him and he was terrified to be found out.

With each step backward he convinced himself that it was all right. It was all right, it was fair, it was just, it was acceptable, regardless of whether Daniel had done it on purpose. It was recompense for the fact that Robbie had wasted Daniel's time and hadn't a clue about how to love anyone properly yet, any better than he knew other practical things like how to use a drill or fix a flat tire. Although Robbie thought he'd known how to love somebody or that he could figure it out. Surely he could. He'd always been an excellent student.

Daniel was going home and Robbie probably should be going home, too. He and Maize would be doing that soon enough. But what would they be going home to? A silly *internship* that was the employment equivalent of blue balls, and no job at all for Maize. No boyfriends, no significant new relationships, no parties or meetings or avenues where they fully belonged, no serious prospects, no commitment to graduate school or rigorous self-education or anything else. And empty rooms just like these in his mother's house, only smaller and shabbier.

At least he and Maize had each other. If they didn't have romance or jobs or money or position or good housing just yet, they had their friendship. Friendship and company while they flailed.

He decided he'd give his notice at the newspaper as soon as he got back to the city. He would keep looking until he found a real job, even if it meant scrubbing toilets with a toothbrush. He would send out his résumé. He would interview like a demon. He would do anything he needed to move ahead. And Maize would be there watching him.

But for now he could only take steps backward. With each step down the hallway Daniel grew smaller and smaller through the half-opened guest room door until Robbie turned to face his old bedroom, and then Daniel disappeared.

✦✦

"Are you sure you don't want me to come back next week?" Robbie said to his mother. "To protect you from the big burly moving men?"

"Nah," his mother said as she engaged her blinker and made a left turn toward the train station. "If those jokers think they can try anything with me, they should think again." She drove half a block without saying anything, glancing in her rearview mirror and catching Maize's eyes staring from the backseat. "Right, Maizie? Two tough girls."

"You bet," Maize said. She made a fist. "One false move and it's brass knuckles to the jaw."

"But I could help you set up the new house," Robbie said.

"You've done plenty already," his mother said. Then like a child reminded to show good manners she said, "And thank you. I appreciate it." She looked over at Robbie and nodded. "I can't tell you how much."

A few minutes before they'd piled into this car, while Robbie was supposed to be packing, he'd overheard his mother pull Maize aside and ask what had really gone down with Daniel. His mother didn't believe Robbie's excuse—muttered into his collarbone—that Daniel had to attend to someone's medical emergency in the city. Daniel wasn't even a real doctor yet.

"It might have been me," he'd heard his mother say to Maize. "We had this thing about my stupid wedding dress. Sometimes I can't keep my mouth shut."

"I don't think so," Maize had said. Robbie told her everything the night Daniel left. "I think it was a lot of things. I'm guessing it was all of us."

A statement that struck Robbie as kind yet overly generous. It had been his fault far more than anyone else's. No one else was to blame. When he'd recounted his final moments with Daniel to Maize—omitting his unmet pleas for help—she'd said, "I'm really sorry it didn't work out between you and him," and Robbie had replied, "Not between me and him, Maizie. Between him and *me*. Between everybody and me." He'd shaken his head and murmured, "I have to do better next time. If there is a next time."

"You will," Maize had said. She'd opened her arms as if about to give him a reassuring hug but then she'd pointedly stopped herself. Robbie appreciated her not smoothing it over with an embrace. "I know you will."

Now as they sat at the train station parking lot in the idling car, Robbie's mother fished through her purse. She withdrew letter envelopes stuffed with cash. "This is for you, Maizie," she said. "You're a champ as usual." She turned to Robbie and handed him an identical envelope. "And this is for Daniel. Please make sure he gets it right away. I don't want him to think I'm a deadbeat."

"All right," Robbie said. He wasn't sure how he'd get the final payment to Daniel. Maybe he'd leave the envelope at the front desk of Daniel's dorm, hoping the security guard wouldn't lift it, or he'd get a money order for the amount and mail it to him with a note that said nothing more than *From my mother, with thanks.* In any case it would have to be delivered without them seeing each other again. Daniel had made it clear he didn't want that. It was one of many things Robbie would have to figure out when he got back to the city.

In the meantime Robbie's mother was shoving a third cash envelope at him and saying, "This is for you, Robbie."

"What? No," he said. "Don't be foolish. I'm your son. Helping you out is my job."

"Only a little," his mother said. "Actually, not so much anymore. So take it. You're a good boy." Her eyes welled as she stared at him but then she looked away. "Besides, if an old broad like me can't take care of herself by now, who the hell can?"

"Nobody," Maize said.

Robbie shoved the envelope back at her and said, "Spend it on yourself. I've still got some of Grandma's bonds, remember?"

"Take it. I'm the parent. Take it," his mother said. "Do as I say."

Robbie turned around to Maize and said, "You see what I have to put up with?" but she merely smiled.

"You can use it to repaint your apartment or something," his mother said. "Didn't you say you wanted to do that? Now would be the right time, with its being empty."

"We did mean to repaint," Maize said, "but we couldn't decide on colors. We got scared. White's boring but the wrong choice could be hideoso."

"Our apartment's already depressing enough," Robbie said.

"You know something?" his mother said. "You should call your father and ask him about it. Your father always had a very good sense of color. Probably still does."

When Robbie merely nodded his mother looked forward through the windshield and swallowed hard. "Get your father's advice the next time you talk to him, Robbie. I'm sure he can help you."

Maize said, "Yeah."

In a dim voice Robbie said, "He's never seen our place."

"I'm sure he'd like to help you with it, anyway," his mother said. "He's your father. And he's always loved giving his opinions regardless of whether anyone asked for them." She coughed out a laugh.

The car continued to idle with the air conditioner running full blast. When it got close to departure time Robbie and Maize decided they'd better wait on the platform. Robbie's mother insisted on watching from the car until she knew they were safely on board.

"That's hardly necessary. What could happen to us here?" Robbie said. "You think we'll get rolled by a roving band of golf ladies from Westport?"

"No," his mother said. "But still."

The train was late in arriving. Robbie and Maize sat in the plexiglass-enclosed waiting room, with their backs to his mother's shadowy figure just a few yards behind them. Every few minutes one of them turned and waved to her and she waved back. When the train finally came they waved one last time and took a place on the three-seater side of the cabin, piling their bags on the empty seat beside them so no one would sit there. It was as if they were marking the spot where Daniel had been on the way up.

◆ ◆

The train didn't accelerate after it pulled away from the station, as Maize would have expected. It lumbered along as towns came into view beyond the window and slid away one after the other, slow enough for her to catch sight of landmarks in each place like chapters in a book. The train stopped and started and stopped again.

She pictured the apartment they'd be going back to—rooms so bare they echoed, the air inside it sharp and raw and waiting to be filled. For the moment it felt enthralling instead of frightening, or enthrallingly frightening. Her heartbeat thrummed as if she was beginning something.

She glanced out the window as they neared the Grand

Central tunnel. Then she kept staring into the darkness where, here and there, a green light appeared, or an electrical box. Her reflection bloomed on the glass like a figure in a night window and she found she looked exotic and compelling. Although it made no sense—they had nearly no time left—she pulled out her pen and she bent over her journal as the train lights flickered above her.

In the romantic ending of her story, she would fall in love with Eli or a painter or the cop or an editor who wanted to publish every word she wrote, or someone else she hadn't met just yet. She'd be happy or something like it. Wasn't that the ending everyone wanted? Wasn't that the ending she was supposed to want? Perhaps someday she would have it. All she could do today was phone Eli when she got back to the apartment, after she unpacked, and hope he'd take her call.

For the moment she still had Robbie sitting beside her—just one slot over, the way he'd existed in her imagination for so long, even in the years when they were separated—so close that she could feel his breath on her. It seemed like a lot: a true friend traveling next to her and, deep inside her, the fierce and strange impulse to write it all down.

As she wondered again what would happen next and what would become of her, the heat from Robbie's leg pressed against hers and she kept filling the journal's blank page until she reached the bottom of it, where she ran out of space.

Before she could turn the page to scrawl anything else Robbie said, "It won't be long now," as they both moved deeper into the tunnel and the city that lay beyond.

Acknowledgments

For their brilliant advice and invaluable support during the writing of this book, I am grateful to my friends Katherine Dieckmann and Clifford Chase; my astounding agent, Bill Clegg; my inspiring and extraordinary editor, Jonathan Galassi; and Peter and Lucy. I would also like to thank Jesse Coleman, Walter Abish, Concetta Adinolfi, Ryan Chapman, Dean Crawford, Kathy Daneman, Raffaella De Angelis, Robert DeMaria, Jr., Shaun Dolan, Frank Frattaroli, Elisa Gerarden, Daniel Halpern, John Hawkes, Matt Hudson, Ann E. Imbrie, Toni Y. Joseph, Rabbi Jennifer Krause, Jannay Morrow, Judith Nichols, Mary O'Donnell, Chris Peterson, Chris Pomeroy, Alice Quinn, Edmund Rung, Emily Russell, Paul Russell, Jeff Seroy, Ira Silverberg, Brett Singer, Elsieliese Thrope, Keith and Rosmarie Waldrop, Kimberly Wallace-Sanders, Nancy Willard and Eric Lindbloom, Amy Wilner, my family, everyone at FSG, and the late Jerome Badanes, for generosity in many forms.